7th Heaven

7th Heaven

James Patterson's Women's Murder Club Series

7th Heaven (coauthor Maxine Paetro)
The 6th Target (Maxine Paetro)
The 5th Horseman (Maxine Paetro)
4th of July (Maxine Paetro)
3rd Degree (Andrew Gross)
2nd Chance (Andrew Gross)
1st to Die

A complete list of books by James Patterson is on pages 482-3.
For more information about James Patterson, go to
www.jamespatterson.com.

7th Heaven

A NOVEL BY

James Patterson

AND

Maxine Paetro

**Doubleday Large Print
Home Library Edition**

LITTLE, BROWN AND COMPANY

NEW YORK   BOSTON   LONDON

Little, Brown and Company
Hachette Book Group USA
237 Park Avenue, New York, NY 10017
Visit our Web site at www.HachetteBookGroupUSA.com

ISBN-13: 978-0-7394-9205-5

Printed in the United States of America

**This Large Print Book carries the
Seal of Approval of N.A.V.H.**

To our spouses and children:
Susie and Jack, John and Brendan

Our thanks and gratitude to these top professionals, who were so generous with their time and expertise: Dr. Humphrey Germaniuk, Captain Richard Conklin, Chuck Hanni, Dr. Allen Ross, Philip R. Hoffman, Melody Fujimori, Mickey Sherman, and Dr. Maria Paige.

And special thanks to our excellent researchers, Ellie Shurtleff, Don MacBain, Lynn Colomello, and Margaret Ross, and to Mary Jordan, who keeps it all together.

THE CHRISTMAS SONG

One

TINY LIGHTS WINKED on the Douglas fir standing tall and full in front of the picture window. Swags of Christmas greenery and dozens of cards decked the well-appointed living room, and apple logs crackled in the fireplace, scenting the air as they burned.

A digitized Bing Crosby crooned "The Christmas Song."

"Chestnuts roasting on an open fire. Jack Frost nipping at your nose…"

Henry Jablonsky couldn't see the boys clearly. The one called Hawk had snatched off his glasses and put them a mile away on the fireplace mantel, a good thing, Jablonsky had reasoned at the time.

It meant that the boys didn't want to be identified, that they were planning to let them go. *Please, God, please let us live and I'll serve you all the days of my life.*

Jablonsky watched the two shapes moving around the tree, knew that the gun was in Hawk's waistband. He heard wrapping paper tear, saw the one called Pidge dangling a bow for the new kitten.

They'd said they weren't going to hurt them.

They said this was only a robbery.

Jablonsky had memorized their faces well enough to describe to a police sketch artist, which he would be doing as soon as they got the hell out of his home.

Both boys looked as though they'd stepped from the pages of a Ralph Lauren ad.

Hawk. Clean-cut. Well-spoken. Blond, with side-parted hair. Pidge, bigger. Probably six two. Long brown hair. Strong as a horse. Meaty hands. Ivy League types. Both of them.

Maybe there really was some goodness in them.

As Jablonsky watched, the blond one,

Hawk, walked over to the bookshelf, dragged his long fingers across the spines of the books, calling out titles, his voice warm, as though he were a friend of the family.

He said to Henry Jablonsky, "Wow, Mr. J., you've got *Fahrenheit 451.* This is a classic."

Hawk pulled the book from the shelf, opened it to the first page. Then he stooped down to where Jablonsky was hog-tied on the floor with a sock in his mouth.

"You can't beat Bradbury for an opening," Hawk said. And then he read aloud with a clear, dramatic voice.

"'It was a pleasure to burn. It was a special pleasure to see things eaten, to see things blackened and *changed.*'"

As Hawk read, Pidge hauled a large package out from under the tree. It was wrapped in gold foil, tied with gold ribbon. Something Peggy had always wanted and had waited for, for years.

"To Peggy, from Santa," Pidge read from the gift tag. He sliced through the wrappings with a knife.

He had a knife!

Pidge opened the box, peeled back the layers of tissue.

"A Birkin bag, Peggy. Santa brought you a

nine-thousand-dollar purse! I'd call that a no, Peg. A definite no."

Pidge reached for another wrapped gift, shook the box, while Hawk turned his attention to Peggy Jablonsky. Peggy pleaded with Hawk, her actual words muffled by the wad of sock in her mouth. It broke Henry's heavy heart to see how hard she tried to communicate with her eyes.

Hawk reached out and stroked Peggy's baby-blond hair, then patted her damp cheek. "We're going to open all your presents now, Mrs. J. Yours too, Mr. J.," he said. "Then we'll decide if we're going to let you live."

Two

HENRY JABLONSKY'S STOMACH HEAVED. He gagged against the thick wool of the sock, pulled against his restraints, smelled the sour odor of urine. Heat puddled under his clothes. Christ. He'd wet himself. But it didn't matter. The only thing that mattered was to get out alive.

He couldn't move. He couldn't speak. But he could reason.

What could he do?

Jablonsky looked around from his place on the floor, took in the fire poker only yards away. He fixed his vision on that poker.

"Mrs. J.," Pidge called out to Peggy, shaking

a small turquoise box. "This is from Henry. A Peretti necklace. Very nice. What? You have something to say?"

Pidge went over to Peggy Jablonsky and took the sock out of her mouth.

"You don't really know Dougie, do you?" she said.

"Dougie who?" Pidge laughed.

"Don't hurt us—"

"No, *no,* Mrs. J.," Pidge said, stuffing the sock back into his captive's mouth. "No don'ts. This is *our* game. *Our* rules."

The kitten pounced into the heap of wrapping paper as the gifts were opened; the diamond earrings, the Hermès tie, and the Jensen salad tongs, Jablonsky praying that they would just take the stuff and leave. Then he heard Pidge speak to Hawk, his voice more subdued than before, so that Jablonsky had to strain to hear over the blood pounding in his ears.

"Well? Guilty or not guilty?" Pidge asked.

Hawk's voice was thoughtful. "The J.'s are living well, and if that's the best revenge…"

"You're kidding me, dude. That's totally bogus."

Pidge stepped over the pillowcase filled with the contents of the Jablonskys' safe. He spread the Bradbury book open on the lamp table with the span of his hand, then picked up a pen and carefully printed on the title page.

Pidge read it back. "Sic erat in fatis, man. It is fated. Get the kit-cat and let's go."

Hawk bent over, said, "Sorry, dude. Mrs. Dude." He took the sock out of Jablonsky's mouth. "Say good-bye to Peggy."

Henry Jablonsky's mind scrambled. *What? What was happening?* And then he realized. He could speak! He screamed *"Pegg-yyyyy"* as the Christmas tree bloomed with a bright yellow glare, then went up in a great exhalation of flame.

VOOOOOOM.

Heat rose and the skin on Henry Jablonsky's cheeks dried like paper. Smoke unfurled in fat plumes and flattened against the ceiling before curling over and soaking up the light.

"Don't leave us!"

He saw the flames climbing the curtains, heard his dear love's muffled screams as the front door slammed shut.

Part One

BLUE MOON

Chapter 1

WE SAT IN A CIRCLE around the fire pit behind our rental cottage near the spectacular Point Reyes National Seashore, an hour north of San Francisco.

"Lindsay, hold out your glass," Cindy said.

I tasted the margarita—it was good. Yuki stirred the oysters on the grill. My border collie, Sweet Martha, sighed and crossed her paws in front of her, and firelight made flickering patterns on our faces as the sun set over the Pacific.

"It was one of my first cases in the ME's office," Claire was saying. "And so I was 'it.' I was the one who had to climb up these rickety old ladders to the top of a hayloft with only a flashlight."

Yuki coughed as the tequila went down her windpipe, gasping for breath as Cindy and I yelled at her in unison, "Sip it!"

Claire thumped Yuki's back and continued.

"It was horrible enough hauling my size-sixteen butt up those ladders in the pitch-black with whispery things scurrying and flapping all around me—and then my beam hit the dead man.

"His feet were hovering above the hay, and when I lit him up, I swear to God he looked like he was levitating. Eyes and tongue bugged out, like a freakin' *ghoul.*"

"No way." Yuki laughed. She was wearing pajama bottoms and a Boalt Law sweatshirt, her hair in a ponytail, already drunk on her one margarita, looking more like a college kid than a woman nearing thirty.

"I yelled down into the dark well of that barn," Claire said, "got two big old boys to come up and cut the body down from the rafters and put Mr. Levitation into a body bag."

Claire paused for dramatic effect—and right then my cell phone rang.

"Lind-say, *no,*" Cindy begged me. "Don't take that call."

I glanced at the caller ID, expecting it to be my boyfriend, Joe, thinking he'd just gotten home and was checking in, but it was Lieutenant Warren Jacobi. My former partner and current boss.

"Jacobi?"

Yuki shouted, "Don't stop, Claire. She could be on the phone all night!"

"Lindsay? Okay, fine," Claire said, and then she went on. "I unzipped the body bag...and a bat flew out of the dead man's clothes. I peed my pants," Claire squealed behind me. "I really did!"

"Boxer? You there?" said Jacobi, gruff in my ear.

"I'm on my own time," I growled into my cell phone. "It's Saturday, don't you know that?"

"You're going to want this. If not, tell me and I'll give it to Cappy and Chi."

"What is it?"

"The biggest deal in the world, Boxer. It's about the Campion kid. Michael."

Chapter 2

MY PULSE SHOT UP at the mention of Michael Campion's name.

Michael Campion wasn't just a kid. He was to Californians what JFK Jr. had been to the nation. The only child of our former governor Connor Hume Campion and his wife, Valentina, Michael Campion had been born into incredible wealth. He'd also been born with an inoperable heart defect and had been living on borrowed time for the whole of his life.

Through photos and newscasts, Michael's life had been part of ours. He'd been a darling baby, a precocious and gifted child, and a handsome teenager, both funny and smart.

His father had become a spokesman for the American Heart Association, and Michael was their adored poster boy. And while the public rarely saw Michael, they cared, always hoping that one day there would be a medical breakthrough and that California's "Boy with a Broken Heart" would be given what most people took for granted—a full and vigorous life.

Then, back in January of this year, Michael had said good night to his parents, and in the morning his bedroom was empty. There was no ransom note. No sign of foul play. But a back door was unlocked and Michael was gone.

His disappearance was treated as a kidnapping, and the FBI launched a nationwide search. The SFPD did its own investigation, interviewing family members and retainers, Michael's teachers and school friends, and his virtual online friends as well.

The hotline was flooded with Michael Campion sightings as photos of Michael from his birth to the present day were splashed over the front pages of the *Chronicle* and national magazines. TV networks and cable news ran documentary specials on Michael Campion's doom-shadowed life.

The tips had led nowhere, and months later, when there'd been no calls from a kidnapper, and no trace of Michael had surfaced, terror attacks, wildfires, politics, and new violent crimes pushed the Michael Campion story off the front page.

The case was still open, but everyone assumed the worst. That a kidnapping had gone terribly wrong. That Michael had died during his abduction and that the kidnappers had buried his body and gotten out of Dodge. The citizens of San Francisco mourned along with Michael's famous and beloved family, and while the public would never forget him, they put the book of his life aside.

Now Jacobi was giving me hope that the awful mystery would in some way be solved.

"Michael's body has been found?" I asked him.

"Naw, but we've got a credible lead. Finally."

I pressed the phone hard against my ear, ghost stories and the first annual getaway of the Women's Murder Club forgotten.

Jacobi was saying, "If you want in on this, Boxer, meet me at the Hall—"

"I can be there in an hour."

Chapter 3

I MADE THE ONE-HOUR DRIVE back to the Hall of Justice in forty-five minutes, took the stairs from the lobby to the third floor, and strode into the squad room looking for Jacobi.

The forty-by-forty-foot open space was lit with flickering overhead fluorescent tubing, making the night crew hunched over their desks look like they'd just crawled out of their graves. A few old guys lifted their eyes, said, "Howsit goin', Sarge?" as I made my way to Jacobi's glassed-in corner office, with its view of the on-ramp to the 280 freeway.

My partner, Richard Conklin, was already

there; thirty years old, six feet two inches of all-American hunk, one of his long legs resting on the edge of Jacobi's junkyard of a desk.

I pulled out the other chair, bashed my knee, swore loudly and emphatically as Jacobi sniggered, "Nice talk, Boxer." I sat down, thinking how this had been a functional workspace when Jacobi's office had been *mine.* I took off my baseball cap and shook out my hair, hoping to hell that the guys wouldn't smell tequila on my breath.

"What kind of lead?" I asked without preamble.

"It's a tip kind of lead," Jacobi said. "Anonymous caller using a prepaid cell phone— untraceable, naturally. Caller said he'd seen the Campion kid entering a house on Russian Hill the night he disappeared. The house is home to a prostitute."

As Jacobi made room on his desk for the prostitute's rap sheet, I thought about Michael Campion's life at the time he'd disappeared.

There'd been no dates for Michael, no parties, no sports. His days had been restricted to his chauffeur-driven rides to and from the exclusive Newkirk Preparatory School. So it didn't sound exactly crazy that he'd visited a prostitute. He'd probably paid off his driver and escaped the plush-lined prison of his parents' love for an hour or two.

But what had happened to him afterward?

What had happened to Michael?

"Why is this tip credible?" I asked Jacobi.

"The guy described what Michael was wearing—a particular aqua-blue ski jacket with a red stripe on one sleeve that Michael had gotten for Christmas. That jacket was never mentioned in the press."

"So why did this tipster wait three months before calling it in?" I asked Jacobi.

"I can only tell you what he *said.* He said he was leaving the prostitute's house as Michael Campion was coming in. That he didn't drop the dime until now because he has a wife and kids. Didn't want to get caught up in the hullabaloo, but that his conscience had been needling him. Finally got to him, I guess."

"Russian Hill is a nice neighborhood for a pross," Conklin said.

And it was. Kind of like the French Quarter meets South Beach. And it was within walking distance of the Newkirk School. I took a notebook out of my handbag.

"What's the prostitute's name?"

"Her given name is Myrtle Bays," Jacobi said, handing me her sheet. The attached mug shot was of a young woman with a girlish look, short blond hair, and huge eyes. Her date of birth made her twenty-two years old.

"A few years ago she legally changed her name," said Jacobi. "Now she calls herself Junie Moon."

"So Michael Campion went to a hooker, Jacobi," I said, putting the rap sheet back down on his desk. "What's your theory?"

"That the kid died in flagrante delicto, Boxer. In English that means 'in the saddle.' If this tip pans out, I'm thinking maybe Ms. Myrtle Bays, AKA Junie Moon, killed Michael with his first roll in the hay—and then she made his body disappear."

Chapter 4

A YOUNG MAN in his twenties with spiky blond hair and a black sport coat whistled through his teeth as he left Junie Moon's front door. Conklin and I watched from our squad car, saw the john lope across Leavenworth, heard the tootle as he disarmed his late model BMW.

As his taillights disappeared around the corner, Conklin and I walked up the path to the front door of what's called a Painted Lady: a pastel-colored, gingerbread-decorated Victorian house, this one flaking and in need of repair. I pressed the doorbell, waited a minute, pressed it again.

Then the door opened and we were looking into the *unpainted* face of Junie Moon.

From the first moment, I saw that Junie was no ordinary hooker.

There was a dewy freshness about her that I'd never seen before in a working girl. Her hair was damp from the shower, a cap of blond curls that trailed into a wisp of a braid that had been dyed blue. Her eyes were a deep, smoky gray, and a thin white scar cut through the top lip of her cupid's-bow mouth.

She was a beauty, but what grabbed me the most was Junie Moon's disarming, childlike appearance. Junie pulled the sash of her gold silk dressing gown tightly around her narrow waist as my partner showed her his shield, said our names and "Homicide. Mind if we come in?"

"Homicide? You're here to see *me*?" she asked. Her voice matched her appearance, not just young, but sweetened with innocence.

"We have some questions about a missing person," Rich said, launching his amazing, babe-catcher smile.

Junie Moon invited us in.

The room smelled sweet, floral, like lavender and jasmine, and the light was soft, coming from low-watt bulbs under silk-draped lampshades. Conklin and I sat on a velvet upholstered loveseat while Junie took a seat on an ottoman, clasped her hands around her knees. She was barefoot, her nail polish the pale coral color of the inside of sea-shells.

"Nice place," Conklin said.

"Thank you. I rent it. Furnished," she said.

"Have you ever seen this man?" I asked Junie Moon, showing her a photo of Michael Campion.

"You mean for real? That's Michael Campion, isn't it?"

"That's right."

Junie Moon's gray eyes grew even more huge. "I've never seen Michael Campion in my entire life."

"Okay, Ms. Moon," I said. "We have some questions we'd like to ask you at the police station."

Chapter 5

JUNIE MOON SAT ACROSS FROM US in Interview Two, a twelve-by-twelve-foot gray-tiled room with a metal table, four matching chairs, and a video camera affixed to the ceiling.

I'd checked twice to be sure. The camera was loaded and running.

Junie was now wearing an open-weave pink cardigan over a lace-trimmed cami, jeans, and sneakers, no makeup, and—I'm not overstating this—she looked like she was in the tenth grade.

Conklin had started the interview by reading Junie Moon her Miranda rights in a charming, "no big deal," respectful manner. She initialed the acknowledgment of rights form without complaint, but still, it irked the hell out of me. Junie Moon wasn't under arrest. We didn't have to Mirandize her for a noncustodial interview, and Conklin's warning might very well inhibit her from telling us something we urgently needed to know. I swallowed my pique. What was done was done.

Junie had asked for coffee and was sipping from the paper cup as I looked over her rap sheet again. I mentioned her three arrests for prostitution, and she told me that since she'd changed her name, she hadn't been arrested for anything.

"I feel like a new person," she said.

There were no track marks on her arms, no bruises that I could see, and that made it even less understandable. What was the draw? What was the hook?

Why would a pretty girl like Junie turn pro?

"I took my name from an old Liza Minnelli movie," she was telling Conklin. "It was called *Tell Me That You Love Me, Junie Moon.* A lot of my clients ask me to tell them that," she said with a wistful smile.

Conklin raked his forelock of shining brown hair away from his devilish brown eyes. I was sure that Rich had never seen the movie or read the book. "Is that so?" he said. "That's cool."

"So, Junie," I said, "most of your clients are prep school kids?"

"Tell me the truth, Sergeant Boxer. Should I get a lawyer? Because I think you're trying to say that I have sex with underage boys, and that's not true."

"You ask for their driver's licenses before you take off your pants?"

"We're not interested in your, ah, social activities, Junie," Conklin said, breaking in. "We're only interested in Michael Campion."

"I told you," she said, her voice trembling just a bit. "I've never met him, and I think I would *know.*"

"Understand," I said, "we're not blaming you for anything. We know Michael was sick. Maybe his heart gave out while he was with you—"

"He was never a client," Junie insisted. "I would have been honored, you know, but it just didn't happen."

Conklin turned off the dazzling smile, said,

"Junie. Work with us and we'll leave you and your business alone. Keep stonewalling us and vice is going to nail you to the wall."

We played patty-cake with Junie for about two hours, using every legal technique in the book. We made her feel safe. We leaned on her, lied to her, reassured her, and threatened her. And after all that, Junie still denied any knowledge of Michael Campion. In the end, I played our only card, slamming my hand down on the table for emphasis.

"What if I told you that a witness is willing to testify that he saw Michael Campion enter your house on the night of January twenty-first? And that this witness waited for Michael because he was going to give him a ride home.

"But that never happened, Junie, because *Michael never left your house.*"

"A witness? But that's *impossible,*" said the young woman. "It has to be a mistake."

I was desperate to crack open this one miserable lead, but we were getting no traction at all. I was starting to believe that Jacobi's anonymous tipster was yet another crank caller—and I was seriously considering waking Jacobi and peppering him with a few choice words—when Junie looked down at the table. Her eyes were moist and her face seemed pinched, actually transformed by grief.

"You're *right,* you're *right,* and I can't take this anymore. If you turn that thing off, I'll tell you what happened."

I exchanged startled looks with Conklin. Then I snapped out of it. I reached up to the video camera and switched it off. "You can't go wrong if you tell us the truth," I said, my heart going *ga-lump, ga-lump.*

I leaned forward, folded my hands on the table.

And Junie began to tell us everything.

Chapter 6

"IT HAPPENED just like you said," Junie said, looking up at us with an anguished expression I read as fear and pain.

"Michael died?" I asked her. "He is, in fact, *dead?*"

"Can I start at the beginning?" Junie asked Conklin.

"Sure," Rich told her. "Take your time."

"See, I didn't know who he was at first," Junie said. "When Michael called to make the date, he gave me a fake name. So when I opened the door and there he was—oh, my God. The boy in the bubble. He'd come to see *me!*"

"What happened next?" I asked.

"He was really nervous," Junie said. "Shifting from one foot to the other. Looking at the window like someone could be watching him. I offered him a drink, but he said no, he didn't want to forget anything. He said that he was a virgin."

Junie bowed her head and tears spilled out of her eyes, dropped to the table. Conklin passed her the box of tissues, and we looked at each other in shock as we waited her out.

"A lot of boys are virgins when they come to me," she said at last. "Sometimes they like to pretend that we're having a date, and I make sure it's the best date they ever had."

"I'm sure," Conklin murmured. "So is that what happened with Michael? He pretended he was on a date?"

"Yeah," Junie said. "And as soon as we got into the bedroom, he told me his real name—and I told him mine!

"He got a real kick out of that, and then he started telling me about his life. He was a champion chess player on the Internet, did you know that? And he didn't act like a celebrity. He was super *real.* I started to think we were on a date, too."

"You got around to having sex with him, Junie?" I asked.

"Well, sure. He put the money on the night table, and I took off his clothes, and we had, you know, just started when—when he had to stop. He said he was in pain," Junie said, touching her chest with the flat of her palm. "And I knew about his heart, of course, but I hoped it would pass."

And then she broke down, put her arms on the table, her head in her arms, and sobbed as though she'd really cared.

"He got worse," Junie choked out. "He was saying, 'Call my dad,' but I couldn't *move.* I didn't know *how* to call his father. And if I had, what would I say? That I was a prostitute? His dad was *Governor Campion.* He would've put me in jail forever.

"So I held Michael in my arms and sang to him," Junie told us. "I hoped he'd start to feel better," she said, lifting her tearstained face. "But he got worse."

Chapter 7

THE MUSCLE TWITCHING in Conklin's jaw was the only outward sign that he was as stunned by Junie's confession as I was.

"How long did it take for Michael to die?" he asked Junie Moon.

"I don't know. Maybe a couple of minutes. Maybe a little more. It was awful, *awful*," Junie said, shaking her head at the memory. "About then, that's when I called my boyfriend."

"You called your *boyfriend*?" I shouted. "Is he a *doctor*?"

"No. But I needed him. And so Ricky came over, and Michael had passed away by then, so we put him into the bathtub. And then Ricky and I talked for a long time about what to do."

I wanted to scream, *You moron! You might have saved him! Michael Campion might have lived.* I wanted to shake her. Slap her bimbo face—so I got a grip on myself, sat back, and let Conklin keep the ball rolling.

"So what did you do with his body, Junie? Where is Michael now?"

"I don't know."

"What do you mean, you don't know?" I said, getting up from my chair, making a racket with it, taking a couple of laps around the table.

Junie started speaking quickly, as if by talking fast she'd get to the end of her story and it would all be over.

"After a few hours, Ricky decided to cut up his body with a knife. It was the most horrible thing I could ever imagine—and I grew up on a farm! I was throwing up and crying," Junie said, looking as though she might do it *now.*

I pulled out my chair again, put my butt in the seat, determined not to scare the little hooker even as she shocked me to the bone.

"But once we started cutting, there was no way back," Junie said, pleading to Conklin with her eyes. "I helped Ricky put Michael's body into about eight garbage bags, and then we piled the bags into Ricky's truck. It was like five in the morning. And no one was around."

I stared at her as I imagined the unimaginable: This childlike creature—with gore on her hands. The body of Michael Campion in bloody chunks.

I heard Conklin say, "Go on, Junie. We're with you. Get it all off your chest."

"We drove up the coast a few hours," Junie said, now telling the story as if she were recalling a dream. "I fell asleep, and when I woke up, Ricky was saying, 'This is the end of the line.' We were parked in the back of a McDonald's, and there were some Dumpsters back there.

"That's where we left the garbage bags."

"What town? Do you know?" I asked.

"Not really."

"Think," I snapped.

"I'll *try.*"

Junie gave us her boyfriend's name and address, and I wrote it all down. Rich passed her a pad of paper and asked her if she'd like to make her statement official.

"Not really," she said, seeming empty and exhausted. "So...will you drive me home now?"

"Not really," I repeated back at her. "Stand up and put your hands behind your back."

"You're *arresting* me?"

"Yes. We are."

Even on the tightest notch, the cuffs were loose around her wrists.

"But—I told you the truth!"

"And we appreciate it," I said. "Thank you very much. You're under arrest for tampering with evidence and interfering with a police investigation. That should hold you for now."

Junie was crying again, telling Conklin how sorry she was and that it wasn't her fault. I was scanning the map in my mind, imagining the towns along the coast, the six hundred McDonald's restaurants in Northern California.

And I was wondering if there was a chance in the world that we'd ever recover Michael Campion's remains.

Chapter 8

AT JUST AFTER MIDNIGHT, I was sitting on a kitchen stool watching Joe put pasta on to boil. Joe is a big, gorgeous guy, over six feet, dark hair, bright blue eyes, and now he was standing at the stove in his blue boxers, his hair rumpled and his dear face creased with sleep. He looked husband-y and he loved me.

I loved him, too.

That's why Joe had just moved to San Francisco from DC, ending our tumultuous long-distance relationship in favor of starting something new and maybe permanent. And although Joe had rented a fantastic apartment on Lake Street, a month after his move he'd brought over his copper-bottomed cook-ware and started sleeping in my bed five nights a week. Luckily, I'd been able to move up to the third floor of my building to give us a little more room.

Our relationship had gotten richer and more loving, exactly what I'd hoped for.

So I had to ask myself—why was the en-gagement ring Joe had given me still in its black velvet box, diamonds blazing in the dark?

Why couldn't I just say yes?

"What did Cindy tell you?" I asked him.

"Verbatim? She said, 'Here's *Martha.* Lind-say got a break in the *Campion* case and she's *on* it. Tell. Her. She wrecked our *week-end,* and I'm calling her in the morning for a *quote.* And she'd better give me a *good* one.'"

I laughed at Joe's imitation of Cindy, who is not only my friend, but also the top reporter on the *Chronicle*'s crime desk.

"It's either tell her everything," I said, "or tell her nothing. And for now, it's nothing."

"So, fill me in, Blondie. Since I'm wide-awake."

I took a deep breath and told Joe all about

Junie Moon; how she'd denied everything for two hours before telling us to turn off the camera, then talking about her "date" with Michael and his apparent heart attack; and how instead of calling 911, Junie had sung Michael Campion a lullaby as his heart bucked to a halt and killed him.

"Oh, for God's sake."

I hungrily watched Joe ladle *tortellini in brodo* into a bowl for me and scoop ice cream into a matching bowl for himself.

"Where's the body?" Joe asked me, pulling out a stool and sitting beside me.

"That's the sixty-million-dollar question," I said, referring to the reported size of the Campion fortune. I told Joe the rest of it: Junie's dazed speech about Michael Campion's dismemberment, the subsequent run up the coast with her boyfriend, and the eventual body dump behind a fast food restaurant— *somewhere.*

"You know, Conklin read Junie her rights when we brought her in for questioning," I mused. "And it pissed me off.

"Junie wasn't in custody, and I was sure if she was Mirandized, she wouldn't talk. And frankly, I *believed* what she said at first, that everything she knew about Michael Campion she'd read in *People* magazine. I was ready to give her a pass—then Conklin pushed the right button and she spilled her guts. It was a good thing that he'd read her her rights."

I shook my head thinking about it. "Rich has such confidence for a young cop, not to mention an astonishing way with women," I said, warming to the subject. "And it's not just that he's great-looking, it's that he's very respectful. And he's very *smart.* And women just want to tell him everything..."

Joe reached for my empty bowl and stood up, abruptly.

"Honey?"

"It's getting so I feel like I know this guy," Joe said over the sound of water running in the sink. "I'd like to meet him sometime."

"Sure—"

"What do you say we go to bed, Lindsay?" he said, cutting me off. "It's been a long night."

Chapter 9

AT AROUND EIGHT the next morning, we found Ricky Malcolm jiggling his key into the front door of a shabby apartment house on Mission Street. He made us as cops and tried to take off, so we scuffled with him on the sidewalk and convinced him to come to the Hall.

"You're not under arrest," I'd said, escorting him to our car. "We just want to hear your side of the story."

Ricky was in "the box" now, glaring at me with his weird, wide-spaced green eyes, tattooed arms crossed over his chest, his face blanched with the nocturnal pallor of a man who hadn't seen broad daylight in years.

Within the forest of tattoos on Malcolm's right arm was a red heart with the initials *R.M.* The heart was impaled on the hook of a crescent moon. Malcolm looked predatory and violent, and now I was wondering if Junie's story of Michael Campion's death was true.

Had Campion really died of natural causes?

Or had this freak walked in on Michael and Junie—and killed him?

Malcolm's sheet showed three arrests, one conviction, all for possession. I slapped the folder closed.

"What can you tell us about Michael Campion?" I asked him.

"What I read in the papers," he said.

The interview went on in this vein for a couple of hours, and since Conklin's charms had no effect on Ricky Malcolm, I took the lead. I was trying to get him to say anything, even lies that we could use to trip him up later, but Ricky was stubborn or cagey or both. He denied any knowledge of Michael Campion, alive or dead.

I blinked first.

"I think I understand what happened, Ricky,"

I said. "Your girlfriend was in big trouble, and so you had to help her out. Pretty understandable, I guess."

"What are you talking about?"

"The body, Ricky. You remember. When Michael Campion died in Junie's bed."

Malcolm snorted. "Is she saying that actually happened? And that I had something to do with it?"

"Junie *confessed,* you understand," Conklin said. "We know what happened. The kid was *dead* when you got there. That wasn't your fault, and we're not putting that on you."

"This is a joke, right?" Malcolm said. "Because I don't know what the hell you're talking about."

"If you're innocent, help us," I said. "Where were you on January twenty-first from midnight until eight that morning?"

"Where were *you?*" he shot back. "You think I remember where I was three months ago? I can tell you this. I wasn't helping Junie out of a jam with a dead john. You guys really crack me up." Malcolm sneered. "Don't you know that Junie's playing you?"

"Is that right?" I said.

"Yeah! She's *romantic,* you know? Like a

girl in the 'I Can't Believe It's Not Butter' commercial. Junie wants to *believe* that she did Michael Campion before he croaked—"

I heard the tap on the glass I'd been waiting for.

Malcolm was saying to Conklin, "I don't care what she told you. I didn't cut anyone. I never dumped any freaking body parts anywhere. Junie just likes the attention, man. You should know by now when a whore is lying to you. Charge me, dude, or I'm outta here."

I opened the door, took the papers from Yuki's hand. We exchanged grins before I closed the door and said, "Mr. Malcolm, you're under arrest for tampering with evidence and interfering with a police investigation."

I fanned the search warrants out on the table. "By this time tomorrow, *dude,* you won't have a secret in the world."

Chapter 10

WHILE RICKY MALCOLM SLEPT in a holding cell on the tenth floor at 850 Bryant, I opened the door to his second-floor, one-bedroom apartment over the Shanghai China restaurant on Mission. Then Conklin, McNeil, Chi, and I stepped inside. A faint stink of decomposing flesh hit me as soon as I crossed the threshold.

"Smell that?" I said to Cappy McNeil. Cappy had been on the force for twenty-five years and had seen more than his share of dead.

He nodded. "Think he left one of those bags of body parts behind?"

"Or maybe he just kept a souvenir. A finger. Or an ear."

McNeil and his partner, the lean and resourceful Paul Chi, headed for the kitchen while Conklin and I took the bedroom.

There was a pull-shade in the one window. I gave it a yank and it rolled up with a bang, throwing Ricky Malcolm's boudoir into a dim morning light. The room was a study in filth. The sheets were bunched to one side of the stained mattress, and cigarette butts floated inside a coffee mug on the nightstand. Dinner plates balanced on the dresser and the television set, forks congealed in the remains of whatever Malcolm had eaten in the last week or two.

I opened the drawer in the nightstand, found a couple of joints, assorted pharmaceuticals, a strip of Rough Riders. McNeil came into the room, looked around, said, "I like what he's done with the place."

"Find anything?"

"No. And unless Ricky dismembered Campion with a four-inch paring knife, the blade's not in the kitchen. By the way, the smell is stronger in here."

Conklin opened the closet, searched pockets and shoes, then went to the dresser. He tossed out T-shirts and porn magazines, but I was the one who found the dead mouse under a steel-toed work boot behind the door.

"Whoaaa. I think I found it."

"Nice door prize," McNeil cracked.

Four hours went by, and after turning over every stinking thing in Malcolm's apartment, Conklin sighed his disappointment.

"There's no weapon here."

"Okay, then," I said. "I guess we're done."

We stepped out into the street as the flat-bed truck pulled up to the curb. CSIs hooked up Malcolm's '97 Ford pickup, and we stood by as the truck rattled noisily up the hill on the way to the crime lab. McNeil and Chi took off in their squad car, and Conklin and I got into ours.

Conklin said, "I'll bet you a hundred bucks, or dinner— your choice, Lindsay—"

I laughed at his girl-magnet smile.

"I'll bet you Michael Campion's DNA is somewhere inside the bed of that truck."

"I don't want to bet," I said. "I want you to be right."

Chapter 11

JUNIE MOON'S PAINTED LADY looked tired and dull that afternoon as the sky darkened and a fine rain swept the city. Conklin lifted up the crime scene tape that was strung across Junie's front door and I ducked under it, signed the log, and entered the same room where Conklin and I had interviewed the fetching young prostitute late the night before.

This time we had a search warrant.

The sound of hammers slamming into ceramic tile led us to the bathroom on the second floor, where CSIs were tearing up the floors and walls in order to get to the bathtub plumbing. Charlie Clapper, head of our CSU, was standing in the hallway outside the bathroom door. He was wearing one of his two dozen nearly identical herringbone jackets, his salt-and-pepper hair was neatly combed, and his lined face was somber.

"Curb your expectations, Lindsay. There's enough splooge in this whorehouse to tie up the lab for a year."

"We just need one hair," I said. "One drop of Michael Campion's blood."

"And I'd like to see Venice before it sinks into the sea. And as long as we're wishing on stars here, I'm still pining for a Rolls Silver Cloud."

There was a leaden sound as the CSI working behind and under the tub dismantled the trap. As the tech bagged the plumbing, Conklin and I went back to Junie's bedroom.

It wasn't the pigpen Ricky Malcolm slept in, but Junie wasn't a tidy homemaker either. There were dust balls under the furniture, the mirrored walls were smudged, and the dense gray carpet had the oily look of a floor mat in a single dad's minivan.

A CSI asked if we were ready, then closed the curtains and shut off the overhead light. She waved the wand end of the Omnichrome

1000 in a side-to-side pattern across the bedspread, carpet, and walls, each pass of her wand showing up pale blue splotches indicating semen stains everywhere. She shot me a look and said, "If the johns saw this, they'd never take off their clothes in this girl's house, guaranteed."

Conklin and I walked downstairs toward the sound of the vacuum cleaner, watched the CSIs work, Conklin shouting to me over the vacuum's motor, "Three months after the fact, what do we expect? A sign saying, 'Michael Campion died here'?"

That's when we heard the clank of metal against the vacuum cleaner nozzle. The CSI turned off the motor, stooped, pulled a steak knife from under the skirt of a velvet-covered sofa—just where Conklin and I had been sitting last night.

The investigator held out the steak knife with his gloved hand so that I could see the rust-colored stain on the sharp, serrated blade.

Chapter 12

I WAS STILL SAVORING the discovery of the knife when my cell phone rang. It was Chief Anthony Tracchio, and his voice was unusually loud.

"What is it, Tony?"

"I need the two of you in my office, *pronto.*"

After a short volley of useless quibble, he hung up.

Fifteen minutes later, Conklin and I walked into Tracchio's wood-paneled corner suite and saw two well-known people seated in the leather armchairs. Former governor Connor Hume Campion's face looked swollen with rage, and his much younger wife, Valentina, appeared heavily sedated.

The front page of the Sunday *Chronicle* was on Tracchio's desk. I could read the headline upside down and from ten feet away: SUSPECT QUESTIONED IN CAMPION DISAPPEARANCE.

Cindy hadn't waited for my quote, damn it.

What the hell had she written?

Tracchio patted his Vitalis comb-over and introduced us to the parents of the missing boy as Conklin and I dragged chairs up to his massive desk. Connor Campion acknowledged us with a hard stare. "I had to read this in the *newspaper*?" he said to me. "That my son died in a *whorehouse*?"

I flushed, then said, "If we'd had anything solid, Mr. Campion, we would have made sure you knew first. But all we have is an anonymous tip that your son visited a prostitute. We get crank tips constantly. It could have meant nothing."

"*Could have meant?* So what's in this paper is *true*?"

"I haven't read that article, Mr. Campion, but I can give you an update."

Tracchio lit up a cigar as I filled the former

governor in on our last eighteen hours: the interviews, our futile searches for evidence, and that we had Junie Moon in custody based on her uncorroborated admission that Michael had died in her arms. When I stopped talking, Campion shot out of his seat, and I realized that while we had assumed Michael was dead, the Campions hadn't given up hope. My sketchy report had given the Campions more of a reality check than they'd expected.

It wasn't what they wanted to hear.

Campion turned his red-faced glare on Tracchio, a man who'd become chief of police by way of an undistinguished career in administration.

"I want my son's body returned to us if every dump in the state has to be picked through by hand."

"Consider it done," Tracchio said.

Campion turned to me, and I saw his anger collapse. Tears filled his eyes. I touched his arm and said, "We're on this, sir. Full-time. We won't sleep until we find Michael."

Chapter 13

JUNIE MOON SLIPPED into the interview room at the women's jail wearing an orange jumpsuit and new worry lines in her youthful face.

She was followed by her attorney, Melody Chado, a public defender who would make a reputation for herself with this case, no matter how the jury decided. Chado wore black—tunic, pants, jet-black beads—and was all business. She settled her client in a chair, opened her black leather briefcase, and looked at her watch several times as we waited. There were only four chairs in the small room, so when my good friend Assistant

District Attorney Yuki Castellano entered a moment later, there was standing room only.

Yuki put down her briefcase and leaned against the wall.

Ms. Chado appeared to be just out of law school. She was probably only a couple of years older than her client, who looked so vulnerable I felt a little sorry for her—and that pissed me off.

"I've advised my client not to make any statements," Ms. Chado said, setting her young face with a hard-ass expression that I found hard to take seriously. "This is your meeting, Ms. Castellano."

"I've talked with the DA," Yuki said. "We're charging your client with murder two."

"What happened to 'illegal disposal of a body'?" Chado asked.

"That's just not good enough," Yuki snapped. "Your client was the last person to see Michael Campion alive. Ms. Moon never called medical emergency or the police—and why not? Because she didn't care about Campion's life or death. She only cared about herself."

"You'll never get an indictment for murder," Chado said. "There's enough reasonable doubt in your theory to fill the ocean."

"Listen to me, Junie," Yuki said. "Help us locate Michael's remains. If it can be determined in autopsy that his heart attack would have killed him no matter what you did, we'll drop the murder charge and pretty much get out of your life."

"No deal," Chado interjected. "What if she helps you find his body and it is so decomposed that his heart is just rotted meat? Then you'll have a demonstrable connection to my client and she'll be *screwed.*"

I reevaluated Melody Chado as she fought with Yuki. Chado had either had a great education, grown up in a family of lawyers — or both. Junie fell back in her chair, turned a shocked face toward her breathless attorney. I guessed that Chado's description had blown off whatever romance was left of Junie's memory of Michael Campion.

"I want to hear about the knife, Junie," Rich said, steering the interview to our only piece of evidence.

"The knife?" Junie asked.

"We found a knife under your sofa. Looks like bloodstains on the blade. It'll take a few days to get the DNA results, but if you help us, Ms. Castellano will take that as another sign of your cooperation."

"Don't answer," said Melody Chado. "We're *done.*"

Junie was looking at Rich, and she was talking over her attorney. "I thought the knife went into one of the garbage bags," she said to my partner. "So I don't know what knife you found. But listen, I remember the name of the town."

"Junie, that's enough. That's all!"

"I think it was Johnson," Junie said to Rich. "I saw a sign when we got off the highway."

"Jackson?" I asked. "Was it Jackson?"

"Yes. That's right."

"You're sure about that? I thought you said you drove up the coast."

"I'm pretty sure. It was late, I got confused. I wasn't trying to remember," she told me, her eyes downcast. "I was trying to forget."

Chapter 14

THE TOWN OF JACKSON was known for its cowboy cookouts and craft fairs. It also had a sizable dump. It was just after noon, and the smell of rot was rising as the sun cooked the refuse. Gulls and buzzards circled the trash dunes that filled our view out to the foothills.

Sheriff Oren Braun pointed out the square acre of landfill he'd had cordoned off—the approximate section where waste had been unloaded at the end of January.

"Soon as I got the call from the governor I had my boys on it," Braun told me and Conklin. "'Pull out the stops,' that's what he said."

We were looking for eight black plastic

garbage bags in a sea of black plastic garbage bags. A hundred yards uphill, a dozen members of the sheriff's department were picking very slowly through the three thousand tons of refuse piled twenty feet high, and the dump foreman was assisting the dog handler, who followed behind his two cadaver dogs as they trotted over the site.

I was trying to maintain some optimism, but that was tough to do in this grim landscape. I mumbled to Rich, "After three months out here, all that'll be left of Michael's corpse will be ligaments and bones."

And then, as if I'd telepathically cued them, the dogs alerted.

Conklin and I joined the sheriff in stepping cautiously toward the frenzied, singing hounds.

"There's something in this bag," their handler said.

The hounds had located a plastic shopping bag, the thin supermarket kind. I stooped down, saw that the plastic had been ripped, that the contents were wrapped in newspaper. I parted the newspaper wrapper. Saw the decomposing remains of a newborn child. The baby's skin was loose and greenish, the soft tissues eaten by rats, so that it was no longer possible to tell if it was a boy or a girl. The date on the newspaper was only a week old.

Someone hadn't wanted this child. Had it been smothered? Was it stillborn? At this stage of decomposition, the ME might never know. Rich was crossing himself and saying a few words over the baby's remains when my Nextel rang.

I walked downhill as I answered the call, glad to turn my eyes from the terrible sight of that dead child.

"Tell me something good, Yuki," I begged her. "Please."

"Sorry, Lindsay. Junie Moon has recanted her confession."

"*No.* Come on! Michael *didn't* die in her arms?" My roiling innards sank. Right now, all we *had* was Junie's confession.

How could she take that back?

"Yeah. Now she says that she had nothing to do with Michael Campion's death and disappearance. She's saying that her confession was coerced."

"Coerced? By whom?" I asked, still not getting it.

"By you and Conklin. The mean ol' cops made her confess to something that never, ever happened."

Chapter 15

SUSIE'S CAFÉ IS KIND OF a cross between Cheers and a tiki hut bar on a beach in St. Lucia. The food is spicy, the steel drums are live, the margaritas are world-class, and not only do the waitresses know our names, they know enough to leave us alone when we're into something—as Cindy and I were now.

We were in our booth in the back room, and I was glaring at Cindy over my beer.

"You understand? Talking to you off the record is 'leaking.' Just saying to you that I was working a new *lead* on the Campion case could jam me up!"

"I swear, Lindsay, I didn't use what you

said. I didn't need a quote from *you* because
I got the story from *upstairs.*"

"How is that possible?"

"Management has a source and I did an
interview and I am not telling you with *whom,*"
she said, setting down her beer mug hard on
the table. "But the point is, you can hold your
head up, Linds, because you told me nothing. Okay? That's the *truth.*"

I'm several years older than Cindy, and
we've had a big sister, little sister thing since
she crashed my crime scene a few years
back and then helped me close the case.

It's hard to be friends with reporters when
you're a cop. Their rationalized "public's need
to know" gives bad guys the heads-up and
messes up jury pools.

You can't truly trust reporters.

On the other hand, I love Cindy, and I
trusted her 99 percent of the time. She sat
across from me in her snow-white silk sweater,
blond curls bouncing like mattress springs,
her two overlapping front teeth making her
pretty features look even prettier. She looked
totally innocent of my accusation, and she
was holding her ground.

"Okay," I said through clenched teeth.

"Okay and I'm sorry?"

"Okay. I'm sorry."

"Good. You're forgiven. So, can you tell me what's happening on this case?"

"You're a funny girl, Cindy," I said, laughing and waving my hand so that Yuki and Claire could see us from the doorway.

Claire was so far along in her pregnancy she couldn't fit in the booth anymore. I got up, moved a chair to the head of the table for Claire, as Yuki slipped in beside Cindy. Lorraine took our orders, and as soon as she'd left us, Yuki said to Cindy, "*Whatever* I say, even if it's in the public domain, it's *off* the record."

Claire and I cracked up.

"What a pain. See, people think it's actually an *advantage* that I know you guys," Cindy said, sighing dramatically.

"The hearing to suppress Junie Moon's confession? It went great," Yuki told us. "Since Junie had been Mirandized when she confessed, the judge says it's admissible."

"Excellent," I said, letting out my breath. "A break for the good guys."

"Yuki, you're trying her for a murder and you don't have a body?" Claire asked.

"It's a circumstantial case, but circumstantial cases are won all the time," Yuki said.

"Look, I'd be happier with physical evidence. I'd be happier if Ricky Malcolm made any kind of a corroborating statement.

"But the powers that be are piling on the pressure. Plus, we can win."

Yuki stopped to gulp down some beer, then carried on.

"The jury is going to believe Junie's confession. They're going to believe her, and they're going to hold her responsible for Michael Campion's death."

Chapter 16

I WAS AT MY DESK in the squad room the next day when Rich came in after lunch smelling of garbage.

"Tough morning in Jackson?"

"Yeah, but I think the sheriff's digging for his fifteen minutes of fame before the Feds take over the search. He's got it under control."

I pinched my nose as Rich pulled out his chair, folded his long legs under his side of the desk, and opened his container of coffee.

"Phone records show that yes, Junie did call Malcolm at 11:21 on the night Michael went missing. And she called him *every* night at about that time."

"Girl stays in touch with her boyfriend."

"And Clapper called," I told my partner. "The prints on the knife are Malcolm's."

"Yeah? That's excellent!"

"But the blood is bovine," I said.

"It's a steak knife. He ate a steak."

"Yep. It gets worse."

"Hang on." Rich dumped a couple of sugars into his coffee, stirred, slugged it down. "Okay. Hit me."

"There's no blood or tissue in the bathtub, and the hair we sent out came back with no match. Furthermore, there's no sign that anyone tried to cover up the blood. No bleach."

"Great," my partner said, scowling. "What is this? The perfect crime?"

"There's more and worse. There's no trace of blood in or on Malcolm's vehicle, no hairs consistent with Michael's."

"So I was wrong about the truck. You should have bet me, Lindsay. We'd be having dinner tonight—on me."

I grinned and said, "You would have showered first, I suppose."

But my mood could hardly be lower. I was going to have to call the Campions and tell them that we still had no physical evidence, and that Junie Moon had recanted her confession and we'd had to kick Ricky Malcolm.

"You want to call Malcolm and tell him he can have his truck back?"

Rich picked up his phone, called Malcolm, got no answer.

We took a drive out to the crime lab at Hunter's Point Naval Yard, opened all the car windows on the way, and let the wind air out my partner's clothes. At the lab, I signed a release for the truck, and after three more unanswered calls to Ricky Malcolm, we drove to his apartment.

Rich yelled, "Police," and knocked loudly on Malcolm's door until a small Chinese man came out from the restaurant downstairs.

He shouted up to us, "Mr. Malcolm gone. He paid his rent and leave on motorcycle. You want to see mess upstairs?"

"We've seen it, thanks."

"He's gone, all right," I muttered to Conklin as we got into the squad car. "Ricky Malcolm. Sleaze. Slob. Easy rider. Criminal freakin' mastermind. Coming soon to a town near you."

Chapter 17

I WAS RIPPED out of a dream and my lover's arms by Jacobi's voice on the phone saying, "Get dressed, Boxer. Conklin is five blocks away. He's picking you up at your door."

Jacobi clicked off before giving me details, but this much I knew: someone had died.

It was just after midnight when Conklin nosed our squad car onto the lawn of a smoldering house in the 3800 block of Clay Street in Presidio Heights. Four fire rigs and an equal number of patrol cars were already parked in front of the Greek Revival, the wind whipping smoke into a vortex at an inside corner of the house. Dazed bystanders clustered across the street, watching the firefighters douse the charred remains of what had once been a beautiful home in this upscale neighborhood.

I pulled my canvas jacket closed, ducked under the water spouting from a fire hose just as the generators on the front lawn fired up. Conklin was ahead of me as we mounted the front steps. He badged the cop at the door and we entered the scorched carcass of the house.

"Two victims, Sarge," said Officer Pat Noonan. "First doorway on your right. DRT."

Dead right there.

I asked, "Has the ME been called?"

"She's on her way."

It was darker inside the house than out. The room Noonan indicated had been a large den or family room. I flicked my flashlight beam over piles of furniture, bookshelves, a large TV. Then my light caught a pair of legs on the floor.

They weren't attached to a body.

I screamed, "Noonan! Noonan! What the hell is this?" I waved my torchlight around, catching a second body a few feet from the torso of the first, just inside the doorway.

Noonan came into the den with a firefighter behind him, a young guy with the name Mackey stenciled on his turnouts.

"Sarge," Mackey said, "it was me. I was trying to reel in my line, but it caught. That's how I discovered the DB."

"So you *dragged* the body?"

"I, um, didn't know that if I picked up the body by the legs, it would fall apart," Mackey said, his voice cracking from smoke inhalation and probably fear.

"Did you move the entire victim, Mackey, or just the legs? Where was the body lying?"

"He, she, or it was in the doorway, Sarge. Sorry."

Mackey backed out of the room, and he was right to get away from me. What the fire hadn't destroyed, the water and the firefighters had. I doubted we'd ever know what had happened here. I heard someone call my name, and I recognized his voice as the glare of a handheld lantern came toward me.

Chuck Hanni was an arson investigator, one of the best. I'd met him for the first time a few years ago when he'd come to a fire directly from a Rotary Club dinner.

He'd been wearing pale khakis at the time, and he'd walked through a smoking house from the least burned rooms to the fire's point of origin. He'd taught me a lot about crime detection at a fire scene that night, but I still didn't know how he'd kept those khakis clean.

"Hey, Lindsay," Hanni said now. He was wearing a jacket and tie. There were comb marks in his fine black hair and burn scars running from his right thumb up into his sleeve. "I've got a working ID on this couple."

My partner stood up from where he'd been crouched beside one of the victims.

"Their names are Patty and Bert Malone," Conklin said, something in his voice I couldn't read. The corpses were so burned, they were featureless. He saw the question in my eyes.

"I've been in this house before," Conklin told us. "I used to know these people."

Chapter 18

I STARED AT MY PARTNER as embers fell from the ceiling of the den and the crackle of water against smoking wood competed with the radio static and the shouts of the fire-fighters.

"I was close to their daughter when I was in high school," Conklin said. "Kelly Malone. Her parents were great to me."

"I'm so sorry, Rich."

"I haven't seen them since Kelly went off to the University of Colorado," Conklin said. "This is going to kill her."

I put my hand on his shoulder, knowing that we were going to treat the Malones' deaths as homicides unless it was proven otherwise. Upstairs, the fire crew was doing mop-up and overhaul, dismantling the second-story ceiling, putting out hot spots under the eaves.

"The security system was off," Hanni said, joining us. "The fire department got the call from a neighbor. The fire started in this room," he said, pointing out the furniture that had been burned low to the ground.

He looked around the room at the mounds of plaster and debris. "After we sift through all this, I'll let you know if I find anything, but I think you can pretty much kiss off any notes or fingerprints."

"But you'll try anyway, right?" Conklin said.

"I said I would, Rich."

Last thing we needed was for Conklin to get into a fight. I asked him what the Malones were like.

"Kelly said her dad could be a prick," Rich said, "but when you're eighteen, that could've meant he wouldn't let her stay out with me past eleven."

"Tell me whatever else you remember."

"Bert sold luxury cars. Patty was a homemaker. They had money, obviously. They entertained a lot. Their friends seemed nice—regular parents, you know."

"Wouldn't be the first time regular people turned out to be twisted," Hanni muttered.

A sweep of headlights drew my eyes toward the broken plate glass window. The coroner's van joined the fleet of law enforcement and fire department vehicles on the street.

Noonan called out to me. "I checked out the bedroom on the second floor, Sarge. There's a safe in the closet. The lock and the safe are intact, but the door is open—and the safe is empty."

Chapter 19

"ROBBERY WAS THE MOTIVE for *this*?" Conklin shouted as Claire stepped into the den with her assistant in tow.

Before Claire could say, "Who died?" I reached out to her for a hug, said into her ear, "Conklin knew the victims."

"Gotcha," she said.

As Claire unpacked her scene kit, I told her about the manhandled corpse. Then I stepped out of her way as she took pictures of both bodies with her old Minolta, two shots from every angle.

"There are two doors to this room," she said as her camera flashed. "Chuck, you say that this room was the point of origin. But the victims stayed in here. Why was that?"

"They could've been caught by surprise," Hanni said. He was cutting samples from the carpet, putting fibers into K-packs.

"If they were drinking and fell asleep, maybe a cigarette dropped down into the couch cushions."

Hanni explained what was still so hard to believe—that a fire could fill a room this size with smoke in less than a minute, that sleeping people could wake up coughing, be unable to see, get disoriented.

Chuck said, "Someone says, 'Let's go this way.' Other person says, 'No, it's this way.' Maybe someone falls. Smoke inhalation gets them. Boom, they're down, and they're unconscious. These two people were dead inside a couple of minutes."

Conklin came back into the room holding a book in his gloved hand. "I found this on the staircase."

He handed the book to me. "*Burning in Water, Drowning in Flame.* Charles Bukowski. Is this poetry?"

I opened the book to the title page, saw an inscription written there in ballpoint pen.

"This is Latin," I said to my partner, sounding out the words. "Annuit Cœptis."

"That's pronounced *chep-tus*," Conklin said. "It's a motto inscribed on the dollar bill right above that symbol of the pyramid thing with the eye. Annuit Cœptis. 'Providence favors our undertaking.'"

"You know Latin?"

He shrugged. "I went to Catholic school."

I said, "So, what do you think, Rich? Is the firebug leaving us a message? That God's okay with this?"

Conklin looked around at the destruction, said, "Not the God I believe in."

Chapter 20

AT THREE THAT MORNING, Hanni, Conklin, and I watched the fire department board up the Malones' windows and put a lock on the front door. The onlookers were back in their beds, and as the sounds of hammering cracked through the otherwise silent neighborhood, Hanni said, "There was a fire four months ago in Palo Alto, reminds me of this one."

"How so?"

"Big, expensive house. The alarm was turned off. Two people died in the living room, and I had the same question in my mind: Why didn't they leave?"

"Panic, disorientation, like you were saying."

"Yeah, it happens. But since I wasn't called in until a couple of days after the fire, I couldn't know for sure. Drives me crazy when the fire department decides the fire's accidental without an arson investigator present. Anyway, the bodies were cremated at the funeral home by the time I was called."

"You thought the fire was suspicious?" Conklin asked.

Hanni nodded. "I still think so. The victims were good people, and they had money. But no one could come up with a motive for anyone to kill Henry and Peggy Jablonsky—not revenge, not insurance fraud, not even 'I hate your face.' So I was left with a bad feeling and no way to tell if the fire was arson or a spark flew out of the fireplace and lit up the Christmas tree."

"I guess you didn't find a book with Latin written inside," I said.

"By the time I got there, the 'evidence eradication unit' had tossed a mountain of soaked household goods into the front yard. I guess I wasn't looking for a book."

Hanni took his car keys out of his pocket. "Okay, guys, I'm done. See you in a few hours."

Rich and I stood back from his van as the arson investigator drove off.

"Were you able to reach Kelly?" I asked my partner.

"Got her answering machine. I didn't know what to say." He shook his head. "I finally said, 'It's Rich. Conklin. I know it's been a long time, Kelly. But. Um. Could you call me right away?'"

"That's good. That's fine."

"I don't know. She'll either think I'm a psycho for calling her at one in the morning to say hello after twelve years. Or, if she knows that I'm a cop, I just scared the hell out of her."

Chapter 21

THE ME'S OFFICE is in a building connected to the Hall of Justice by a breezeway out the back door of the lobby. Claire was already working in the chilly gray heart of the autopsy suite when I got there at 9:30 that morning. She said, "Hey, darlin'," barely looking up as she drew her scalpel from Patty Malone's sternum to her pelvic bone. The dead woman's hands were clenched and her legless body was carbonized.

"She hardly looks like a person," I said.

"Bodies burn like candles, you know," Claire said. "They become part of the fuel." She clamped back the burned tissue.

"Did the blood tests come back from the lab?"

"About ten minutes ago. Mrs. Malone had had a couple of drinks. Mr. Malone had antihistamine in his blood. That could have made him sleepy."

"And what about carbon monoxide?" I was asking as Chuck Hanni came through reception and back to where we stood over the table.

"I picked up the Malones' dental records, Claire," he said. "I'll put them in your office."

Claire nodded, said, "I was about to tell Lindsay that the Malones lived long enough to get a carbon monoxide in the high seventies. The total body X-rays are negative for projectiles or obvious broken bones. But I did find something you're going to want to see."

Claire adjusted her plastic apron, which just barely spanned her ever-thickening girth, and turned to the table behind her. She pulled back the sheet exposing Patricia Malone's legs and touched a gloved finger to a thin, barely discernible pink line around one of the woman's ankles.

"This unburned skin right here?" said Claire. "Same thing on Mr. Malone's wrists. The skin was *protected* during the blaze."

"Like from a ligature?" I asked.

"Yes, ma'am. If it was just the ankles, I'd say maybe Mrs. Malone was wearing socks, but on her husband's wrists, too? I'm saying these are from ligatures that burned away in the fire. And I'm calling the cause of death asphyxia from smoke inhalation," Claire said. "Manner of death, homicide."

I stared at the fire-ravaged body of Patty Malone.

Yesterday morning she'd kissed her husband, brushed her hair, made breakfast, maybe laughed with a friend on the telephone. That night she and her husband of thirty-two years had been tied up and left to die in the fire. For some period of time, maybe hours, the Malones had known they were going to die. It's called psychic horror. Their killers had *wanted* them to feel fear before their horrible deaths.

Who had committed these brutal murders—and why?

Chapter 22

JACOBI AND I would have cared about the Malones' deaths even if Conklin hadn't known them. The fact that he had been close to them once made us feel as if we'd known them, too.

Jacobi was my partner today, standing in for Conklin, who was picking up Kelly Malone at the airport. We stood on the doorstep of a Cape Cod in Laurel Heights only a dozen blocks from where the Malone house waited for the bulldozer. I rang the bell and the door was opened by a man in his early forties wearing a sweatshirt and jeans, looking at me like he already knew why we were there.

Jacobi introduced us, said, "Is Ronald Grayson at home?"

"I'll get him," said the man at the door.

"Mind if we come in?"

Grayson's father said, "Sure. It's about the fire, right?" He opened the door to a well-kept living room with comfy furniture and a large plasma-screen TV over the fireplace. He called out, "Ronnie. The police are here."

I heard the back door slam hard, as if it were pulled closed by a strong spring.

I said, "*Shit.* Call for backup."

I left Jacobi in the living room, ran through the kitchen and out the back door. I was on my own. Jacobi couldn't run anymore, not with his bad lungs and the twenty pounds he'd put on since his promotion to lieutenant.

I followed the kid in front of me, watched him leap the low hedge between his house and the one next door. Ronald Grayson wasn't an athlete, but he had long legs and he knew the neighborhood. I was losing ground as he took a hard right behind a detached garage.

I yelled out, *"Stop where you are. Put your hands in the air,"* but he kept running.

I was in a jam. I didn't want to shoot at him, but clearly the teenager had a reason for running. Had he set that fire?

Was this boy a killer?

I called in my location and kept running, clearing the garage in time to see Grayson Jr. cross Arguello Boulevard and slam into the hood of a patrol car. He slid down to the pavement. A second cruiser pulled up as two uniforms got out of the first. One officer grabbed the kid by the back of his shirt and threw him over the hood, while another kicked the boy's legs apart and frisked him.

That's when I noticed that Ronald Grayson's face had turned blue.

"Oh, Christ!" I yelled.

I pulled Grayson off the car and bent him over. I grabbed the kid from behind, wrapped my right hand around my left fist, found the spot under his rib cage, and gave him three hard abdominal thrusts. He coughed, and three small bags fell from his mouth to the asphalt. The bags were filled with rock cocaine.

I was heaving, too. And I was furious. I cuffed the kid roughly, arrested him for possession with intent to sell. And I read him his rights.

"You *idiot*," I panted. "I have a *gun.* Get it? I could have shot you."

"Fuck *you.*"

"You mean 'thank you,' don't you, asshole?" said one of the uniforms. "The sergeant here just saved your worthless life."

Chapter 23

JACOBI AND I already knew two things about Ronald Grayson: that he'd had crack in his possession when we arrested him, and that this kid had called in the Malone fire.

Had he also *set* that fire?

Sitting in the interrogation room across from Ronald Grayson, I thought about another teenager, Scott Dyleski. Dyleski was sixteen when he'd broken into a woman's home in Lafayette, stabbed her dozens of times, and mutilated her body because in his twisted mind, he imagined that she'd taken delivery of his drug paraphernalia and was keeping it from him. Dyleski was wrong, psychotic, and the murder should never have happened.

But it had.

And so, as I looked at fifteen-year-old Ronald Grayson with his clear skin and dark hair, drumming his fingers on the tabletop as though *we* were wasting *his* time, I wondered if he had doomed Pat and Bert Malone to horrific deaths so he could steal their stuff in order to buy drugs. I used my most patient and friendly tone of voice.

"Ron, why don't you tell us what happened?"

"I have nothing to say."

"That's your right," Jacobi grumbled menacingly.

Jacobi is five eleven, over two hundred pounds of well-marbled muscle, with lumpy features, hard gray eyes, gray hair, and a shiny gold badge. I would have expected the kid to show either fear or deference, but he seemed unfazed by our bad lieutenant.

"I don't want to talk to you about the cocaine, you little shit," Jacobi said, breathing into Grayson's face. "But, man-to-man, tell us about the fire and we'll help you with the coke charge. Do you understand me? I'm trying to *help* you."

"Leave me alone, you fat fuck," Grayson said.

Before Jacobi could smack the back of the kid's head, his father, Vincent Grayson, and his lawyer blew through the door. Grayson was livid. "Ronnie, don't say anything."

"I didn't, Dad."

Grayson turned his fury on Jacobi. "You can't talk to my son unless I'm with him. I know the law."

"Save it, Mr. Grayson," Jacobi growled. "Your imbecile son is under arrest for using and dealing, and I haven't talked to him about the drugs at all."

The lawyer's name was Sam Farber, and from his business card I gathered that he had a one-man practice doing wills and real estate closings.

"I'm telling *you* and *you* and *you*," Jacobi said, pointing his finger at the kid, his father, and the lawyer in turn. "I'll lobby the DA on Ronald's behalf if he helps us with the fire. That's our only interest in him right now."

"My client is a good Samaritan," Farber said, dragging up a chair, squaring his leather briefcase with the edge of the table before opening it. "His father was with him when he made the call to 911. That's all he had to do with it, end of story."

"Mr. Farber, we all know that the person who calls in the fire has to be cleared of setting it," I said. "But Ronald hasn't convinced us that he had nothing to do with it."

"Go ahead, Ron," said Farber.

Ron Grayson's eyes slid across mine and up to the camera in the corner of the room. He mumbled, "I was in the car with my dad. I smelled smoke. I told Dad which way to drive. Then I saw the fire coming out of that house. I dialed 911 on my cell and reported it. That's all."

"What time was this?"

"It was ten thirty."

"Mr. Grayson, I asked your son."

"Look. My son was sitting next to me in the car! The guy at the gas station can vouch for Ronnie. They cleaned the windshields together."

"Ronnie, did you know the Malones?" I asked.

"Who?"

"The people who lived in the house."

"Never heard of them."

"Did you see anyone leaving the house?"

"No."

"Ever been to Palo Alto?"

"I've never been anywhere in Mexico."

"Do you have enough, Inspectors?" Farber said. "My client has cooperated fully."

"I want to take a look at his room," I said.

Chapter 24

SHRINKS SAY THAT ARSON is a masculine sexual metaphor; that setting the fire is the arousal phase, the blaze itself is the consummation, and the hoses putting out the blaze are the release. It may be true, because almost all arsonists are male, and half of them are teenage boys.

Jacobi and I left young Ronnie Grayson in lockup and returned to the Grayson house with Ron's father. We parked again in the driveway of the small house, wiped our feet on the welcome mat, and said hello to Grayson's mother, who looked frightened and eager to please. We turned down an offer of coffee, then excused ourselves so that we could thoroughly search Ronald Grayson's bedroom.

I had a few objects in mind, specifically a reel of fishing line, fire accelerant, and anything that looked like it had belonged to the Malones.

Ronnie's dresser was of the hand-me-down Salvation Army kind: chipped wood, four big drawers and two small ones. There was a lamp on the top surface, some peanut jars full of coins, a pile of scratched-off lottery tickets, a car magazine, and a red plastic box holding the kid's orthodontic retainer. There was a night-light in the socket near the door.

Jacobi grunted as he tipped the mattress over, then took the drawers from the dresser and systematically dumped them onto the box springs of Ronnie's bed. The search resulted in a half-dozen girlie magazines, a small bag of pot, and a crusty pipe. Then we opened his closet and upended his hamper of dirty laundry.

We examined it all, the tighty-whiteys, the jeans, and the dirty socks, all smelling of sweat and youth, but not of gasoline or smoke. I looked up to see that Vincent Grayson was now watching from the doorway.

"We're almost done here, Mr. Grayson," I said, smiling. "We just need a sample of Ronnie's handwriting."

"Here," Grayson said, picking up a spiral notebook from the stack of books on the night table.

I opened the notebook and could see without having to turn it over for handwriting analysis that Ron Grayson's elaborate, artsy lettering was not a match for the Latin inscription I'd seen on the flyleaf of the book of poetry left on the Malones' stairs. Ron Grayson had a solid alibi, and I had to reluctantly accept that he'd told us the truth. But what bothered me about this boy, more than his being a smart-ass punk with a drug habit, was that he hadn't asked about the Malones.

Was it because he'd lied about knowing them?

Or because he just didn't care?

"What about my son?"

"He's all yours," said Jacobi over his shoulder just before he slammed the screen door on his march out of the house.

I said to Grayson, "Ron will be in your custody until he's arraigned on the coke charge, and we'll speak to the DA on his behalf like we said we'd do.

"But I'd ground Ronnie, if I were you, Mr. Grayson. He's breaking the law and doing business with criminals. If he were my son, I wouldn't let him out of my sight for a minute."

Chapter 25

FOR THE NEXT FOUR HOURS, Jacobi and I rang doorbells in the Malones' neighborhood, badging the rich and richer, scaring them brainless with the questions we asked. Rachel Savino, for instance, lived next door to the Malones in a sprawling Mediterranean-style house. She was an attractive brunette of about forty, wearing tight slacks, a tighter blouse, the break in the tan line on her ring finger telling me she was a recent divorcée.

She wouldn't let us inside her door.

Savino eyed my dusty blue trousers, man-tailored shirt, and blazer, and did a double take when she noticed my shoulder holster. She barely acknowledged Jacobi. I guess we didn't look like residents of Presidio Heights. So Jacobi and I stood on her terra-cotta steps while her pack of corgis jumped and yelped around us.

"Have you ever seen this young man?" I asked, showing her a Polaroid of Ronald Grayson.

"No. I don't think so."

"Have you seen anyone hanging around or driving by who may have seemed out of place in the neighborhood?" asked Jacobi.

"Darwin! Shut up! I don't think so, no."

"Any kids or cars that don't belong here? Anyone ring your bell who seemed out of place? Any suspicious phone calls or deliveries?"

No. No. No.

And now she was asking questions. What about the fire at the Malones'? Was it an accident as she had assumed? Were we suggesting that it was deliberately set?

Had the Malones been *murdered*?

Jacobi said, "We're just doing an investigation, Ms. Savino. No need to get your bowels in an—"

I cut him off. "What about your dogs?" I asked. "Did they set up any kind of an uproar last night at around ten thirty?"

"The fire trucks made them crazy, but not before."

"Do you find it unusual that the Malones didn't arm their security system?" I asked.

"I don't think they even locked their *doors*," she said. And that was her final word. She opened her door, let in the pack, then closed it firmly behind her, locks and bolts clicking into place.

Over four hours and a dozen interviews later, Jacobi and I had learned that the Malones were churchgoing, well liked, generous, friendly, and got along well together, and not one soul knew of anyone who hated them. They were the perfect couple. So who had killed them, and why?

Jacobi was grousing about his aching feet when my cell phone rang. Conklin, calling from the car.

"I looked up that pyramid symbol on the dollar bill," he said. "It has to do with the Masons, a secret society that goes back to the 1700s. George Washington was a Mason. So was Benjamin Franklin. Most of the Founding Fathers."

"Yeah, okay. How about Bert Malone? Was he a Mason?"

"Kelly says no way. She's with me now, Lindsay. We're heading over to her parents' house."

Chapter 26

WE PULLED UP to the curb at the same time Conklin's car arrived. His passenger-side door swung open before he'd come to a full halt and a young woman sprang out, dashed across the lawn toward the remains of the Malone house.

Conklin called out to her, but she didn't stop. For a second she turned her face into our headlights and I saw her clearly. She was a whip-slim thirty-year-old in tights, a tiny skirt, a brown leather jacket. Her hair was copper-red, worn in a braid down her back long enough to sit on. Wisps of hair had escaped the braid, haloing her face in our headlights. Halo was the right word.

Kelly Malone had the face of a Madonna.

Conklin ran to catch up to her, and by the time Jacobi and I reached them, Conklin had opened the fire department lock on the front door. With dusky light filtering in through the caved-in roof, we walked Kelly Malone through the skeleton of her parents' house. It was a wrenching tour, Conklin staying close to Kelly's side as she cried out, "Oh, *God,* oh, *God.* Richie, no one could have hated them this much. I just don't believe it."

Kelly avoided the library where her parents had died. Instead she walked upstairs into a smoky cone of light. Conklin was beside Kelly when she crossed the threshold into what remained of the master suite. The ceiling had been punched out with pike poles. Soot and water had destroyed the furnishings, the carpeting, and the photos on the walls.

Kelly lifted a wedding portrait of her parents from the floor, wiped it with her sleeve. The glass hadn't broken, but water had seeped in along the edges.

"I think this can be restored," she said, tears cracking her voice.

"Sure. Sure, that can be done," Conklin said.

He showed Kelly the open safe in the closet, asked her if she knew what her parents had kept there.

"My mom had some antique pieces that my grandmother left her. I guess the insurance company will have a list."

Jacobi asked, "Miss Malone. Anyone you can think of who might have had a grudge against your parents?"

"I haven't lived here since I was eighteen," she said. "My dad could throw his weight around at the dealership, but if there'd been any serious threats, my mom would've told me.

"Are you sure this wasn't an accident?" she asked, turning pleading eyes on my partner.

Conklin said, "I'm sorry, Kelly. This was no accident."

He put his arms around her and Kelly sobbed against his chest. Her pain was breaking my own heart. Still, I had to ask. "Kelly, who stands to benefit the most from your parents' death?"

The young woman recoiled as if I'd struck her.

"Me," she shouted. *"I* do. And my *brother.*

You *got* us. We hired a hit man to kill our parents and torch the house so that we could inherit our parents' *money.*"

I said, "Kelly, I'm sorry. I wasn't implying that you had anything to do with this." But she talked only to Conklin after that.

As I stood downstairs with Jacobi, I overheard Rich tell Kelly about the note in Latin written on the flyleaf of a book.

"Latin? I don't know anything about that. If Mom or Dad wrote anything in Latin, it would have been the first and only time," said Kelly Malone.

Chapter 27

HAWK HAD TRAPPED the roach under an eight-ounce drinking glass upended on top of the worktable he used as a desk in his room at home. The roach was a *Blatta orientalis,* the oriental cockroach, about an inch long and shiny black, commonly found in all the swank houses of Palo Alto.

But although this bug was common, he was special to Hawk.

"You're doing very well, Macho," Hawk said to the roach. "It's not much of a bug's life, I have to admit, but you're worthy of the challenge."

Behind Hawk, Pidge lay on Hawk's bed

reading background material on an upcoming class project: a three-dimensional fax, something that had probably been inspired by the "beam me up, Scotty" technology from *Star Trek* and was now becoming manifest in the real world.

How it worked was, a machine scanned an object at point A, and an identical object was created by a laser carving out a replica from another material at point Z. But Pidge knew all of this. He'd seen the demo. So what he was doing was busywork while he waited for Hawk to get his lazy ass in gear.

"You're behind on the dialogue," Pidge grumbled. "Instead of talking to that bug, you should do the dialogue before your stupid parents come home."

"Why don't you like Macho?" Hawk asked. "He's been living on air and whatever body oil might have been on the desk for, um, sixteen days. Haven't you, Macho? It's damned admirable, Pidge. Seriously."

"Seriously, bro, you're an asshole."

"You're missing the nobility of the experiment," Hawk continued, unfazed. "A creature descended from insects that've been around since the first ass crack of time. Macho is living on *air*. And if he lives for four more days,

I'm going to release him. That's the deal I made with him. I'm thinking up his reward right now.

"Macho," Hawk said, bending over to examine his captive. He tapped on the glass. The roach's antennae waved at him. "I'm thinking chocolate brownie, dude."

Pidge got up off the bed, strode to the desk, reached over Hawk's shoulder, and removed the glass. He made a fist, pounded it down on the bug, squashing it on the Formica table. One of Macho's legs moved in a postterminal reflex.

"*Hey!* Why'd you *do* that, man? Why'd you—"

"Ars longa, vita brevis. Art is long, dude. Life is short. Write the dialogue for the freaking chapter, bug man, or I'm outta here."

Chapter 28

CONKLIN AND I had been working pawn-shops all day, hoping one of Patricia Malone's pieces of jewelry would turn up—and if it did, maybe we'd have a lead we could work with. The last shop on our list was a hole between two bars on Mission, the Treasure Coop.

I'm not sure the owner heard the bell ring over the door when Conklin and I came in, but he picked up our reflection from one of the dozens of mirrors hanging on the walls and came out from the back of the store. His name was Ernie Cooper. He was a slablike man from the Vietnam era and seemed to fill up his store. Cooper had a gray ponytail and an iPod in his shirt pocket, cords dangling from his ears. There was the bulge of a gun under his jacket.

While Conklin showed Cooper the insurance company's photos of Patricia Malone's Victorian jewelry, I looked around at the innumerable trophies, guitars, and out-of-date computers, and at the stuffed monkey with a lamp coming out of its back perched on a plant stand. A collection of fetal pigs was lined up on one of the four counters, which were filled with wedding bands, watches, military medals, and junk gold chains.

Ernie Cooper whistled when he saw the photos.

"What's all this worth, a couple hundred thou?"

"Something like that," Conklin said.

"Nobody brings this kind of stuff to me, but who am I looking for, anyway?"

"Maybe him," Conklin said, slapping down a photocopy of the Polaroid of Ronald Grayson.

"I can keep this?" Cooper asked.

"Sure, and here's my card," Rich said.

"Homicide."

"That's right."

"So, this was what? Armed robbery?"

Conklin smiled. "If this kid comes in, if *any-one* comes in with this stuff, we want to know."

I noticed a small black-and-white snapshot stuck to the cash register. It was a photo of Ernie Cooper coming down the steps of the Civic Center Courthouse, and he was wearing the uniform of the SFPD. Cooper saw me looking at the photo, said, "I notice your shield says Boxer on it. I used to work with a guy by that name."

"Marty Boxer?"

"That's the guy."

"He's my father."

"No kidding? I couldn't stand him, no offense."

"No offense taken," I said.

Cooper nodded, rang up a "no sale," and put the photocopies of Grayson's picture and the Malone jewelry along with Conklin's card inside the cash register, under the tray.

"I've still got the instincts, maybe even better than when I was on the Job. I'll put out the word. If I hear anything," Ernie Cooper said, shoving the cash drawer shut, "I'll be in touch. That's a promise."

Chapter 29

THE SKY HAD TURNED GRAY while Conklin and I were inside Ernie Cooper's pawnshop. Muted thunder grumbled as we walked to Twenty-first Street, and by the time we got into the squad car, the first fat drops of rain splattered against the windshield. I cranked up the window, pinching the web between my thumb and forefinger. I shouted, "Damn," with more vehemence than was absolutely necessary.

I was frustrated. So was Rich. The long workday had netted us exactly nothing. Rich fumbled with the keys, his brow wrinkled, exhaustion weighing him down like a heavy coat.

"You want me to drive?"

My partner turned off the ignition and sighed, threw himself back into the seat.

"It's okay," I said. "Give me the keys."

"I can drive. That's not the problem."

"What is?"

"It's you."

Me? Was he mad at me for questioning Kelly?

"What did *I* do?"

"You just *are,* you know?"

Aw, no. I tried to ward off this conversation by imploring him with my eyes and thinking, *Please don't go there, Richie.* But the pictures flashed into my mind, a strobe-lit sequence of images of a late work night in LA that had turned into a reckless, heated clinch on a hotel bed. My body had been screaming yes, yes, yes, but my clearer mind slammed on the brakes—and I'd told Richie no.

Six months later, the memory was still with us inside the musty Crown Victoria, crackling like lightning as the rain came down. Richie saw the alarm on my face.

"I'm not going to *do* anything," he insisted. "I would never do anything—I'm just not good at keeping what I feel to myself, Lindsay. I know you're with Joe. I get it. I just want you to know that I've got this arrow through my heart. And I would do anything for you."

"Rich, I can't," I said, looking into his eyes, seeing the pain there and not knowing how to make it right.

"Aw, jeez," he said. He covered his face with his hands, screamed, "Aaaaaargh." Then he pounded the steering wheel a couple of times before reaching for the keys and starting up the car again.

I put my hand on his wrist. "Rich, do you want another partner?"

He laughed, said, "Delete the last forty-two seconds, okay, Lindsay? I'm an idiot, and I'm sorry."

"I'm serious."

"Forget it. Don't even think about it."

Rich checked the rearview mirror and turned the car into the stream of traffic. "I just want to remind you," he said, cracking a strained smile, "when I worked with Jacobi, nothing like this ever happened."

Chapter 30

THE POPULATION OF COLMA, California, is heavily skewed toward the dead. The ratio of those below the ground to those breathing air is about twelve to one. My mom is buried at Cypress Lawn in Colma, and so is Yuki's mom, and now Kelly Malone and her brother, Eric, were burying their parents here, too.

It would appear to the casual observer that I was alone.

I'd put flowers at the base of a pink granite stone engraved with "Benjamin and Heidi Robson," two people I didn't know. Then I sat on a bench a hundred feet from where the grass-scented breeze puffed out the tent flaps where the Malones' funeral was in progress.

My Glock was holstered under my blue jacket, and the microphone inside my shirt connected me to the patrol cars at the entrance to the cemetery. I was watching for a gangly kid named Ronald Grayson, or someone else who looked out of place, a stranger with a penchant for torture and murder. It didn't happen every time, but some killers just had to see the end of the show, give themselves a psychic round of applause.

I hoped we'd get lucky.

As I watched, Kelly Malone stood in front of the group of fifty, her back to the pair of coffins. And I saw Richie, his eyes on Kelly as she gave her eulogy. I couldn't hear any of the words, just the sound of a lawn mower in the distance and soon enough, the squeal of the winch lowering the coffins into the ground. Kelly and her brother each tossed a handful of earth into their parents' graves and turned away.

Kelly went into Rich's arms and he held her.

There was something touching and familiar about the way they fit together, as if they were still a couple. I felt a painful pull in my gut and tried to shut it down. When Kelly and Rich left the tent and walked with the priest in my direction, I turned before they came close enough to see my eyes.

I spoke into the collar of my shirt, said, "This is Boxer. I'm coming in."

Chapter 31

LOCATED TWO BLOCKS AWAY and across the street from the Hall of Justice, MacBain's Beers O' the World Pub is the eatery of choice for lawyers and cops, anyone who doesn't mind sitting at a table the size of a dinner napkin and shouting over the noise.

Cindy and Yuki had a table by the window, Yuki with her back against the doorjamb, Cindy's chair rocking whenever the man sitting behind her moved his rump. Cindy was mesmerized by the perpetual motion of Yuki's hands as she talked. Yuki had twenty minutes to eat and run, and she'd stepped up her usual warp-speed conversational style to fit the time allowed.

"I begged for this case," Yuki said, folding one of Cindy's french fries into her mouth, telling Cindy what she'd told her many, many times before. "Three people were in line ahead of me, and Red Dog is letting me run with it because of Brinkley."

Red Dog was Yuki's boss, Leonard Parisi, the red-haired and legendary bulldog deputy DA, and Brinkley was Alfred Brinkley, "the Ferry Shooter," and Yuki's first big case for the DA's office. The Brinkley trial had been heated, the public enraged that a mentally disabled man with a gun had mowed down five citizens who'd been enjoying a Saturday afternoon ferry ride out on the bay.

"It's so ironic," Yuki said to Cindy. "I mean, with Brinkley, I had nothing *but* evidence. The gun, the confession, two hundred eye-witnesses, the fricking videotape of the shootings. With Junie Moon it's just the opposite." She stopped talking long enough to slurp her diet cola through a straw down to the bottom of the glass.

"We've got *no* murder weapon, *no* body, *no* witnesses—just a recanted confession from a girl who is so dim it's hard to believe she's bright enough to boil eggs. I don't dare lose, Cindy."

"Take it easy, hon. You're not going to—"

"I could. I could. But I'm not going to do it. And now, Junie's got a new lawyer."

"Who?"

"L. Diana Davis."

"Oh man, oh man, oh man."

"Yep. Cherry on top. I'm up against a big-time feminist bone crusher. Oh! I forgot. This writer is doing a book on Michael Campion. He's been following me around all week. His name is Jason Twilly, and he wants to talk to you."

"Jason Twilly? The author of those true-crime blockbusters?"

"Yep. That's the one."

"Yuki. Jason Twilly is a giant. He's a star!"

"That's what *he* says." Yuki laughed. "I gave him your number. He just wants some background on me. I don't care what you tell him as long as you don't tell him that I'm freaking *out*."

"You're a piece a' work, ya know?"

Yuki laughed. "Oops. Gotta go," she said, putting a twenty under a corner of the bread basket.

"Got a meeting with Red Dog," Yuki said.

"There were three people in line in front of me, Cindy. You know, if he'd assigned this case to anyone but me, I would've offed myself. So I only have one option. I have to *win.*"

Chapter 32

CINDY ENTERED THE BAR inside the St. Regis Hotel at the corner of Third and Mission in the vibrant SoMa district. Jason Twilly was staying there for the course of the trial, and it was definitely the place to be.

Twilly stood as Cindy approached his table. He was tall, thin, a young forty-three, with striking features Cindy recognized from his book jackets and recent profile in *Entertainment Weekly.*

"Jason Twilly," he said, stretching out his hand.

"Hi, I'm Cindy Thomas." She slipped into the chair Twilly pulled out for her. "Sorry I'm late."

"No problem. I was glad to have a minute to do some quiet thinking."

She'd researched Twilly before this meeting, adding to what she already knew—that he was very smart, calculating, talented, and a little ruthless. One journalist had written that Twilly was picking up where Truman Capote left off with *In Cold Blood*, noting that Twilly had a rare talent for getting into the minds of killers, humanizing them so that readers regarded the killers almost as friends.

Cindy wanted to let herself enjoy the ambience of the place and the fun of being with Jason Twilly, but she couldn't let down her guard. She was worried for Yuki, wondered how Twilly would depict her and if it was a good or bad thing for her friend that Twilly's next book would be about Michael Campion. Even though Yuki didn't seem to care, Cindy knew that Twilly would use anything she said to benefit himself.

"I just finished *Malvo*," Cindy said, referring to Twilly's bestselling account of the DC sniper who, with his manipulative partner, had killed ten people and terrified the capital in a month-long crime spree.

"What did you think?" Twilly smiled. It was a charming smile, lopsided, the left side of his mouth twitching up, making the corners of his eyes crinkle.

"Made me think about teenage boys in a whole new way."

"I'm going to take that as a compliment," Twilly said. "What can I get you to drink?"

Twilly called the waitress over, ordered wine for Cindy, mineral water for himself, and told Cindy that since Yuki was going to be prosecuting Junie Moon, he wanted to get some sense of her from her closest friend.

"I spoke with some of her professors at Boalt Law," Twilly told Cindy. "And a couple of her former colleagues at Duffy and Rogers."

"She was really on the fast track to partnership there," Cindy said.

"So I've heard. Yuki told me that after her mother was killed at Municipal Hospital, she lost her taste for civil cases and went over to the prosecutorial side."

"Exactly."

"So what does that make her? Fierce? Vengeful?"

"You're baiting me," Cindy said, laughing. "Did Yuki strike you as vindictive?"

"Not at all," Twilly said, giving her another of his electrifying smiles. "Well, maybe the fierce part is true," he said. "I've seen Yuki in action at the Brinkley thing."

Twilly told Cindy that he already had a contract from his publisher to do the unauthorized biography of Michael Campion when, suddenly, Michael disappeared.

"It looked like an unsolved mystery until the cops found a suspect and indicted Junie Moon," Twilly said. "And when I heard that Yuki Castellano was going to try Moon for Michael's murder, it just couldn't get any better. It should be a hell of a trial. And what I love about Yuki Castellano is that she's passionate and she's fearless."

Cindy nodded in agreement, said, "L. Diana Davis had better bring her best game."

"That's interesting," said Twilly. "Because what I was thinking is that it's good that Yuki has a friend like you, Cindy. I mean, with all due respect to Yuki, Davis is going to slaughter her."

Part Two

HABEAS CORPUS
(Produce the Body)

Chapter 33

YUKI PUSHED THROUGH the swarm of reporters and cameramen who had surrounded her from the moment she parked her car. She hoisted her handbag higher on her shoulder, clutched her briefcase, and headed toward the street, the press moving along with her, shouting out questions about how she thought the trial would go, and if there was anything she wanted to say to the public.

"Not now, people," she said. "I don't want to keep the court waiting." She lowered her head, pushed her way out to the intersection, saw the fleet of satellite vans and setups on Bryant: local news, cable news vans, and crews from the networks, all there to cover the trial of Junie Moon.

The light changed and Yuki crossed the street encased in a mob of reporters. She headed toward the Hall of Justice and into the thicker crowd that had gathered at the foot of the granite steps. Len Parisi had told her he'd field the media, but right now he was locked in a pileup on the freeway, an oil truck having tipped over, blocking all lanes, cars slamming into each other in the slick.

Parisi didn't know when he'd get to court, and so Yuki had spent a half hour going over her opening with him again on the phone, and that's why she'd cut the time too close. She marched up the courthouse steps, eyes front, said, "Can't talk now, sorry," to a gang of reporters at the heavy steel-and-glass front doors to the Hall of Justice. And then, to her chagrin, *she couldn't open the doors.*

A reporter from KRON held the door for her, then winked and said, "See ya later, Yuki."

Yuki tossed her briefcase and handbag on the security desk, walked through the metal detectors without incident, accepted "luck of the Irish" wishes from the guard, and made

for the stairs, taking them quickly to the second floor.

The golden oak-paneled courtroom was
packed to the walls. Yuki took her seat at
the prosecution table, exchanged looks with
Nicky Gaines, her second chair. He was
big-eyed and sweaty, looked as apprehen-
sive as she was.

"Where's Red Dog?" he asked.

"He's in a traffic jam."

The bailiff cut the murmur in the courtroom
by calling out, "All rise," and Judge Bruce
Bendinger entered the room through a panel
behind the bench, took his seat between Old
Glory and the California state flag.

Bendinger was sixty, gray-haired, recovering from knee replacement surgery. His shirt
collar above his robe was pink, his striped
satin tie was a vibrant ultramarine. Yuki noted
Bendinger's rumpled brow and thought the
normally easygoing judge looked a bit frayed
before the trial had even begun. His knee
must be giving him hell.

Yuki half listened as Bendinger instructed
the jury. She used the moment to sneak a
look at Junie Moon's formidable, take-
no-prisoners attorney, L. Diana Davis.

Davis was in her fifties, with twenty years'

experience as a champion of abused and victimized women. This morning she appeared in one of her trademark red suits, wearing bright lipstick and chunky jewelry, her short hair in crisp, silver waves. Davis looked ready for prime time, and Yuki didn't doubt for a minute that she would get it—full frontal TV cameras, bouquets of microphones at every recess.

And that's when Yuki realized that it wasn't just the pressure of the trial and the scorching focus of the media that was freaking her out; it was Junie Moon, sitting now beside her attorney, looking so fawnlike and vulnerable in her cream-colored suit and lace collar that she was almost transparent.

"Are you ready, Ms. Castellano?" Yuki heard the judge say.

Yuki said, "Yes, Your Honor." She pushed back her chair and stepped to the lectern, checking that her one-button jacket was closed, feeling her spine prickle as two hundred pairs of eyes focused on her. Yuki paused for a moment in the well of the courtroom.

She smiled at the jurors and then began the most important opening statement of her career.

Chapter 34

"LADIES AND GENTLEMEN," Yuki said from the lectern. "A great deal is known about the life of Michael Campion. Sadly, this trial is about his *death.* On the night of January twenty-first, Michael Campion, an eighteen-year-old boy, went to the home of the defendant, Junie Moon—and he was never seen again.

"Ms. Moon is a prostitute.

"I mention her profession because Ms. Moon met Michael Campion *because* she's a prostitute. The People will introduce witnesses, classmates of the victim, who will tell you that Michael had long planned to visit Ms. Moon because he wanted to lose his virginity. On January twenty-first, he did visit her.

"And Michael Campion not only lost his *virginity,* he lost his *life.*

"It shouldn't have happened.

"Michael shouldn't have died. And if the defendant had behaved responsibly, if she'd acted *humanely,* Michael might be here with us today.

"What happened to Michael Campion after he entered Ms. Moon's house was told to us in detail by the defendant herself," Yuki said, pointing to Junie Moon. "She told us. She admitted to the police that she let Michael Campion die and that she treated his remains like *garbage.*"

Yuki walked the jury through Junie Moon's admission of guilt, her description of Michael Campion's death, grisly dismemberment, and disposal in a Dumpster. Then she turned her back on the defendant, left her notes on the lectern, and took thoughtful, measured steps to the jury box.

She no longer cared that Red Dog wasn't in the seat beside her or that half the room was filled with salivating reporters, and she didn't care that Junie Moon looked as innocent as a flower girl at a summer wedding.

She was focused purely on the jury.

"Ladies and gentlemen," she said. "The police developed information leading to the defendant three full months after Michael Campion disappeared. His remains were not recovered because it was just too late.

"The defense will tell you, 'No body, no crime,'" Yuki said. "The defense will say that the police must have bullied Ms. Moon, because she has since recanted her confession. The defense will say that the People have no case. *That's. Not. True.* We don't have to have physical evidence.

"We have circumstantial evidence, and lots of it."

Yuki walked the length of the jury box, trailing her hand along the railing, feeling the power and flow of her opening and that the jury was not only with her, they were waiting for every word. And she would give them everything they wanted.

"Ms. Moon is charged with tampering with evidence and with murder in the second degree," Yuki told the jurors. "In order to prove murder, we have to prove *malice.* This is how the law is worded. Malice can be inferred in that the person acted in such a way that you could construe them to have had 'an abandoned and malignant heart.' Think about that.

"An abandoned and malignant heart.

"The defendant told us that Michael Campion asked her to call for help and that she didn't do it—because it was more important to protect *herself.* She let him die when she might have saved him. That's the clearest possible example of an abandoned and malignant heart. That's why the People are charging Junie Moon with murder.

"And in the course of this trial, we will prove Junie Moon guilty beyond reasonable doubt."

Chapter 35

L. DIANA DAVIS put her hands on both sides of the lectern and wiggled it until it was centered on the jury box. Then she looked up at the jurors, said, "Good morning. I want to thank the prosecution for giving my opening statement for me.

"Saved us all a lot of time."

Davis warmed to the laughter in the gallery and was glad to see that a few of the jurors had joined in. She put one hand on her hip, smiled, and went on.

"Remember the advertising slogan? 'Where's the beef?' That's what I want to know, and you're going to want to know it, too. As the

People just told you, ladies and gentlemen, this is a noncase. If the young man in question weren't a celebrity, I doubt the DA would have the nerve to bring this case to trial.

"Ms. Castellano is right when she says no body, no crime.

"Not only is there no body, there's no weapon, and in this day of advanced forensic science, there isn't even a microscopic trace of evidence at the so-called crime scene. Oh, yes," Davis said as if it were an aside. "After an *intense,* and I would say mind-blowing, interrogation by the police, my client confessed to a crime she didn't commit.

"An expert witness will talk about this syndrome of false confessions, a sign of emotional battery, which is what happened to Ms. Moon. And Ms. Moon will tell you about the night of January twenty-first herself. All the prosecution has to present to you is the retracted confession of a terrified young woman who was intimidated by the interrogation of an aggressive, motivated team of homicide inspectors who had an agenda: to hang the disappearance of the governor's son on *someone.*

"They picked Junie Moon.

"Over the next few days, you will hear the preposterous case against her. There will be no DNA evidence, and Henry Lee won't be coming here with photos of blood spatter to tell you how this so-called crime went down.

"Even Ricardo Malcolm, Ms. Moon's former boyfriend, won't be called to testify for the prosecution, because he told the police that Junie never *met* Michael Campion. He said nothing happened.

"So what did happen to Michael Campion?

"We know—everyone in the free world knew—Michael Campion had a serious, congenital, and potentially fatal heart condition, and that he was living on borrowed time. After he left his house on the night of January twenty-first, *something* happened. We don't know what that something *was,* but it's not our job or yours to speculate.

"When you've heard this case in its entirety, the prosecution will ask you to find Ms. Moon guilty beyond reasonable doubt. And common sense will tell you that Ms. Moon is *not* guilty of any of the charges against her.

She's *not* guilty of tampering with evidence. She *didn't* help dismember a body in her bathtub or dispose of that body.

"And as sure as I'm standing in front of you, Junie Moon is *not* guilty of *murder.*"

Chapter 36

THE BAILIFF CALLED MY NAME and I got up from the bench in the hallway, stiff-armed the double doors of the vestibule to the courtroom, and strode up the aisle. Heads turned as I approached the witness stand. And I was reminded again that the case against Junie Moon would hang in large part on my testimony. And that L. Diana Davis was going to do her best to crush me.

I swore to tell the truth and took my seat, and my good friend Yuki asked me preliminary questions, setting up my time and grade as a police officer.

Then she asked, "Sergeant Boxer, did you

interview the defendant on April nine-teenth?"

"Yes. Inspector Richard Conklin and I first interviewed her in her house, and then later at the southern division of the SFPD, on the third floor of this building.

"Did she seem afraid or anxious or intimidated?"

"Actually, no. She seemed quite comfortable. In fact, she agreed to come to the Hall for questioning."

"At that time, did you ask her about Michael Campion?"

"We did."

"And what was her response?" Yuki asked.

"At first she told us that she had never met Michael Campion. Approximately two hours later, she asked us to shut off the video camera."

"And what happened after that?"

In answer to Yuki's questions, I told the jury what Junie had told me and Conklin — how the victim had expired, that she had called Ricky Malcolm, and what the two of them had done with Michael Campion's body.

"Did you have any reason to doubt this story?" Yuki asked.

"No. I found her quite credible."

"Did you interview the defendant at any other time?"

"Yes. We met with Ms. Moon a few days later at the women's jail. We hoped Ms. Moon might remember the name of the town where she and her boyfriend disposed of Mr. Campion's remains."

"And did she remember?"

"Yes. The town of Jackson, about three and a half hours northeast, in Amador County."

"So to be clear, this was a second interview?"

"Correct."

"Was the defendant under duress?"

"*Objection.* Calls for speculation," Davis sang out.

"Sustained," Judge Bendinger snapped.

"I'll rephrase," Yuki said. "Did you threaten the defendant? Deny her food or water or sleep?"

"No."

"She gave you this information of her own volition?"

"Yes."

"Thank you, Sergeant," Yuki said to me. "I have no further questions."

And then L. Diana Davis was in my face.

Chapter 37

TO MY SURPRISE, L. Diana Davis was petite, maybe five three, and I guessed that her close-up shots on the small screen and her reputation had made her seem larger than life.

"Sergeant Boxer," Davis said. "You've been a homicide inspector for over ten years. You've investigated countless homicides. You've interrogated innumerable suspects, and you knew that eventually you'd be sitting in a courtroom telling us what happened in the case against Junie Moon. Isn't that true?"

"Yes."

"So how did you get the defendant to confess, Sergeant? Tell her that accidents happen? That she wasn't culpable?"

I knew damned well to keep my answers short and blunt, but looking at Davis's expression, half kindly grandma, half bulldog, I felt a need to let my mouth do the talking.

"I may have said things like that. Interrogations aren't one size fits all. Sometimes you've got to raise your voice. Sometimes you've got to be sympathetic. And sometimes you've got to lie to a subject," I said. "There are legal boundaries for interrogations, and my partner and I stayed within those boundaries."

Davis smiled, turned, and walked toward the jury, turned back to face me.

"Is that so?" she said. "Now, you've testified that the defendant asked you to turn off the tape during your interrogation at the police station."

"That's right."

"So let me get this straight, Sergeant. You videotaped everything—up to the point when Ms. Moon 'confessed.' That confession is not on the tape."

"The defendant seemed reluctant to talk

because the camera was running. So when she asked me to turn it off, I did so. And then she told us what happened."

"So what are we to make of the fact that you recorded everything this young woman had to say *except her confession?* I guess you're suggesting that the defendant was being cagey when she asked you to shut off the camera," Davis said, shrugging her shoulders, sending a nonverbal message to the jury that she thought I was full of crap. "You're saying she was sophisticated enough to confess off the record."

"There is no such thing—"

"Thank you, Sergeant. That's all I have for this witness," said Davis.

Yuki shot to her feet, said, "Redirect, Your Honor."

"Proceed, Ms. Castellano," said the judge.

"Sergeant Boxer, are you required to tape a confession?"

"Not at all. A confession's a confession, whether it's written or verbal, on tape or off. I'd rather have a taped confession, but it's not required."

Yuki nodded.

"Did you have any idea what Ms. Moon

was going to tell you when she asked you to turn off the video camera?"

"Had no idea. I turned off the camera because she *asked* us to—and I thought it was the only way we were going to get the truth. And you know what, Ms. Castellano? It *worked*."

Chapter 38

YUKI WISHED ALL of her witnesses were as good as Rich Conklin. He was solid. He was believable. Made you think of a young military officer, a mother's good son. It didn't hurt that he was also good to look at. In answer to her questions, Conklin affably told the jury that he'd been with the SFPD for five years and that he'd been in the homicide division for the last two.

"Did you interview the defendant on the night of April nineteenth?" Yuki asked Conklin.

"Sergeant Boxer and I talked with Ms. Moon together."

"Did you have any preconceived notions about her guilt or innocence before you talked to her?"

"No, ma'am."

"Did you read Ms. Moon her Miranda rights?"

"Yes, I did."

"As I understand it, Ms. Moon wasn't in custody when you Mirandized her, so why did you warn her that anything she said could be used against her?"

"It was a gamble," Conklin told Yuki.

"When you say it was a gamble, could you explain what you mean to the jury?"

Conklin brushed his forelock of brown hair away from his eyes. "Sure. Suppose I say to a suspect, 'I want to interview you. Can you come down to the station?'

"And the suspect comes in of his or her own volition. That person doesn't have to answer our questions and can leave at any time. I don't have to Mirandize that person when we sit down to talk because they're not in custody."

Conklin sat back comfortably in his seat and continued, "But, see, if that subject then starts to get wary, he or she could ask for a lawyer, who would end the interview. Or that subject could simply leave. And we'd have to let her go because that person is not under arrest."

"If I understand you, Inspector, you were taking a precaution, so that if Ms. Moon incriminated herself, you'd already be covered by having told her that anything she said could be used against her?"

"That's right. I was thinking how Ms. Moon was our only witness, maybe a suspect in a serious crime, and I didn't want to take a chance that *if* she had something to do with Michael Campion's disappearance, we'd have to stop the interview and Mirandize her. That might have *ended* the interview. And we not only wanted the truth, we wanted to find Michael Campion."

"And did Ms. Moon ask for a lawyer?"

"No."

"Did she give you the details of Michael Campion's death and the disposal of his body?"

"Yes, she did."

"Inspector Conklin, what was her demeanor as she confessed to you and Sergeant Boxer?"

"She seemed sad and remorseful," Conklin said.

"And how did you determine that?"

"She cried," said Conklin. "She said she was sorry, and that she wished she could change everything that happened."

Chapter 39

"INSPECTOR CONKLIN," Davis said, smiling. "You sound like a very smart police officer."

Yuki tensed. She could almost see Davis setting the trap, baiting it, tying the trap to a tree. Conklin just looked at Davis until she spoke again.

"Isn't it true that from the beginning, the defendant denied that she'd ever met Michael Campion?"

"Yes, but ninety-nine times out of a hundred, a suspect is going to say they didn't do it."

"You've interviewed a hundred homicide suspects?"

"Figure of speech," Conklin said. "I don't know how many homicide suspects I've interviewed. Quite a few."

"I see," Davis said. "Is it a figure of speech to say that you and Sergeant Boxer tricked and bullied my client until she confessed?"

"Objection!" Yuki called out from her seat.

"Sustained."

"I'll rephrase. As we all know, Ms. Moon's 'confession,'" Davis said, making the universal symbol for quote marks with the first two fingers of each hand, "wasn't on tape, isn't that right?"

"That's right."

"So we don't know the tenor of that interview, do we?"

"I guess you just have to trust me," Conklin said.

Davis smiled, wound up for the pitch. "Inspector, did you take notes of Ms. Moon's statement?"

"Yes."

"I asked to see those notes during discovery," Davis said, "but I was told you no longer had them."

Conklin's cheeks colored. "That's right."

"I want to make sure I understand what you're telling us, Inspector," Davis said in the snotty tone she'd perfected over decades and was using now in an attempt to under-mine and humiliate Conklin.

"You were investigating a probable murder. As you told us, Ms. Moon was your primary witness, or maybe a suspect. You had no taped record, so you made a written record. That was so you could tell the court and the jury what the defendant said, right? And then you threw the notes away—can you tell us why?"

"I used my notes as the basis for my re-port. Once my report was typed, I didn't need them anymore."

"No? But what's a better record of that in-terview? The notes you took that night? Or the report you filled out a couple of days later? You're supposed to keep those notes, aren't you, Inspector?...Inspector?

"Your Honor, please direct the witness to answer my question."

Yuki clenched her fists under the table. She hadn't known Conklin had destroyed his notes, but while it wasn't kosher, homicide cops did it all the time.

Judge Bendinger shifted in his seat, asked Conklin to answer the question.

Reluctantly, Conklin said, "My notes would be more of a verbatim account, but—"

"But still, you felt it was appropriate to throw them out? Is there a shortage of storage space at the Hall of Justice? Were the file cabinets full, maybe?"

"That's ridiculous."

"It is, isn't it?" Davis asked, letting the question hang in the dead silence of the courtroom.

"Do you remember *where* you threw the notes? In the *garbage* perhaps, or out your car window? Maybe you flushed them down the *toilet?*"

"Your Honor," Yuki said. "Defense counsel is badgering the witness—"

"Overruled. The witness may answer," said Judge Bendinger.

"I *shredded* them," Conklin said, the cords in his neck straining against the white collar of his shirt.

"Please tell the jury why you shredded your notes."

Yuki saw the flash in Conklin's eye but was helpless to stop him from snapping, "The reason we get rid of our notes is so that shyster lawyers like *you* don't *twist* things around—"

Yuki stared at Conklin. She'd never seen him blow up before. Davis had manipulated him, and she was going to nail him to the wall.

"Inspector Conklin, is that how you behaved when you interviewed my client? Lose your temper like that?"

"*Objection,* Your Honor," Yuki called out.

"On what grounds?"

"Defense counsel is *objectionable.*"

Bendinger was unable to stifle a laugh. "Overruled. Watch it, Ms. Castellano."

Davis smiled, faced Conklin, one hand on her hip. "Only one more question, Inspector. Any other important evidence you *shredded* that would have exonerated my client?"

Chapter 40

STILL FEELING STUNG by Davis's cross-examination of Rich Conklin and the stress of the entire horrid day, Yuki left the Hall of Justice by the back door and walked several blocks out of her way, checking her Black-Berry as she walked.

She deleted messages, made notes for the file, sent an e-mail to Red Dog, who was now back in his home office asking for a report. She entered the All Day parking lot from the rear and had just opened the door of her brownish-gray Acura sedan when she heard someone call her name.

Yuki turned, frisked the crowded lot with

her eyes, saw Jason Twilly loping toward her against traffic on Bryant, calling out, "Yuki, hey, hang on a minute." Yuki reached into the car, put her briefcase on the passenger seat, and turned back to face the superstar writer, who was closing in.

Twilly looked fantastic, Yuki thought, as she watched him maneuver through the crowded parking lot. She liked everything about the way he put his act together: the cut of his hair, the Oliver Peoples glasses framing his intense dark brown eyes. Today he was wearing a fine blue shirt under a well-fitted gray jacket, and his pants were buckled with a plain Hermès belt that must've cost seven hundred dollars.

Twilly pulled up to where she stood with her car door opened between them, not even blowing hard from his run.

"Hey, Jason. What's wrong?"

"Not a thing," he said, eyes locking on hers. "I just wanted to tell you that I thought you rocked today."

"Thanks."

"No, I mean it. You're great on your feet, and it's smart the way you're handling the press. Davis is out there campaigning on the front steps and you're—"

"The defense has to spin this," Yuki said. "I have to prove Junie Moon is guilty, and that's not going to happen in front of the Hall."

Twilly nodded his agreement, said, "You know, I wanted to tell you that I overheard a conversation in the hallway, and what I heard is that Junie's a little slow, below average IQ."

"I don't get that impression," said Yuki, wondering what the hell Twilly was getting at. Was he working an angle? Or was her six months in the DA's office making her cynical?

Twilly set down his briefcase on the asphalt, took a soft leather eyeglass case from his breast pocket, removed a small square of cloth, and massaged the pollution off his Oliver Peeps.

"I gathered that Davis is going to get an expert shrink to tell the jury that Junie is dumb and suggestible and that the brutal cops could make her say anything."

"Well, thanks for the heads-up, Jason."

"No problem. Look, Yuki," he said, adjusting his glasses over the bridge of his nose. "I'm dying to pick your very lovely mind. Would you have dinner with me? Please?"

Yuki shifted her weight in her narrow, pointy shoes, thought of the nice cold Coors waiting for her at home. The ton of work she had to do.

"No offense, Jason. When I'm trying a case, I like to be alone at the end of the day. I need the solitude and the time to clear my head—"

"Yuki. You've got to eat, so why not let me treat you to a lavish expense account dinner? Caviar, lobster, French champagne. Anyplace you want to go. You'll be home by eight, and no business talk either. Just romance," Twilly said, giving her his full frontal, lopsided grin.

He was charming and he *knew* it.

Yuki laughed in the face of such practiced seduction, and then she surprised herself.

She said yes.

Chapter 41

STEVEN MEACHAM AND HIS WIFE, Sandy, were watching *48 Hours Mystery* on TV in their expansive home in Cow Hollow when the doorbell chimed.

Steve said to Sandy, "Are we expecting someone?"

"Hell no," Sandy said, thinking of the door-to-door canvassing that had been going on because of the heated school board elections. She took a sip from her wineglass. "If we ignore them, they'll go away."

"I guess I can always give 'em a couple of shots to the ribs, make 'em take us off the list," Meacham said, feinting and punching the air, then slipping his bare feet into his loafers.

He walked to the front door, peered through the fanlight, saw two good-looking boys standing outside, kids about the age of his son, Scott.

What was this?

The heavier of the two wore a peachy-colored T-shirt under a camouflage vest, his hair covering his shirt collar, more Banana Republic than Republican, and definitely not a Jehovah's Witness. The other boy was dressed traditionally in a glen plaid jacket over a lavender polo shirt, hair long in front like a kid from an English boarding school. The boys had unopened liquor bottles in hand.

Meacham turned off the security alarm, opened the door a crack, said, "May I help you fellows with something?"

"My name is Hawk, Mr. Meacham," said the one in the sport jacket. "This is Pidge. Uh, those are our pledge names," he said apologetically. "We're friends of Scotty's, you know, and we're pledging Alpha Delta Phi?"

"No kiddin'? Scotty didn't call..."

"No, sir, he doesn't know we're here. We have to do this on the sneak."

"Pledges, huh?"

Meacham fondly remembered his own fraternity days. "So, when's the initiation?" he asked.

"Next week, sir," said Pidge. "If we make it. We have to ask you about Scotty, things people don't know about him, and we need to score a baby picture, preferably a naked one..."

Meacham laughed, said, "Okay, okay, come on in." He threw open the door to his spacious home with its heart-stopping view of the bay.

"Honey, we've got company," he called to his wife, leading the two boys through the foyer. "Hawk, like Ethan Hawke? Or some sort of bird theme, probably."

Meacham accepted the bottles from the boys with thanks, then he opened the inlaid wooden liquor cabinet in the living room. He took out glasses as the boys introduced themselves to his wife, who said, "It's quite nice of you to bring something, but it really wasn't necessary."

"Cointreau," Meacham said. He poured from the bottle, handed the glasses around. "To the Greeks."

Actually, Meacham was trying to cut down on the booze, but Sandy was already half sloshed. She swished her drink in the glass, took a sip, said, "Honey bear, why don't you show the boys Scotty's room? I'll get out the photo albums."

"I'll stay with you, Mrs. Meacham," Pidge said. "Help you pick out the right picture."

Sandy was lost in the photo album in her lap when Pidge's shadow fell across her face. She looked up, did a double take through her unfocused eyes, finally putting it together. *Pidge was holding a gun.*

She took in a deep breath, but Pidge raised a finger to his lips, then said, "Don't scream, Sandy. Just do what I tell you and everything will be fine."

Chapter 42

"THIS ISN'T FUNNY ANYMORE," Steve Meacham said to the two boys, wincing as Hawk jammed the gun between his shoulder blades.

"Go stand by your wife, Mr. M.," said Hawk. "This is kind of a scavenger hunt, you know? We're not going to hurt you guys. Not unless you *make* us."

Meacham went to his wife's side, looking at each of the two guns in turn, sending his mind toward his own gun, which was wrapped in a towel at the top of the linen closet. He glanced at Sandy's face, saw that she was sobering up, trying to figure out what was happening.

He wished he knew.

He turned back to Pidge, said, "This is just a fraternity prank, right, fellas?"

"Yes, sir," Hawk said at his back. "I need you both to lie on the floor, facedown."

"Well, I'm not going to do that, you crazy boy," Sandy said, whipping her head around, eyes flashing furiously. "Get out of here, both of you, now, and tell Scotty I want to hear from him tonight, I don't care what time—"

Pidge walked behind Sandy, cocked his arm, and whacked her on the back of the head with the gun butt. Sandy yowled, went down into a crouch, hands covering her head. Steven saw blood seep between her fingers. Steven started toward Sandy, but the chilling metallic clicks of hammers being cocked stopped him where he stood.

Steven wanted to keep denying the wordless terror that was flooding his mind—but he couldn't block it out anymore. *These kids were going to kill them—unless, somehow . . .*

"I don't want to shoot you, lady," Pidge said. "Drop all the way to the floor. You, too, buddy. Hurry up now."

Steven got to his knees, pleaded. "We'll do what you say. Take it all," he said. "Take everything we have. Just don't, please, don't hurt us."

"Good attitude," Pidge said, shoving Sandy Meacham to the floor with his foot, standing behind her as her husband lay facedown on the Persian carpet.

"Hands behind your backs, if you'll be so kind," Pidge said. He took a reel of fishing line out of his back pocket, wrapped the monofilament fiber tightly around the Meachams' wrists. Then he tugged off their shoes, stripped off Sandy's socks, and began winding fishing line around Steven Meacham's ankles.

"I'll let you in on something," Pidge said. "Actually, we're not fraternity types like Scotty." He tugged down Sandy's elastic-waisted pants and underwear in one motion. Sandy yelped.

"Where's your safe, Mr. M.? What's the combination?" Hawk asked.

"We don't *have* a safe," Meacham said.

"Hawk, go back upstairs," said Pidge. "I'll keep these folks company."

He slapped Sandy's buttocks playfully, laughing as Meacham cried out, *"There's some money inside the humidor on my dresser.* You can have it. Take it all!"

Pidge turned up the TV volume to high, balled Sandy's socks, jammed a woolen gag into each of the Meachams' mouths. As Sandy whimpered and squirmed, he slapped her buttocks again, this time almost tenderly; then reluctantly, Pidge tied her ankles together with the fishing line. That done, he broke the neck of the second bottle of Cointreau against the mantelpiece. He poured liquor on a pile of newspapers by the upholstered chair, into a basket of yarn, doused the Meachams' hair and their clothing, Meacham shouting against the sock in his mouth, starting to gag.

"I wouldn't do that," Pidge said, reasonably. "You could drown on your own vomit. That would be nasty, bud."

Hawk came down the stairs into the living room, a cigar in his mouth, jangling a lumpy pillowcase.

"Swag," he said, grinning. "About five grand in the humidor. Oh, and I got a book."

Pidge bent to Sandy Meacham, who was moaning half naked at his feet. He twisted the diamond rings off her fingers, then shouted into Steven Meacham's ear.

"What is it you people like to say? Living

well is the best revenge? Well, enjoy your revenge. And thanks for the stuff."

"Ready?" Hawk asked.

Pidge finished writing the inscription and
capped the pen.

"Veni, vidi, vici, bro," Pidge said, lighting
matches and dropping them where he'd
poured the Cointreau.

VOOOOOOM.

Flames flared up around the room. Smoke
billowed, darkening the air. The Meachams
couldn't see the two young men wave
good-bye as they left by the front door.

Chapter **43**

THE SMELL OF BURNED FLESH hit us before we crossed the threshold into the smoking ruins of the Meacham house in Cow Hollow. It had once been an architectural masterpiece. Now it was a crypt.

Arson investigator Chuck Hanni stepped out of the shadows to greet us. He looked uncharacteristically tired and grim.

"My second job tonight," he explained.

"The first one was like this?" Conklin asked.

"Nope. Meth lab explosion," Hanni said. "Victim was blown out of the house and into the back of her pickup truck." He shook his head. "Now *this* is exactly like the Malone fire."

We followed Hanni into what was once the Meachams' living room. I imagined the space as it once was—the cathedral ceiling, the massive fireplace, and the mirror above the mantel. Now it was all smoke-blackened gilt and carbon-streaked marble. The bodies were lying close together in three inches of black water, flat on their stomachs, hands curled in a pugilistic attitude, the result of tendons tightening as their bodies burned.

"If there were ligatures on the victims, they've burned up," Hanni said, hunching down beside the bodies. "No point in dusting for prints. Maybe tomorrow, in the light of day.… Anyway," Hanni went on, "I found this on the kitchen counter." He handed a book to Conklin. I read the title: *A History of Yachting.* "Got a signature in there for you, Rich. It's in Latin."

Conklin cracked open the book to the title page and read out loud. "Radix omnium malorum est cupiditas."

"What's it mean?" Hanni asked him.

Conklin tried to hunch it out, saying, "Something, something, bad is love? I don't know. What the hell. My tenth-grade Latin is exhausted."

"Aren't we all?" Claire said, stepping into the room, a crew of two assistants trailing behind her. "What have we got here?"

She walked to the bodies, rolled the smaller of the two, and a rush of air came from the victim's mouth. *Paaahhhhhh.*

"Look here," Claire said to Chuck, showing him a liquor bottle that had been partially hidden by the victim's body.

Hanni picked it up with a gloved hand.

"Maybe we'll get some prints after all," he said.

Conklin and I left Claire and Hanni with the bodies of the victims and went outside. The first officer pointed out an attractive woman standing at the front of the now-thinning crowd at the edge of the lawn.

"That's the woman who called it in. Her name is Debra Kurtz," the cop told me. "She lives directly across the street."

Kurtz was in her late forties, five four or so, a tad too thin, maybe anorectic, wearing black spandex running gear. Mascaraed tear tracks marked her cheeks. I introduced myself and Conklin, asked Kurtz if she'd known the deceased.

"Steve and Sandy Meacham were my closest friends," she said. "I called 911 when

I saw the fire. God, oh, God, it was already too late."

"Mind coming down to the station with us?" I asked. "We need to know everything we can about your friends."

Chapter 44

DEBRA KURTZ WAS DRINKING day-old coffee in the smaller, cleaner of our two interview rooms. "The Meachams were the greatest couple in the world," she told us tearfully.

"Any reason you can think that anyone would want to hurt them?" I asked.

"I'm going to the soft drink machine downstairs," Conklin said to Kurtz. "Can I get you something else?"

She shook her head no.

When Conklin was gone, Kurtz leaned across the table and told me about Sandy's drinking and that both Sandy and Steven had

had casual affairs. "I don't think that means anything, but just so you know."

Kurtz told me that the Meachams had two children; a boy, Scott, nineteen or so, away at college, and a girl, Rebecca, older and married, living in Philadelphia. Kurtz choked up again, as though something painful was stuck in her gut—or her conscience.

"Is there something else you want to tell me, Debra? Something going on between you and Steven Meacham?"

"Yes," she said quietly. "Yes, there was."

Kurtz watched the door as she talked, as if she wanted to finish talking before Conklin returned. She said, "I hated myself for cheating on Sandy. It's hard to explain, but in a way I loved her as much as I loved Steve."

I pushed a box of tissues over to her side of the table as Conklin came back into the interrogation room. He was holding a computer printout.

"You have a rap sheet, Ms. Kurtz," said Conklin, pulling out a chair. "That kinda surprised me."

"I was in *grief,*" the woman told us, her gray eyes flooding anew. "I didn't hurt anyone but myself."

Conklin turned the pages toward me.

"You were arrested for burglary."

"My boyfriend talked me into it, and I was stupid enough to go along. Anyway, I was acquitted," Kurtz said.

"You weren't acquitted," said Conklin. "You got probation. I think you made a deal to flip on your boyfriend, am I right? Oh, and then there's the arson."

"Randy, my husband Randy, was *dead.* I wanted to cut my heart out," she said, pounding her chest with her fist. "I set fire to our house because it was the only way I could *see* what I *felt.* The bottomless *grief.*"

I leaned back in my chair. I think my mouth may have dropped open. Debra Kurtz reacted to the shock on my face.

"It was my own *house,*" she shouted. "I didn't even file an insurance claim. I only hurt myself, do you understand? I only hurt *myself!*"

"Had Steven Meacham broken off your affair?"

"Yes. But it was weeks ago, and it was mutual."

"You weren't a little angry?" Conklin asked. "Didn't feel a little bottomless *grief?*"

"No, no, whatever you're thinking, I didn't

set fire to the Meachams' house. I didn't *do* it. I didn't *do* it."

We asked Debra Kurtz where she was when the Malone house burned, and we asked her if she knew her way around Palo Alto. She had alibis, and we wrote everything down. What she told us added up to a crazy woman with a burning desire to both destroy and self-destruct.

It added up, and yet it didn't add up at all. And now it was half past five in the morning.

"You have any trips planned, Debra?" Conklin said, in his charming way.

She shook her head. "No."

"Good. Please don't leave town without letting us know."

Chapter 45

JOE WAS STILL ASLEEP when I crawled into bed. I gently shoved Martha out of my spot and snuggled up to Joe's back, wanting to wake him up so that I could tell him what was bugging me. Joe turned toward me, pulled me close to his body, buried his face in my smoky hair.

"Have you been barhopping, Blondie?"

"House fire," I said. "Two dead."

"Like the Malones?"

"*Just* like the Malones."

I threw an arm across his chest, rested my face in the crook of his neck, exhaled loudly.

"Talk to me, honey," Joe said.

Excellent.

"It's about this woman, Debra Kurtz," I said, as Martha got back up on the bed, turned around a couple of times, then curled into the hollow behind my legs, pinning me in.

"Lives across the street from the victims. She called in the fire."

"Firebugs often do."

"Right. Says she got up for a glass of water, saw the flames. Called the fire department, then joined the crowd watching them put the fire out."

"She was still standing there when you arrived?"

"She'd been there for hours. Said she was best friends with the female victim, Sandy Meacham, and she'd also been sleeping with the second victim, Sandy's husband—"

"Weird definition of best friend."

I had to laugh. "Sleeping with her best friend's husband until he dumped her. This Debra Kurtz has a key to the victims' house. She also has a sheet. An old arrest for burglary. And guess what else? Arson."

"Hah! She knows her way around the system. So she what? Sets fire to the house across the street—and just waits for the cops to take her in?"

"That's what I'm saying, Joe. The whole package is too much. Kurtz had the means, the motive, the opportunity. 'Hell hath no fury'—plus once a firebug, you know, it's a hard rush to kick."

"She strike you as a killer?" Joe asked me.

"She struck me as a pathetic narcissist, in need of attention."

"You got that right."

I gave Joe a kiss. Then I gave him a few more, just loving the feeling of his rough cheek against my lips, his mouth on mine, and the fact of him, big and warm and in my bed.

"Don't start something you're too tired to finish, Blondie," he growled at me.

I laughed again. Hugged him tight. Said, "Ms. Kurtz insists she didn't do it. So what I'm thinking is..." My thoughts drifted back to the victims, soot-blackened water lapping around their bodies.

"What you're thinking," Joe prompted.

"I'm thinking either she set this fire because she's so completely self-destructive, she wants to get caught. Or she did it and maybe she didn't plan for her friends to die. Or else..."

"Your gut is telling you that she didn't do it. That she's just a total wackjob."

"There ya go," I said to my sweetheart. "There…ya…go…"

When I woke up, my arms were entwined around Martha, Joe was gone, and I was late for my meeting with Jacobi.

Chapter 46

I MET CLAIRE at her car after work. I moved a pair of galoshes, a flashlight, her crime scene kit, a giant bag of barbecued potato chips, and three maps into the backseat and then climbed up into the passenger side of her Pathfinder. I said, "Richie got a translation of that Latin phrase that was written inside that yachting book."

"Oh yeah? And what did it mean?" she said, pulling her seat belt low across her belly, stretching it to the limit before locking it in place.

I cinched my seat belt, too, said, "It roughly translates as 'Money is the root of all evil.' I'd like to get my hands on the sucker who wrote that and show him the victims all crispy and curled up on your table. Show him what real evil is."

Claire grunted. "You got that right," she said, and pulled the car out onto Bryant heading us north, apparently deciding to take the 1.8 miles to Susie's like she was racing the Daytona 500. She jerked the wheel around a slow-cruising sightseer, stepping on the gas. "You're saying 'him,'" Claire pointed out. "So that Debra Kurtz person is off your list?"

"She has an alibi," I told Claire through clenched teeth. I grabbed the dashboard as she cleared the yellow light. "Also, her alibis check out for the nights of the Malone fire and the Jablonskys in Palo Alto."

"Humph," Claire said. "Well, about the two legible fingerprints on that bottle found at the scene. One belongs to Steven Meacham. The other didn't match to anybody. But I've got *something* for you, girlfriend. Sandy Meacham had a good-sized blunt-force wound to the skull. Looks like she got clobbered with maybe a gun butt."

I thought about that—that the killer had gotten violent—then I told Claire how the canvass of the Meacham neighborhood had netted us no leads whatsoever. She gave me the results of the blood screen—that Sandy Meacham had been drinking, and that the Meachams had both died of smoke inhalation.

It was all interesting, but none of it added up to a damned thing. I said so to Claire as she pulled into the handicapped zone right in front of Susie's Café.

She looked at me and said, "I *am* handicapped, Linds. I'm carrying fifty pounds of baby fat, and I can't walk a block without huffing."

"I'm not going to write you up for *this,* Butterfly. But as for the land speed record you just set in a business district…"

My best friend kissed my cheek as I helped her down out of the Pathfinder. "I love that you worry about me."

"Lotta good it does," I said, hugging her, cracking open the door to Susie's.

As we plowed through the gang at the bar toward the back room, the plinking steel-band version of a Bob Marley classic surrounded us, as well as the divine aromas of roasting chicken, garlic, and curry. Cindy and Yuki were already at our booth, and Lorraine dragged up a chair for Claire. She dropped laminated menus that we knew by heart onto the table and took our order for a pitcher of tap and mineral water for Claire.

And then with Cindy urging her on—"Yu-ki, *tell* them, *tell* them"—Yuki "volunteered" her news.

"It's nothing," she said. "Okay. I had a date. With Jason Twilly."

"And you were careful what you said to him," Cindy said, sternly. "You remembered that he's a *reporter.*"

"We didn't talk about the case at all," Yuki said, laughing. "It was *dinner.* A very nice dinner, no kissing or anything, so all you guys calm down, okay?"

"Was it fun? Are you going to see him again?"

"Yeah, yeah, if he asks me, I suppose I will."

"Jeez. First date in what, a year?" I said. "Think you'd be more excited."

"It hasn't been a year," Yuki said. "It's been sixteen months, but never mind that. What're we toasting?"

"We're toasting Ruby Rose," said Claire, lifting her water glass.

"Who?" we all asked in unison.

"Ruby Rose. She's right here," Claire said, patting her belly. "That's the name Edmund and I picked out for our little baby girl."

Chapter 47

WHEN I RETURNED home from Susie's, the sun was still hanging above the horizon, splashing orange light on the hood of a squad car parked right outside my apartment.

I bent to the open car window, said, "Hey there. Something wrong?"

"You got a couple of minutes?"

I said, "Sure," and my partner opened the car door, unfolded his long legs, and walked over to my front steps, where he sat down. I joined him. I didn't like the look on Rich's face as he opened a pack of cigarettes and offered me one.

I shook my head no, then said, "You don't smoke."

"Old habit making a brief return visit."

I'd kicked tobacco once or twice myself, and now I felt the pull of the many-splendored ritual as the match sparked, the tip of the cigarette glowed, and Rich released a long exhalation into the dusky air.

"Kelly Malone is calling me every day so I can tell her that we've got nothing. Had to tell her about the Meachams."

I murmured sympathetically.

"She says she can't sleep, thinking how her parents died. She's crying all the time."

Rich coughed on the smoke and waved his hand to tell me that he couldn't talk anymore. I understood how helpless he felt. The Malones' deaths were shaping up to be a part of a vicious serial killing spree. And we were clueless.

I said, "He's going to screw up, Richie, they almost always do. And we're not in this alone. Claire, Hanni—"

"You like Hanni?"

"Sure. Don't you?"

Conklin shrugged. "Why does he know so much and so little at the same time?"

"He's doing what we're doing. Wading

through the sludge. Trying to make sense of the senseless."

"Good word for it. Sludging. We're *sludging,* and the killer is laughing—but hell, I'm a bright guy. I can translate Latin platitudes into English! That's worth *something.* Isn't it?"

I was laughing with Rich as he joked himself out of his blue mood when I saw a black sedan crawling slowly up the street in search of a parking spot. It was Joe.

"Oh, look. Stay and meet Joe," I said. "He's heard a lot about you."

"Nah, not tonight, Linds," said Rich, standing up, grinding out the butt of his cigarette on the pavement. "Maybe some other time. See you in the morning."

Joe's car stopped.

Richie's car pulled out of the spot.

Then Joe's car pulled in.

Chapter 48

"YOU EVER USE THIS THING?" Joe was asking me about the stove.

"Sure I do."

"Uh-huh? So what's this?"

He pulled a user's manual and some Styrofoam packing out of the oven.

"I use the stove *top*," I said.

He shook his head, laughed at me, asked if I could open the wine and start the salad. I said I thought I could handle that. I uncorked the chardonnay, tore a head of romaine into a pretty blown-glass bowl Joe had given me, and sliced up a tomato. I reached around Joe for the olive oil and spices, patted his cute behind. Then I settled onto a stool near the counter, kicked off my shoes.

I sipped my wine and with a Phil Collins CD playing in the background, listened to Joe talk about three accounts he'd landed for his new disaster-preparedness consultancy and his upcoming meeting with the governor. Joe was happy. And I was glad that he was using his modern, larger, fancier apartment as his office—and making himself at home right here.

And my apartment was a darned cute place, I have to say. My four cluttered but cozy rooms are on the third floor of a nice old Victorian town house, and there's a deck off the living room where the sun sets on my sliver view of the bay. It was becoming *our* sliver view of the bay.

I topped up Joe's wineglass, watched him stuff a couple of tilapias with crabmeat and slide the pan into the oven. He washed his hands and turned his handsome self to me.

"The fish will be ready in about forty-five minutes. Want to go outside and catch the last rays?"

"Not really," I said.

I put down my glass, hooked my leg around Joe's waist, and pulled him to me, grinning as I saw my better idea flash into Joe's blue eyes. He drew me closer, slid me off the stool, and gathered me up, cupping my butt and grunting theatrically as he carried me down the hallway, saying, "You're a load, Blondie."

I laughed, bit his earlobe, said, "You didn't think 130 was a load when you were younger."

"Like I said. Light as a feather."

He dropped me softly onto the bed, crawled in next to me, took my face in his big hands, and gave me a kiss that made me groan. I wrapped my arms around his neck, and Joe did the almost impossible, pulled off his shirt and kissed me at the same time, tugged off my pants, and also somehow managed to kick the door shut to keep Martha out of our private moments.

"You're amazing," I said, laughing.

"You haven't seen anything, yet, baby doll," my lover growled.

Soon we were both naked, our skin hot and slick, limbs completely wrapped around each other. But as we grappled together, making the delicious climb to ecstasy, an image of another man came winging into my mind.

I fought it hard, because I didn't want him there.

That man was Richie.

Part Three

HOME COOKING

Chapter 49

JASON TWILLY SAT in the front row of the gallery in Courtroom 2C, right behind the elfin Junie Moon, taking notes as Connor Hume Campion answered Yuki Castellano's softball questions. Twilly thought Campion had aged tremendously since his son disappeared. He looked haggard, stooped, as though Michael's death was literally killing him.

As he looked at the governor and Yuki together, Twilly felt a shift in his thinking, and a new structure for his book appeared in his mind. Yuki was Michael Campion's defender, and she was the underdog; feisty and shrewd and at the same time endearing. Like now.

Yuki was using the former governor's celebrity and heartbreak to both move the jury and block the defense.

Twilly would start the book with Yuki's opening statement, flash back through time using poignant moments in the boy's life as told by the governor, flash forward through the trial and the witnesses. Focus on Davis's maternal defense. Linger on the vulnerable Junie Moon. Then end the book with Yuki's closing argument. The verdict, the vindication, hurrah!

Twilly turned his attention back to the governor.

"Mike was born with a conductive defect in his heart," Campion told the court. "It was being managed medically, but of course he could die at any time."

Yuki asked quietly, "And what did Michael know about his life expectancy?"

"Mikey wanted to live. He used to say, 'I want to live, Dad. I have plans.' He knew he had to be careful. He knew that the longer he lived, the more chance—"

Campion stopped speaking as his throat tightened and his eyes watered.

"Mr. Campion, did Michael talk to you about his plans?"

"Oh, yes," Campion said, smiling now. "He was training for an upcoming world chess tournament, on the computer, you know. And he'd started writing a book about living with a potentially fatal illness. . . . It would've made a difference to people. . . . He wanted to get married someday . . ."

Campion shook his head, looked at the jury, and addressed them directly.

"He was such a wonderful boy," he said. "Everyone has seen his pictures, the interviews. Everyone knows how his smile could light up the darkness, how brave he was — but not everyone knows what a good soul he had. How compassionate he was."

Twilly noted that Diana Davis's face was pinched, but she didn't dare object to Campion's meandering testimony about the pain of losing his son. Campion turned and looked squarely at the defendant, spoke directly to her, sadly but not unkindly.

"If only I could have been there when Michael died," Connor Campion said to Junie Moon. "If only I could have held him in my arms and comforted him. If only he'd been with *me,* instead of with *you.*"

Chapter 50

"THE PEOPLE CALL Mr. Travis Cook," Yuki said.

Heads swung toward the double doors at the back of the courtroom, and a young man about eighteen years old, wearing a gray prep school blazer with a crest over the breast pocket, walked up the aisle, came through the gate.

Cook's bushy hair looked patted down rather than combed, and his shoes needed a polish. He looked uneasy as he swore to tell the whole truth and nothing but. Then he stepped up to the witness stand.

Yuki said good morning to her witness and then asked, "How did you know Michael Campion?"

"We went to Newkirk Prep together."

"And when did you meet Michael?"

"I knew him in our freshman year, but, uh, we became better friends last year."

"In your opinion, what caused this friendship to grow?"

"Uh, Michael didn't have many friends, really," Travis Cook said, meeting Yuki's eyes briefly, then looking down again at his hands. "People liked him, but they didn't get too close to him 'cause he couldn't play any sports or hang out or anything. Because of his heart condition."

"But you didn't have the same problem becoming friends with Michael?"

"I have severe asthma."

"And how did that affect your friendship?"

Travis Cook said, "What he had was worse, but I could relate. We talked about how bad it sucked living with these things hanging over us all the time."

"Now, did there come a time when you told Michael about the defendant, Ms. Moon?"

"Yeah."

"Travis, I realize this may be a little uncomfortable, but you've sworn to tell the truth."

"I know."

"Good. And what did you tell Michael about Ms. Moon?"

"That I'd been with her," he mumbled.

"Please speak up so the jury can hear you," Yuki said.

The boy started again. "I told Michael that I'd been with her. A lot of us had. She's a nice girl for someone who...anyway. She's not crude or anything, and so..." Travis sighed. "And so she's a good person to break you in."

"Break you in?" Yuki asked, turning away from the witness, looking at the jurors. "I'm not sure what you mean."

"Do it for the first time. You're not worried about what the girl's going to think of you or anything. I mean, you get to be yourself, have fun, pay her, and leave."

"I see. And what did Michael Campion say when you told him about Ms. Moon?"

"He said he didn't want to die a virgin."

"Travis, did you see Michael the day before he disappeared?"

"I saw him on the lunch line."

"And how did he appear to you?"

"Happy. He said he had a date that night with Junie."

"Thank you, Travis. Your witness," Yuki said to L. Diana Davis.

Davis was wearing a blue double-breasted suit with two rows of four large white pearl buttons and a triple strand of pearls at her throat. Her silver hair was crisp, almost sharp.

She stood up and spoke from the defense table, saying, "I only have one question, Mr. Cook."

The boy looked at her earnestly.

"Did you see Michael Campion go into Junie Moon's house?"

"No, ma'am."

"That's all we have, Your Honor," Davis said, sitting down.

Chapter 51

TANYA BROWN WAS ENJOYING HER-
SELF, giving Yuki a headache at the same
time.

Ms. Brown smiled at the bailiff, tossed her
hair as she swore to tell the truth, and mod-
eled her orange jumpsuit as if it were de-
signed by Versace. She was the third of Yuki's
three jailhouse witnesses, all "in the system"
for dealing drugs, prostitution, or both, and
all of whom had met Junie Moon within the
walls of the county jail. And while the testimony of jailhouse snitches was generally
considered suspect or useless, Yuki was

hoping that the virtually identical statements of these three women would together substantiate Junie Moon's confession.

Yuki asked Tanya Brown, "Did the prosecution offer you anything in exchange for your testimony?"

"No, ma'am."

"We didn't offer to get you transferred, or get you time off or better treatment or more privileges?"

"No, ma'am, you said you weren't going to give me anything." Tanya Brown wiggled her fanny in the witness seat, poured herself a glass of water, smiled at the judge, then settled down.

"All right then, Ms. Brown," said Yuki. "Do you know the defendant?"

"I wouldn't say I know her, *know* her, but we were cellmates one night at the women's jail."

"And did Ms. Moon say why she was arrested?"

"Yeah, everyone gets a turn at that."

"And what did Ms. Moon tell you?"

"She said she was a working girl and that she had a date with Michael Campion."

"And why did that stick in your mind?"

"Are you kiddin'? It was like, *Whoa.* You did the dirty with the golden boy? And like what was that like? And by and by it came out that he died when they were doing it."

"Is that what Ms. Moon told you?"

"Yeah. She said he had a bad heart, and that happened to me once, too, but my john was no golden boy. He was a smelly old man, and he died in the front seat of his Caddy, so I just opened the door—oh, 'scuse me."

"Ms. Brown, did Ms. Moon say what she did when Mr. Campion had a heart attack?"

"She got all weepy-like," said Tanya Brown. "Said she and her boyfriend got rid of his body."

"Did she say anything else?"

"She said Michael was the sweetest boy she ever met and how bad it sucked for him to die on the happiest night of his life."

Yuki thanked the witness, made sure she didn't roll her eyes as she turned her over to L. Diana Davis.

Davis asked Tanya Brown the same question she'd asked each of Yuki's previous two jailhouse witnesses.

"Did Ms. Moon offer you any proof that she'd been with the so-called victim? Did she describe any distinguishing marks on his body, for instance? Show you any souvenirs? A ring, or a note, a lock of his hair?"

"Huh? No, I mean, no, ma'am, she didn't."

"I have no other questions," said Davis dismissively, again.

Chapter 52

TWILLY PHONED YUKI at the office, asked her to have dinner with him at Aubergine, a hot new restaurant on McAllister. "I've got so much work to do," she moaned. Then she relented. "An early dinner, okay? That would be great."

At six the restaurant was filling up with the loud pretheater crowd, but she and Twilly had a small table far from the bar, where it was quiet enough to talk. Twilly's knees bumped against hers from time to time and Yuki didn't mind.

"Davis is like an IED," Yuki said, moving tiny bay scallops on her plate with her fork.

"She blows up in your face at every check-point."

"Her act is getting old. Don't worry," Twilly told her. "She's probably up every night worrying about *you.*"

Yuki smiled at her dinner companion, said, "Hey. That's enough about me." And she asked him to tell her about his first true-crime book.

"Must I? It sold about two hundred copies."

"It did *not.*"

"It *did,* and I know because I bought all of them myself."

Yuki threw back her head and laughed, loosening up finally, feeling pleased that she had Twilly's attention all to herself.

"I wrote it under a pseudonym," Twilly said. "That way if you were to Google me, that bomb won't come up on the list."

"Well, now I know," said Yuki. "So, what was the book about?"

Twilly sighed dramatically, but Yuki could see he was just revving his motor before rolling out a story he loved to tell.

"It's about this country-western singer-songwriter in Nashville," Twilly said. "Joey Flynn. Ever hear of her?"

"Nope."

"Okay, well, about ten years ago, Joey Flynn had cut a couple of records and was making her way up the charts. 'Hot Damn.' You know that song? Or 'Blue Northern'? No? Well, it doesn't matter.

"Joey was married to a carpenter, Luke Flynn, her high school sweetheart, and they'd had four kids before they were twenty-five. One day a fan brought Joey a hundred roses at this saloon where she was singing, and her heart went zing."

"A hundred roses...," Yuki said, imagining it.

Twilly grinned, said, "Joey messed around with this guy for three weeks before Luke found out and confronted her."

"Confronted her how?"

"Rapped on the door at the Motel 6."

"Ouch," said Yuki.

"So that was the end of Joey's affair, and Luke never forgave her. Over time, Joey caught on to the fact that Luke was planning to kill her."

"Really? How?"

"How did she find out? Or how did he plan to kill her?"

Yuki laughed again, said, "Both, and I think

I'm going to have that chocolate mousse cake now."

"You deserve cake for the way you handled the governor today," Twilly said, touching the sleeve of Yuki's blue silk blouse, keeping his hand there for a long moment before he signaled the waiter. After ordering dessert, Twilly went on with his story.

"Five *years* after her fling with that fan, Joey opens the cache in Luke's computer and sees that he's been looking up how to poison someone."

"Oh, my God..."

"Joey writes to her best friend saying that if anything should happen to her, the police should question her husband. Ten days later," Twilly went on, "Joey was dead. Potassium cyanide shows up on the tox screen, and Joey's best friend turns the letter over to the cops, and Luke Flynn is arrested and charged with murder."

"This story reminds me of Nicole Simpson putting those Polaroids of her bruises in a lockbox for her sister in case O.J. hurt her."

"Exactly! So I write a book proposal, get a big advance on a six-figure contract, and I start spending time with Luke Flynn, who's cooling his jets in jail while he awaits trial.

And let me tell you, there's no food like *this* near the prison in Nashville."

"Have the rest," Yuki said, pushing two-thirds of her cake across the table.

"You sure you're done? Okay, then," Twilly said, accepting the cake.

Yuki said, "So what *happened?*"

The waiter dropped the check on the table and Twilly placed his platinum card on it, saying, "I'll give you a lift to your car. Tell you on the way."

"Why don't you follow me home in your car," Yuki said. "The least I can do is make you coffee."

Twilly smiled.

Chapter 53

JASON TWILLY SAT in a loveseat in Yuki's living room, an Irish coffee resting on the low glass table between him and where Yuki was sitting in an upholstered chair six feet away.

Yuki was thinking that Twilly was *too* good-looking, and that she hadn't had sex in so long she wasn't sure she remembered how to do it. Now here was this big-time superstar who would surely break her heart if she let him, and she didn't have time for fun, let alone heartbreak. She had a conference call with Parisi and the DA early in the morning, she had to prepare herself for the next round in this week's trial of the century and go to bed. To sleep.

Twilly was excited, hitting the climax of his story. "So now the DA has the letter Joey Flynn gave to her best friend, and turns out she also told her hairdresser that she was afraid Luke would kill her."

"I'm dyin'," Yuki said. "You better tell me what happened, Jason, because I've got to be in bed in ten minutes and you have to leave."

"Come sit with me for those ten minutes," he said.

Yuki felt her heart banging in her chest. And she felt something else: her deceased mother's clucking presence all around her—in the furniture, in the portrait on the wall—and she knew that her mom would want her to say good night and show the stranger out.

Yuki got up and sat next to Jason Twilly.

Twilly put his arm around her, leaned forward, and kissed her. Yuki moved into the kiss, put her hands in Jason's hair, and was jolted by the hot shock of desire that shot through her body. It was incredible! But somewhere into the second kiss, when Jason ran his hand over her breast, she pulled away, gasping and flustered, her confusion burning off into certainty.

She wasn't ready for this. It was too soon.

Yuki dipped her head, avoided Twilly's eyes as he reached out and tucked a glossy fall of her hair behind her ear.

Then, as if nothing had happened, he said, "The judge ruled the letter Joey wrote to her best friend inadmissible as hearsay, because a defendant, in this case Luke Flynn, had a right to confront his accuser."

"Who was, unfortunately, dead," Yuki said.

"Correct. But he *allowed* the testimony of Joey's hairdresser. Luke's lawyer put up a fight. Said the hairdresser's testimony was also hearsay. The evidence went in anyway, and Luke was convicted."

"That's kind of amazing."

"Bingo," Jason said. "Luke's lawyer appealed to the Tennessee State Supreme Court, and eight months later the conviction was overturned. As we speak, Luke Flynn is living in Louisville with his new wife and kids, making custom kitchen cabinets," Twilly said. "As if Joey Flynn never happened."

"So let me guess: the story fizzled out. And you had to either write the book or give back the advance," Yuki said, starting to breathe normally again.

"Exactly. So I wrote *Blue Northern,* naming it after Joey's song, and it bombed. But *Malvo* was a hit, and so was *Rings on Her Fingers.* And *this* book, the shocking story of the life and death of Michael Campion as told through the voice of the bewitching—oh, God, Yuki…"

Jason pulled Yuki to him and kissed her again, and when she resisted, when she said, "No, I can't," he held her tighter, until Yuki jumped up and pushed him away, putting the coffee table between them again.

Twilly's face darkened. He was angry, and she understood: he'd read her libido, but not how much he was scaring her.

"I'm sorry," she said. "I'm just not—"

"Don't be a sorry mouse, be a happy Jappy," Twilly said, interrupting her. His lopsided smile was forced, and he stood, followed her into the middle of the room, reached for her again as she backed away.

Happy Jappy? What was wrong with him?

Yuki walked across the pale green carpet to the door, opened it, and said, "Good night, Jason."

But Jason Twilly didn't move.

"What the *hell* is wrong with you?" he shouted. "You *flirt* with me, invite me back to your *place,* now — hey! Listen to me," he said, advancing on Yuki, gripping her chin hard with his thumb and forefinger, wrenching her face toward him.

"I said *no,*" Yuki said, pulling out of his grip. "Now get *out* or I'm calling the *police.*"

"Crazy *bitch,*" he said, and smiling coldly, he dropped his hands to his sides.

Yuki's heart galloped as Twilly walked slowly out of her apartment. She slammed the door shut behind him, bolted the lock, and leaned against the inside of her door until she heard the elevator door open and close at the end of the hallway. She went to the window and watched as Twilly stalked out of the Crest Royal and got into his car.

His tires squealed as his black Mercedes shot down Jones Street.

Chapter 54

AFTER A GENUINE PSYCHO KILLER had been arrested in her building, Cindy had thought of adopting a dog for protection. Pit bulls were outlawed in San Francisco, and Cindy didn't want an attack dog or a lap dog, and so her pursuit of the perfect watchdog had ended at Seth on Sixth, the pet store around the corner.

Seth had said, "Take *him.* His name is Horndog."

Horndog was a peach-and-white Moluccan cockatoo, a relative of the bird Robert Blake used to have in his TV series *Baretta.* But Horndog was no movie star. He sulked in his cage plucking feathers from his breast, lifting his head to squawk whenever the door to the pet shop opened.

"He's depressed," Seth said. "He needs a home. Anybody comes into your house, Horndog will let you know."

So Horndog had been renamed Peaches, and now that he was living with Cindy he was no longer depressed. Visibly happier, he now perched on Cindy's shoulder, chewing a pencil into wood chips and softly chuffing to himself. It took a week or two for Cindy to finally translate that muffled mutter; Peaches was saying, repeatedly, "Kill the bitch. Kill the bitch."

"Pretty bird, pretty bird," Cindy answered distractedly, sure that if she said it enough times, she could reprogram her bird.

Tonight Peaches and Cindy were at her computer in her home office. Cindy typed a series of key words into a search engine: "home fires fatalities," "home fires fatalities Bay Area," "home fires cause unknown." But each time she pressed the enter key, too much information flooded her screen.

Cindy scratched the bird under its chin, refreshed her tea with hot water from the kettle, and went back to her desk. The clock icon in

the bottom corner of her screen read 10:
and she was still nowhere. She refined h
search, typed "home fire wealthy couple."

"It's unreal, Peaches," she said, as doze
of links appeared on her screen. "Too mu
information!"

Nearly all of the links led to the same fir
a house outside San Francisco that had bee
torched four years before. As Cindy scanne
the articles, she remembered the story of th
victims, Emil and Rosanne Christiansen, wh
had died before she was assigned to th
crime desk.

Emil Christiansen had been the CFO of a
office machine company that had bee
bought out by a computer company. Th
Christiansens had become instant multim
lionaires. They'd moved out of the city to
woodsy setting up the coast. According
the articles, the house had burned down be
fore firefighters could reach it, and the Chris
tiansens had died.

The fire had been classified accidental b
the firefighters at the scene, but when th
couple's son did an inventory of the remainin
property, he reported that his father's coin co
lection was missing and that his mother's larg
emerald ring and a sapphire-and-diamon

bracelet that was alone worth fifty thousand dollars were gone.

At the bottom of the last article was a quote from the arson investigator, who had told the reporter, "A candle tipped over, papers caught fire, the curtains went up, and so went the house. I haven't found any trace of fire accelerant, so right now I can't say if the fire was accidental or intentional."

Cindy typed, clicked, followed the links, found the medical examiner's report on the Christiansens. The ME had given the cause of death as smoke inhalation and the manner of death "undetermined based upon the fire marshal's report."

"Hey, Peaches. What about the missing jewels? Hmmmm?"

"Kill the bitch. Kill the bitch."

Cindy's mind churned with questions. The Christiansens had been robbed, so why, she wondered, had the arson investigator said he didn't know if the fire was accidental or intentional? And here was a thought: Was it a coincidence that the arson investigator who worked the Christiansen fire was also working on both the Malone and Meacham homicides?

Cindy knew the investigator's name because

Lindsay had talked about him. His name was Chuck Hanni.

She put Peaches back into his cage and covered it. Then she got busy on the phone. First she called her editor.

Then she called Lindsay.

Chapter 55

THE GIRL WAS HEAVY.

She was sitting at the picnic table on campus, right outside the Jamba Juice Bar, facing White Plaza, sipping her Strawberry Whirl through a straw. She was wearing tent clothes: a long prairie skirt and a big red sweatshirt. Her skin was rough and her hair was mousy, and she was, in fact, *perfect.*

Hawk lifted an eyebrow in her direction. Pidge nodded. They walked over to the picnic table and took seats, Hawk sitting next to the girl, Pidge sitting opposite.

Hawk made a phone with his thumb and pinkie.

"Ba-rinnng," he said, making a telephone ring tone.

"Hal-lo," Pidge said, answering the call with his own thumb-and-pinkie phone.

"Pidge. You get outta here, man. I saw her first."

"But I like her better, dude. I *told* you how much I like this woman."

The girl looked up, puzzled by the conversation going on around her. She looked at Hawk, sitting to her left, turned her head, and looked at Pidge. Then she dropped her gaze back to her laptop, where she was blogging an entry in MySpace.

"I don't think she likes either of us, dude," Hawk said into his phone. "You think she's a snob?"

"Let me talk to her," Pidge said. He put his "receiver" down on the table, said to the girl, "Hi. I'm Pidge. I'm a senior. Computer sciences." He pointed to the Gates Building. "My buddy wants to ask you out, but I was telling him that even though he saw you first, I like you better."

"Yeah, yeah," the girl said. "I'm sure you're not just playing me. Some kind of goof you're doing with each other."

Hawk reached out, touched the girl's forearm. "Ow, that really *hurts.* You've got us wrong," Hawk said. "I saw you in the library, don't you remember? I'm not that good at meeting a girl by myself."

"That's the truth," Pidge said. "Hawk's shy. I'm just helping out as his wingman. But when I saw you just now, I thought—and this is the truth now—you're more my type than his."

"What kind of type is that?" the girl asked, warming now to the attention. Herds of bikes whizzed by. The smell of bread baking at Subway floated over the plaza. The sun warmed the top of her head. It was a beautiful day, and now it had gotten *better.*

"You're creative, right? I have a feeling that you must be creative. You're a writer, I'll bet."

"I'm in hum bio."

"Human biology? Cool," said Hawk. "Actually, *I'm* a writer. What's your name?"

"Kara. Kara Lynch."

"I'm Hawk, Kara Lynch. This is my friend Pidge."

"What do you write?" she asked Hawk.

"Pidge and I are working together on a novel," said Hawk. "May I get you another one of those?" he asked. "Strawberry Whirl?"

"Yes. Thanks, Hawk," Kara said, smiling.

When Hawk left, Pidge leaned across the table, said to the girl, "Seriously, Kara. He's not your type. Sure, he's a fuzzy, but I'm a computer genius. Top of my class. If I told you my real name, you'd recognize it. But look, when Hawk gets back, you've got to be ready to choose. Either you've got to step up and ask Hawk out. Or you've got to ask me.

"It's got to be one or the other, so that the two of us don't fight. That wouldn't be good. That would be cruel."

Kara shifted her eyes to Hawk as he came back to the table with the smoothie. Kara thanked him, then said, "I was thinking, Hawk, maybe we could hang out sometime."

Hawk smiled. "Oh, wow, Kara. And I was just thinking you're much more Pidge's type than mine. He's famous at Gates. You'd never forgive yourself if you turned him down."

Kara turned dubiously to Pidge. He rewarded her with a blinding smile. "You have to step up, Kara," he said.

"Uh-huh. Kiss my ass," she said, blushing, putting her eyes back on her laptop.

Pidge said, "I can't do that, Kara. Hawk saw you first." He laughed.

"Ba-rinnng," Hawk said.

"Hal-lo?"

"Like either one of us would go out with a fat slob like her," Hawk said, making sure he said it *loud* so that Kara and the students at the other picnic tables could hear him. The two boys laughed, made a big deal of holding their sides, falling off the benches to the ground.

Pidge recovered first. He stood and tousled Kara's hair playfully. "Mea culpa, Kara mia," he said. "Better luck next time."

He took a bow as tears slid down her cheeks.

Chapter 56

CONKLIN PARKED OUR CAR on the narrow, tree-lined road in Monterey, a small coastal town two hours south of San Francisco. On my right, one wing of the three-story, wood-frame house remained untouched, while the center of the house had burned out to the framing timbers, the roof open to the blue sky like a silent scream.

Conklin and I pushed through the clumps of sidewalk gawkers, ducked under the barricade tape, and loped up the walk.

The arson investigator was waiting for us outside the front door. He was in his early thirties, over six feet tall, jangling the keys and change in his pocket. He introduced himself as Ramon Jimenez and gave me his card with his cell phone number printed on the back. Jimenez opened the fire department lock on the front door so we could enter the center of the house, and as the front door swung open we were hit with the smell of apples and cinnamon.

"Air freshener explosion," Jimenez said. "The crispy critters were found in the den."

As we followed Jimenez into the fire-ravaged shell, I thought about how some cops and firefighters use jargon to show that they're tough—when in fact they're horrified. Others do it because they get off on it. What kind of guy was Jimenez?

"Was the front door locked?" I asked him.

"No, and a neighbor called the fire in. Lots of people don't bother to set their alarms around here."

Broken glass crunched under my shoes and water lapped over the tops of them as I slogged through the open space, trying to get a sense of the victims' lives from the remains and residue of their home. But my knack for fitting puzzle pieces together was blunted by the extent of the destruction. First the fire, then the water and the mop-up, left the worst kind of crime scene.

If there had been fingerprints, they were gone. Hair, fiber, blood spatter, footprints, receipts, notes—forget all of that. Unless a bomb trigger or trace of an accelerant was found, we couldn't even be sure that this fire and the others we were investigating had been set by the same *person.*

The most conclusive evidence we had was the similarity of the circumstances surrounding this fire and those at the Malones' and Meachams' homes.

"The vics were a married couple, George and Nancy Chu," Jimenez told us. "She was a middle school teacher. He was some kind of financial planner. They paid their taxes, were law-abiding, good neighbors, and so forth. No known connections with any bad guys. I can fax you the detectives' notes from the canvass of the neighborhood."

"What about the ME's report?" I asked.

Conklin was splashing through the ruins behind me. He started up the skeletal staircase that still clung to the rear wall.

"The ME wasn't called. Uh, the chief ruled the fire accidental. Nancy Chu's sister had the funeral home pick up the bodies, ASAP."

"The chief didn't see *cause* to call the *ME?*" I shouted. "We're looking at a string of fire-related, probable *homicides* in San Francisco."

"Like I told you," Jimenez said, staring me down with his dark eyes. "I wasn't called either. By the time I got here, the bodies were gone and the house was boarded up. Now everyone's yelling at me."

"Who else is yelling?"

"You know him. Chuck Hanni."

"Chuck was here?"

"This morning. We called him in to consult. He said you were working a couple of similar cases. And before you say I didn't tell you, we might have a witness."

Had I heard Jimenez right? There was a *witness?* I stared up at Jimenez and pinned some hope on the thought of a break in the case.

"Firefighters found the Chus' daughter unconscious out on the lawn. She's at St. Anne's Children's Hospital with an admitting carbon monoxide of seventeen percent."

"She's going to make it?"

Jimenez nodded, said, "She's conscious now, but pretty traumatized. So far she hasn't said a word."

Chapter 57

A TELEPHONE RANG repeatedly in some corner of the second floor of George and Nancy Chu's house. I waited out the sad, echoing bell tones before asking Jimenez the name and age of the Chus' daughter.

"Molly Chu. She's ten."

I scribbled in my notebook, stepped around a mound of water-soaked rubble, and headed for the stairs. I called out to Rich, who was already starting down. Before I could tell him about Molly Chu, he showed me a paperback book that he held by the charred edges.

Enough of the book cover remained so that I could read the title: *Fire Lover,* by Joseph Wambaugh.

I knew the book.

This was a nonfiction account of a serial arsonist who'd terrorized the state of California in the 1980s and '90s. The blurb on the back cover recounted a scene of horror, a fire that had demolished a huge home improvement center, killing four people, including a little boy of two. While the fire burned, a man sat in his car, videotaping the images in his rearview mirror—the rigs pulling up, the firefighters boiling out, trying to do the dangerous and impossible, to knock down the inferno even as two other suspicious fires burned only blocks away.

The man in the car was an arson investigator, John Leonard Orr, a captain of the Glendale Fire Department.

Orr was well known and respected. He toured the state giving lectures to firefighters, helping law enforcement read the clues and understand the pathology of arsonists. And while he was traveling, John Orr set fires. He set the fire that had killed those four people. And because of his pattern of setting fires in

towns where he was attending fire confer-
ences, he was eventually caught.

He was tried, convicted, and stashed in a
small cell at Lompoc for the rest of his life,
without possibility of parole.

"Did you see this book?" Conklin asked
Jimenez.

Jimenez shook his head no, said, "What?
We're looking for books?"

"I found it in the master bathroom between
the sink and the toilet," Conklin said to me.

The pages of the book were damp and
warped, but it was intact. Incredibly, books
rarely burn, because of their density and because the oxygen the fire needs for combustion can't get between the pages. Still holding
the book by the edges, Rich opened the
cover and showed me the block letters printed
with a ballpoint pen on the title page.

I sucked in my breath.

**This was the link that tied the homi-
cides together.**

The Latin phrase was the killer's signature,
but why did he leave it? What was he trying
to tell us?

"Hanni was here," Conklin said quietly.
"Why didn't he find this book?"

I muttered, "Got me," and focused on the handwritten words on the flyleaf, *Sobria inebrietas.* Even I could translate this one: "sober intoxication."

But what the hell did it mean?

Chapter 58

CONKLIN AND I had never had a serious fight, but we bickered during the entire two-hour drive back to the Hall. Rich insisted it was significant that a pro like Hanni had missed "the only clue in the whole damned crime scene."

I liked Chuck Hanni. I admired him. Rich didn't have the same history, the same attachment, so he could be more objective. I had to consider his point of view. Was Hanni a psychopath hiding in plain sight? Or was Conklin so desperate to close the Malone case that he was turning an oversight into a major deal?

I saw that Chuck Hanni was with Jacobi in the glass-walled corner office when Conklin and I entered the squad room. As we wove around the desks toward Jacobi's office, Conklin said to me, "Let me handle this, okay?"

Jacobi waved us into his small office, and Conklin leaned against the wall inside the door. I took a side chair next to Hanni, who squirmed in his seat in order to face me.

"I was telling Jacobi, the Chu fire looks like the work of the same sick asshole who set the others," Hanni said. "Don't you think?"

I was looking at Hanni's familiar face and thinking of the time he'd told me about spontaneous human combustion.

"It's like this, Lindsay," he'd said over beer at MacBain's. "Biggish guy is drinking beer and smoking cigarettes in his La-Z-Boy. Falls asleep. The cigarette drops between the cushions and catches fire. Biggish guy's fat is saturated with alcohol. The chair catches fire and so does the guy, like a freakin' torch.

"After they've been incinerated, the fire extinguishes itself. Nothing else catches, so all that's left is the metal frame of the chair and the guy's charred remains.

"There's your so-called spontaneous human combustion."

I had said "Ewwww," laughed, and bought the next round.

Now Conklin said from behind me, "Chuck, you were at the Chu scene and you didn't let us know about it. What's up with that?"

"You think I was keeping something from you?" Hanni bristled. "I told Jimenez to notify you guys as soon as I saw the victims' bodies."

Conklin took the paperback book from his inside jacket pocket. He reached over me, placed the book, now enclosed in a plastic evidence bag, on top of the pile of junk on Jacobi's desktop.

"This was inside the Chu house," Conklin said, his voice matter-of-fact, but there was nothing innocent about it. "There's block lettering on the first page, in Latin."

Hanni looked at the book in silence for a moment, then muttered, "How did I miss this?"

Jacobi said, "Where'd you find it, Rich?"

"In a bathroom, Lieutenant. In plain sight."

Jacobi looked at Hanni with the hard-boiled stare he'd perfected in twenty-five years of interrogating the worst people in the world. He said, "What about it, Chuck?"

Chapter 59

CHUCK HANNI'S CHAIR scraped the floor as he pushed back from Jacobi's desk. He'd been caught off guard and was now indignant. "What? You think I'm like that Orr prick? Setting fires so I can be a hero? ...Oh, and I planted that book to point suspicion at myself? Look! I gave the ATF a standing ovation when they brought John Orr *down.*"

Conklin smiled, shrugged.

I felt sweat beading up at my hairline. Hanni couldn't be what Conklin was suggesting, but so many kind-faced seeming do-gooders had been convicted of mass murder, I had to know. I kept my mouth shut and let the scene play out.

"Why didn't you tell us about the Christiansen fire?" Conklin said, calmly. "Two wealthy people died. Their stuff was *stolen*—"

"Christ," Hanni interrupted. "I don't sit around reminiscing about old cases—do *you*? Bad enough I see them in my dreams—"

"But the MO was the same," Conklin insisted. "And so I'm wondering if the killer can't kick the habit. Maybe he's still at it, and now he's leaving clues at the crime scene. Like a book inscribed with a few words of Latin."

I watched Chuck's expression, expecting him to bolt, or punch out at Rich, or break down.

Instead he frowned, said, "What do you mean, the killer can't kick the habit? Matt Waters confessed to the Christiansen fire two years ago. He's doing time at the Q. Check it out, Conklin, before you start slinging accusations around."

My face got hot.

Had Cindy gotten this wrong? The Christiansen fire had happened far from San Francisco, but still, I should have double-checked Cindy's research.

Jacobi's intercom had buzzed a few times during this meeting, but he hadn't picked up. Now Brenda Fregosi, our squad assistant, barged into the office, ripped a pink square of paper from a pad, handed it to Jacobi, saying, "What's the matter, Lieutenant? You didn't hear me ring?"

Brenda turned and, swinging her hips, walked back across the gray linoleum to her desk. Jacobi read the note.

"Molly Chu is responding to the hospital shrink," he told us. "She might be ready to talk."

Chuck got out of his chair, but Jacobi stopped him.

"Let's talk, Chuck. Just you and me."

Chapter 60

MY HEART LURCHED when I saw the little girl. Her hair was singed to an inch of frizzed, black fuzz sticking out from her scalp. Her eyebrows and lashes were gone, and her skin looked painfully pink. We approached her bed, which seemed to float under a bower of shiny helium balloons.

Molly didn't look at me or Conklin, but two Chinese women moved aside and a white-haired woman in her seventies with rounded features and sapphire blue eyes stood up and introduced herself as Molly's psychiatrist, Dr. Olga Matlaga.

The shrink spoke to the little girl, saying, "Some police officers are here to see you, sweetheart."

Molly turned toward me when I said her name, but her eyes were dull, as if the life had been sucked out of her, leaving only a stick-figure representation of a child.

"Have you found Graybeard?" she asked me, her voice whispery and slowed by pain-killers.

I cast a questioning look at Dr. Matlaga, who explained, "Her dog, Graybeard, is missing."

I told Molly that we would put out an APB for Graybeard and told her what that meant. She nodded soberly and I asked, "Can you tell us what happened in your house?"

The child turned her face toward the window.

"Molly?" Conklin said. He dragged over a chair, sat so that he was at the little girl's eye level. "Have lots of people been asking you questions?"

Molly reached a hand toward the swinging arm of the table near her bed. Conklin lifted a glass of water, held it so the child could sip through the straw.

"We know you're tired, honey, but if you could just tell the story one more time."

Molly sighed, said, "I heard Graybeard barking. And then he stopped. I went back to my movie, and a little later I heard voices. My mom and dad always told me not to come downstairs when they had guests."

"Guests?" Conklin asked patiently. "More than one?"

Molly nodded.

"And they were friends of your parents?"

Molly shrugged, said, "I only know that one of them carried me out of the fire."

"Can you tell us what he looked like?"

"He had a nice face, and I think he had blond hair. And he was like Ruben's age," Molly said.

"Ruben?"

"My brother, Ruben. He's in the cafeteria right now, but he goes to Cal Tech. He's a sophomore."

"Had you ever seen this boy before?" I asked.

I felt Dr. Matlaga's hand at my elbow, signaling me that our time was over.

"I didn't know him," Molly said. "I could have been dreaming," she said, finally fixing her eyes on me. "But in my dream, whoever he was, I know he was an angel."

She closed her eyes, and tears spilled from under those lashless crescents and rolled silently down her cheeks.

Chapter 61

"HANNI IS IN THE CLEAR," Jacobi said, standing over us, casting a shadow across our desks. "He was working the scene of a meth lab explosion the night of the Meacham fire. He said he told you."

I remembered.

He'd told us that the Meacham fire had been his second job that night.

"I've spoken to five people who were at that meth scene who swear Chuck was there until he got the call about the Meachams," said Jacobi. "And I've confirmed that Matt Waters is doing life for the deaths of the Christiansens."

Conklin sighed.

"Both of you," said Jacobi. "Move on. Find out what the victims have in common. Boxer—McNeil and Chi are reporting to you. So make use of them. Concentrate on the Malones and the Meachams. Those are ours. Here's the name of the primary working the Chus' case in Monterey. Conklin, you might want to smooth things over with Hanni. He's still working these cases."

I was looking at Rich as Jacobi stumped back to his office.

Conklin said, "What? I have to buy Hanni flowers?"

"*That*'ll confuse him," I said.

"Look, it made sense, didn't it, Lindsay? The book was about an arsonist who was an arson investigator and Hanni missed it."

"You made a courageous call, Richie. Your reasoning was sound and you didn't attack him. You brought it into the open with our immediate superior. Perfectly proper. I'm just glad you were wrong."

"So...look. You know him. Should I expect to find my tires slashed?" Conklin asked.

I grinned at the idea of it.

"You know what, Rich. I think Chuck feels

so bad about missing that book, he's going to slash his *own* tires. Just tell him, 'Sorry, hope there are no hard feelings.' Do the manly handshake thing, okay?"

My phone rang.

I held Richie's glum gaze for a moment, knowing how bad he felt, feeling bad for him, then I answered the phone.

Claire said, "Sugar, you and Conklin got a minute to come down here? I've got a few things to show you."

Chapter 62

CLAIRE LOOKED UP when Rich and I banged open the ambulance bay doors to the autopsy suite. She wore a flower-printed paper cap and an apron, the ties straining across her girth. She said, "Hey, you guys. Check this out."

Instead of a corpse, there was a bisected tube of what looked like muscle, about seven inches long. The thing was clamped open on the autopsy table.

"What *is* that?" I asked her.

"This here's a trachea," Claire told us. "Belonged to a schnauzer Hanni found in the bushes outside the Chu house. See how pink it is? No soot in the pooch's windpipe and his carbon monoxide is negative, so I'm saying he wasn't in the house during the fire. Most likely he was in the yard, raised the alarm, and someone put him down with a blow to the head.

"See this fracture here?"

So much for the APB on Graybeard. Whose sad task would it be to tell Molly that her dog was dead? Claire went on to tell us she'd spent the day getting George and Nancy Chu's bodies from the funeral home.

"It's not our jurisdiction, not our case, but I finally got permission from the Chus' son, Ruben. Told him that if I have to testify against the killer and I haven't examined *all* the victims' bodies, I'll get diced into pieces by the attorney for the defense."

I murmured an encouraging "uh-huh" and Claire went on.

"Ruben Chu was a mess. Didn't want his parents to 'suffer any more indignities,' but anyway...I got the release. Both bodies are at X-ray now," Claire added.

"What was your take?" I asked.

"They were burned pretty bad, a few extremities fell off during their travels, but one of George Chu's ankles still had several wraps of intact monofilament fibers on it. So that, my friends, is evidence that they were absolutely, positively tied up."

"Great job, Claire."

"And I got enough blood for the tox screens."

"You gonna keep us guessing, girlfriend?"

"You're saying I live to frustrate you? I'm talking as fast as I can." Claire laughed. She squeezed my shoulder affectionately, then removed a sheet of paper from a manila envelope, put it down on the table next to the dog's trachea.

She ran her finger down the column of data. "High alcohol content in their blood," she said. "Either the Chus had been drinking a lot, or else they'd been drinking high-octane stuff."

"Same as Sandy Meacham?"

"Very much the same," said Claire.

I flashed on the inscription in the book. *Sobria inebrietas.* Sober intoxication. I auto-dialed Chuck Hanni on my cell phone. If I was right, it would explain why he didn't detect the odor of ignitable liquids at either of our fire scenes.

"Chuck? It's Lindsay. Could those fires have been set with booze?"

Chapter 63

THE SUN WENT DOWN and someone in the night crew snapped on the bright overhead lights. Rich and I were still wandering around in the dark. Somewhere, a very smug killer was having his dinner, toasting himself on his success, maybe planning another fire—and we didn't know who he was or when he would strike again.

While Chi and McNeil reinterviewed the Malones' and the Meachams' friends and neighbors, Conklin and I sat at our desks, going over the murder book together. We reviewed Claire's findings, the photos of rubberneckers at the fire scenes, the handwriting expert's comparison of the inscriptions in each of the books left at the fire scenes, and the expert's opinion: "I can't say one hundred percent because it's block lettering, but looks like all the samples were written by the same hand."

We reviewed our own eyeball tours of the crime scenes, trying to reduce all of it to a few illuminating truths, speaking in the kind of short-hand that you use with a partner. And I felt that other connection, too, the one I wouldn't let Rich mention but sometimes just arced across our desks. Like it was doing now.

I got up, went to the bathroom, washed my face, got a cup of coffee for me and one for Conklin, black, no sugar. Sat back down, said, "Now, where were we?"

As the night tour walked and talked around us, Rich ticked off on his fingers what we had: "The couples were all in their forties and well-to-do. The doors to all the houses were unlocked, and the alarms weren't set. No sign of gunfire. The couples all had a child of college age. They were all robbed, but the killer took only jewelry and cash."

"Okay, and here are a few suppositions," I said. "The killer is smart enough and unthreatening enough to talk his way into the houses.

And I'm going to also say that it seems probable that there were *two* assailants; one to tie up the victims, one to hold a gun."

Rich nodded, said, "He or they used fishing line as ligatures because they'd burn off quickly in the fire. And they used an untraceable accelerant. That's careful. They don't leave evidence, and that's smart.

"But I don't think Molly Chu was in the plan," Rich added. "This is the first time another person was in the house with the victims. I'm thinking Molly had already passed out from smoke inhalation when her 'angel' found her and subsequently carried her out. Kind of heroic, wouldn't you say?"

"So maybe the killer thought she didn't see him," I said. "And so he felt safe carrying her out of the house. Yeah, I don't think he wanted the little girl to die, hon."

Rich looked up, grinned at me.

"I, uh. Didn't mean—shit."

"Forget it, babe," said Conklin. "Means nothin'." He grinned wider.

I said, "Shut up," and threw a paper clip at his head. He snatched it out of the air and went on.

"So," he said, "let's say Molly saw one of the killers, okay? And let's say he's a college-age kid as Molly suggested. The Malones, the Meachams, the Chus, and that couple in Palo Alto, the Jablonskys—they all had kids in college. But their kids all went to different schools."

"True," I said. "But a kid, any kid, comes to the door and looks presentable, Mom and Dad might open it.

"Rich, maybe that's the *con.* When I was in school, I was always bringing people home that my mom didn't know. So, what if a couple of kids come to the door and say they're friends with your kid?"

"That would be easy to fake," Rich said. "Local newspapers do stories on kids at school. So-and-so's daughter or son, attending such-and-such school won this-or-that award."

Rich drummed his fingers on the desk, and I rested my chin in my hand. Instead of feeling on the brink of a breakthrough, it seemed that we'd just opened the field of potential suspects to every male college-age kid in California who knew high school Latin—and, by the way, was into robbery, torture, arson, and murder.

I thought about the puzzle pieces. Providence favoring the killers' actions, and money being the root of all evil. There was the sci-fi book *Fahrenheit 451,* and now a book about a high-placed fire official who'd set fires. When John Orr was caught, he'd said, "I was stupid, and I did what stupid people do."

These killers weren't making Orr's mistakes.

They were going out of their way to show just how smart they were. Was saving Molly Chu their one miscalculation?

Rich's phone rang and he swiveled his chair toward the wall. He lowered his voice and said, "We're working on it, Kelly, right now. It's *all* we're doing. I promise, when we know something, I'll call you. We won't let you down."

Chapter 64

YUKI WAS AT the Whole Foods Market six blocks from her apartment, looking over the produce, thinking about a quick stir-fry for dinner, when she thought she glimpsed a familiar figure down the aisle. When she looked again, he was gone. She was hallucinating, she thought, so tired she could conjure up bogeymen anywhere. She dropped a head of broccoli into her cart and moved on toward the meat section.

There she selected a shrink-wrapped tray of tiger prawns—and got the feeling again that Jason Twilly was only yards away.

She looked up.

And there he was, dressed in navy blue pinstripes, pink shirt, wearing a full smirk and standing near the pile of frozen free-range turkeys. Twilly waggled his fingers but made no move toward her, though he didn't turn away. He had no cart, no basket.

The bastard wasn't shopping.

He was stalking her.

Yuki's sudden fury gathered power and momentum, so that she saw only one possible course of action. She shoved her cart to the side of the aisle and marched toward Twilly, stopping a few feet from his sturdy English shoes.

"What are you doing here, Jason?" she said, stretching her neck to look up at his crazy-handsome face with the eight-hundred-dollar eyeglass frames and lopsided smile.

"Leave the groceries, Yuki," he said. "Let me take you out to dinner. I promise I'll behave. I just want to make up to you for our misunderstanding the last time—"

"I want to be very clear about this," Yuki said, cutting him off, using her clipped, rapid-fire style. "Mistakes happen. Maybe the misunderstanding was my fault, and I've apologized. Again, I'm sorry it happened. But you have to understand. I'm not interested,

Jason—in anyone. It's all work, all the time, for me. I'm not available, okay? So please don't follow me again."

Jason's odd, twisted smile blossomed into a full-blown laugh. "Nice speech," he said, clapping his hands, an exaggerated round of mock applause.

Yuki felt a little shock of fear as she backed away. What was wrong with this guy? What was he capable of doing? She remembered Cindy's warning to her to be careful of what she said around Twilly. Would he dirty her reputation when he wrote about the Junie Moon trial?

Whatever.

"Good-bye, Jason. Leave me alone. I mean it."

"Hey, I'm writing a book, remember?" Twilly called out to her as she turned her back on him. She heard his voice as she pushed her cart down the aisle.

She wanted to hide. She wanted to *disappear.*

"You're a *key player,* Yuki. Sorry if you don't like it, but you're the star of my whole freakin' *show.*"

Chapter 65

WE WERE GATHERED on the deck of Rose Cottage, outside of Point Reyes, feeling the blessed night breeze on our cheeks. Yuki flipped on the heater for the hot tub, while Claire tossed a giant salad and made burgers for the grill.

This impromptu getaway was Cindy's idea. She had corralled us in a conference call only hours before, saying, "Since our first attempt at a Women's Murder Club Annual Getaway Weekend was canceled due to someone answering a call to return to work, we should grab this opportunity to drop everything and go *now.*"

Cindy added that she'd booked the cottage and that she would drive.

There was no saying no to Cindy, and for once I was glad to turn the wheel over to her.

Yuki and Claire had both slept in the backseat during the drive, and I'd ridden shotgun with Martha in my lap, her ears flapping in the wind. I listened to Cindy talk over the car's CD player, my mind floating blissfully as we neared the ocean.

Once we'd arrived at the rose-covered hobbit house with its two snug bedrooms plus picnic table and grill in the clearing at the edge of a forest, we'd slapped each other high fives and dropped our bags on our beds. Yuki had left her box of files in her room and come with Martha and me as we took a short run up a moonlit trail to the top of a wooded ridge and back again.

And now I was ready for a meal, a margarita, and a great night's sleep. But when we got back to Rose Cottage, my cell phone was ringing. Claire groused, "That damned thing's been ringin' its buttons off, girlfriend. Either turn it off or give it to me and I'll stomp it to death."

I grinned at my best friend, pulled the phone from my handbag, saw the number on the caller ID.

It was Jacobi.

I stabbed the send button, said hello, and heard traffic noise mixed in with the wail of fire engine sirens.

I shouted, *"Jacobi. Jacobi, what's up?"*

"Didn't you get my messages?"

"No, I just caught this ring on the fly."

The sirens in the background, the fact that Jacobi was calling at all, caused me to imagine a new fire and another couple of charred bodies killed by a psycho looking for kicks. I pressed my ear hard to the phone, strained to hear Jacobi over the street noise.

"I'm on Missouri Street," he told me.

That was my street. What was he doing on *my* street? Had something happened to *Joe?*

"There's been a fire, Boxer. Look, there's no good way to say this. You have to come home right now."

Chapter 66

JACOBI DISCONNECTED the phone call, leaving static in my ear and a god-awful gap between what he'd said and what he'd left out.

"There's been a fire on Missouri Street," I announced to the girls. "Jacobi told me to come home!"

Cindy gave me the keys and we piled into her car. I floored the accelerator and we bumped down the twisting roads of the backwoods of Olema and out to the highway. I called Joe as I drove, ringing his apartment and mine, and I rang his cell, pressed redial again and again, *never* getting an answer.

Where was he? Where was Joe?

I don't ask God for much, but as we neared Potrero Hill, I was praying that Joe was safe. When we reached Missouri at Twentieth, I saw that my street was roped off. I parked in the first empty spot, gripped Martha's leash, and dashed up the steep residential block, leaving the girls to follow behind.

I was winded when I caught sight of my house, saw that it was fenced in by fire rigs, patrol cars, and bystanders filling the narrow street. I frantically scoured the faces in the crowd, saw the two female students who lived on the second floor and the building manager, Sonya Marron, who lived on the ground floor.

Sonya reached through the crowd and gripped my arm, saying, "Thank God, thank God." There were tears in her eyes.

"Was anyone hurt?"

"No," she said. "No one was home."

I hugged her then, relieved at last that Joe had not fallen asleep in my bed. But I still had questions, a ton of them. *"What happened?"* I asked Sonya.

"I don't know. I don't know."

I looked for Jacobi, but I found Claire shouting at the fire captain, "I un-der-*stand* it may be a crime scene, but she's a *cop.* With the SFPD!"

I knew the fire department captain, Don Walker, a thin man with a prominent nose, weary eyes peering out from the soot on his face. He threw up his hands, and then he opened the front door. Claire gathered me under her wing, and along with Yuki, Cindy, and Martha, we entered the three-story apartment house that had been my home for ten years.

Chapter 67

I WAS WEAK-KNEED as we mounted the stairs, but my mind was sharp. The stairs hadn't burned, and the doors to the two lower apartments stood open. The apartments looked untouched by fire. This made no sense.

But it all became clear at the top of the stairs.

The door to my apartment was in shards. I stepped through the shattered door frame and saw the stars and the moon where my ceiling used to be. I lowered my eyes from the night sky, finding it hard to take in the grotesque condition of my little nest. The walls were black, curtains gone, the glass in my kitchen cabinets blown out. My crockery and the food in my pantry had exploded, making the place smell crazily like popcorn and Clorox.

My cozy living room furniture had melted down into hunks of sodden foam and wire springs. And then I knew — the fire had taken everything. Martha whined and I bent to her, buried my face in her fur.

"Lindsay," I heard someone shout. *"Are you okay?"*

I turned to see Chuck Hanni coming out of the bedroom.

Did he have something to do with this?

Had Rich been right all along?

And then I saw Conklin right behind Hanni, and *both* of their faces were sagging with *my* pain.

Rich opened his arms. I held on to him in the smoking black ruins of my home, so glad he was there. But as I rested my head on his shoulder, the stark realization hit me: if Cindy hadn't called with her impromptu getaway plan, I would have been home with Martha when the fire broke out.

I ripped myself away from Rich and called out to Hanni.

My voice was trembling.

"Chuck, what happened here? I have to know. Did someone try to kill me?"

Chapter 68

HANNI SNAPPED ON the portable lights inside what was left of my living room, and in that blinding moment, Joe burst through my splintered door frame. I flung myself at him, and he wrapped me in his arms, nearly squeezing the air out of me.

I said, "I *called* and *called*—"

"I turned off my damned cell at dinner—"

"From now on, you've got to put it on *vibrate*—"

"I'll wear an electric shock collar, Linds. Whatever it takes. I'm *sick* that I didn't know you needed me."

"You're here now."

I broke down and cried all over his shirt, feeling safe and lucky that Joe was okay, that we both were. I only vaguely remember my friends and my partner saying good-bye, but I clearly recall Chuck Hanni telling me that as soon as it was daylight, he'd be all over the building, looking for whatever caused the fire.

Don Walker, the SFFD captain, took off his hat, wiped his forehead with his glove, saying that Joe and I had to leave so he could secure the building.

"Just a minute, Don, okay?" I said, not really asking him.

I went to the bedroom closet and opened the door, stood there in a daze, until I heard Joe say behind me, "You can't wear any of this, honey. It's all a loss. You've got to walk away from it."

I turned and tried to take in the utter ruination of my four-poster bed and photo albums and the treasured box of letters that my mother wrote to me when I was away at school and she was dying.

And then I focused my mind and scanned every inch of floor, looking for something *specific,* a book that might be out of place. I found nothing. I went to my dresser, pulled at the knobs of the top drawer—but the charred wooden drawer pulls crumbled in my hands.

Joe strong-armed the dresser and the wood cracked. He gripped the drawer and heaved it open. I pawed through my underwear, Joe saying patiently behind me, "Sweetie, forget this. You'll get new stuff..."

I found it.

I palmed the velvet cube in my right hand, held it into the light, and opened the box. Five diamonds in a platinum setting winked up at me, the ring that Joe had offered me when he asked me to marry him only a few months ago. I'd told Joe then that I loved him but needed time. Now I closed the lid of the box and looked into his worry-creased face.

"I'd sleep with this under my pillow—if only I had a pillow."

Joe said, "Got lots of pillows at my place, Blondie. Even got one for Martha."

Captain Walker stood at the door waiting for us. I took one last look around—and that's when I saw the book on the small telephone stand just inside my front door.

I'd never seen that book before in my life.

That book wasn't mine.

Chapter 69

I STARED IN SHOCK and disbelief at the large 8½ by 11 paperback, tomato-red with thin white stripes running crosswise beneath the title: *National Guide for Fire and Explosion Investigation.*

I started screaming, "That's *evidence.* That's *evidence.*"

Captain Walker was worn out and he was also out of the loop. He said, "The arson investigator will be back in the morning, Sarge. I'm boarding up your place so it'll be perfectly safe, you understand?"

"NO," I shouted. "I want a *cop.* I want this thing locked up in the evidence room *tonight!*"

I ignored Walker's sigh and Joe's hand on the small of my back. I dialed Jacobi's number on my cell, already decided that if he didn't pick up, I would call Clapper and then I would call Tracchio. And if I didn't get Jacobi or CSI or the chief, I would call the mayor. I was hysterical and I knew it, but no one could stop me or tell me I was wrong.

"Boxer, that you?" Jacobi said. His voice crackled from a poor connection.

"I found a *book* in my apartment," I shouted into the phone. "It's clean. It didn't burn. There could be prints. I want it bagged and tagged, and I don't want to do it myself in case there's any question down the road."

"I'm five minutes away," Jacobi said.

I stood in the hallway with Joe and Martha, Joe telling me that Martha and I were moving in with him. I held tightly to his hand, but my mind was running a slide show of all the fire-razed houses I'd walked through in the last month, and I was feeling the searing shame of having been so professional and so removed. I'd seen the bodies. I'd seen the destruction. But I hadn't *felt* the terrible power of fire until now.

I heard Jacobi's voice and that of the building manager downstairs, then Jacobi's ponderous footsteps as he huffed and wheezed up the stairs. I'd ridden thousands of miles in a squad car with Jacobi. I'd been shot with him, and our blood had pooled together in an alley in the Tenderloin. I knew him better than anyone in the world, and he knew me that way, too. That's why when he arrived at the top landing, all I had to do was point to the book.

Jacobi stretched latex gloves over his large hands, gingerly opened the red cover. I was panting with fear, sure that I'd see an inscription inside, another mocking Latin saying. But there was only a name printed inside the front page.

The name was Chuck Hanni.

Chapter 70

IT WAS 1:03 A.M. and sixty-eight degrees outside.

I was lying next to Joe tucked inside the cool, white envelope of his six-hundred-thread-count sheets, wearing one of his T-shirts, staring up at the time and temperature projected onto his ceiling by a clock made for insomniacs and former G-men who needed to have this critical info the second they opened their eyes.

Joe's hand covered mine. He had listened to my fears and my ranting for hours, but as he drifted off, his grip loosened, and now he was snoring softly. Martha, too, was in the land of nod, her fluttery breaths and dream-yips providing a stereophonic accompaniment to Joe's steady snores.

As for me, sleep was on the far side of the moon.

I couldn't stop thinking how the fire skipped the first two floors but had torched my apartment out to the walls. It was undeniable. I was the target of a vicious, premeditated killer who'd already deliberately burned eight people to death.

Had he thought I was home? Or had he watched me leave with Martha and sent me a warning? How could Chuck Hanni be that person?

I'd had meals with Chuck, worked crime scenes with him, *confided* in him. Now I was reconfiguring him in my mind as a killer who knew everything there was to know about setting fires. And everything there was to know about getting away with murder.

But why would a man who was this smart leave his damned calling card in my apartment?

The signature of a killer was actually his *signature?*

It made no sense.

The pounding in my temples was building

up to a five-alarm headache. If there'd been anything in my stomach, I would have heaved it up. When the phone rang at 1:14, I read the caller ID and grabbed the receiver on the first ring. Joe stirred beside me. I whispered, "It's Conklin," and Joe mumbled, "Okay," and dropped back down into sleep.

"You got something?" I asked my partner.

"Yeah. You're not going to like this."

"Just tell me. Tell me what you've *got,*" I half whispered, half shouted. I got out of bed, stepped over Martha, and walked out into Joe's living room with its night view of Presidio Park, its tall eucalyptus trees swaying eerily in the moonlight. Martha's nails clacked on hardwood as she followed me, slurped water from a bowl in the kitchen.

"About the book..." Rich said.

"You found Latin written inside?"

"No. It's Chuck's book, all right—"

"Man oh man."

"Let me finish, Linds. *He* didn't leave it in your apartment. *I* did."

Chapter 71

MY MIND SCRAMBLED as I tried to under-stand what Conklin was telling me. "Say that *again*," I demanded. When he answered, his voice was contrite.

"I left the book at your place."

"You're kidding me, right?"

He had to be. I couldn't imagine any cir-cumstances under which Conklin would leave a fire and explosion manual in my fire-ravaged apartment.

"What happened is, I got together with Chuck, like you said to do," Rich told me in measured tones. "We had a no-hard-feelings dinner and I picked up the tab. And I told him

I'd like to learn more about fire investigation from him. I mean, he's the pro."

Rich paused for breath and I shouted at him, *"Go on!"*

"We went out to his car, Lindsay, he practically lives in that thing. Pop-Tarts wrappers all over the seats, his computer, clothes hanging from the—"

"Rich, for God's sake!"

"So, just as he finds the fire investigations manual to lend me, Jacobi calls and tells me your apartment went up. I told Hanni, and he said, 'I'll drive,' and I was still holding that book when we entered your place."

"You put it down on the telephone table."

"Didn't think about it again until Jacobi called me," Rich said miserably.

"Has Jacobi already spoken to Hanni?"

"No. He wanted to talk to me first. Hanni knows nothing about this."

It took long seconds for me to sort it all out, put Chuck Hanni back into his role as friend, and realize that the essential truth hadn't changed. I was shivering, and I wasn't cold.

"Linds?" I heard Rich say.

"We still don't know who set fire to my place or to any of the others," I said. "We still don't know anything."

Chapter 72

THERE HAD BEEN a whole blessed week's break while Judge Bendinger returned to physical rehab for his replaced knee. But the break was over. Bendinger was back. And Yuki now felt the tsunami effect of the whole freakin' Junie Moon circus starting all over again, the out-of-control press, the pressure to win.

At nine o'clock sharp, court was called into session.

And the defense began to put on its case.

L. Diana Davis didn't look up as her first witness came through the gate, passing so close she must have felt a breeze as his herringbone jacket nearly grazed her arm. Yuki saw Davis lean in and speak behind her hand to her client, all the while panning the gallery with her eyes. The TV cameras were running, and the reporters were packed in the rows at the back of the room.

Davis smiled.

Yuki whispered to Len Parisi, "There's no place Davis would rather be. Nobody she'd rather defend."

Red Dog smiled. "That beast is inside you, too, Yuki. Learn to love it."

Yuki watched Davis pat her client's hand as Lieutenant Charles Clapper, head of CSU, was sworn in. Then Davis stood and greeted her witness.

"Lieutenant Clapper, how long have you been head of the San Francisco Crime Scene Unit?"

"Fifteen years."

"And what did you do before that?"

"I started with the San Diego PD right outta school, worked vice for five years, homicide for five. Then I joined the Las Vegas CSU before moving to San Francisco and joining the CSU here."

"In fact, you've written books on trace evidence, haven't you?"

"Yes, I've done a couple of books."

"You appear on TV a few times a week, don't you? Sometimes even more times than me," Davis said, smiling widely, getting the laugh she wanted from the gallery.

"I don't know about that," Clapper said, smiling too.

"Very good. And how many homicides have you investigated in the last twenty-five years, Lieutenant?"

"I have no idea."

"Take a wild guess."

"A wild guess? Maybe a couple of hundred a year."

"So it's reasonable to say you may have investigated as many as five thousand homicides, is that right?"

"Roughly."

"I think we can accept 'roughly,'" Davis said, good-naturedly. "And as well as investigating fresh crime scenes, you investigate crimes that happened months or even years ago, is that correct?"

"I've investigated cold cases, yes."

"Now, in April of this year, were you called to the home of the defendant?"

"I was."

"And did it have the appearance of a crime scene?"

"No. The rooms were orderly. There was no evident disturbance, no blood or shell casings, et cetera."

Davis said, "Now, were you told that a man may have been dismembered in the bathtub of the defendant's house?"

"I was."

"And you did all the normal tests for trace evidence, did you not?"

"Yes, we did."

"Come up with anything evidentiary?"

"No."

"Find any evidence that showed that the blood had been cleaned up?"

"Nope."

"No bleach or anything like that?"

"No."

"Lieutenant Clapper, let me just give you the whole laundry list at once and save a little time here. The walls hadn't been repainted, the rugs hadn't been cleaned? You didn't find an implement that could have been used to dismember a body?"

"No."

"So it's fair to say that you and your team

did everything you could do to ascertain the manner in which a crime was committed—or even if a crime *was* committed?"

"We did."

"Based on your experience and your examination of the so-called crime scene, please tell the jury—did you find any evidence, direct or indirect, that links Junie Moon to the alleged murder of Michael Campion?"

"No."

"Thank you. That's all I have for this witness, Your Honor."

Chapter 73

YUKI WAS STILL STEAMING from Red Dog's rebuke. Or maybe she was hot under the collar because he'd been right.

Learn to love the beast.

Yuki slapped her pen down on her notepad, straightened her jacket as she stood, and approached Charlie Clapper at the stand.

"Lieutenant, I won't keep you long."

"No problem, Ms. Castellano."

"You're a member of law enforcement, right?"

"Yes."

"And in the course of your twenty-five-year-long career in vice, homicide, and crime scene investigation, have you been involved in matters concerning prostitutes?"

"Certainly."

"Are you familiar, generally speaking, with the lives of prostitutes and their customs?"

"I'd say so."

"Would you agree that in exchange for a fee, a prostitute engages in sexual relations with any number of men?"

"I'd say that's the job description."

"Now, there are many subsets of that job description, wouldn't you say? From street-walker to call girl?"

"Sure."

"And some prostitutes work mostly out of their homes?"

"Some do."

"And is it your understanding that Ms. Moon falls into that last category?"

"That's what I was told."

"Okay. And would you also agree that as a matter of hygiene and practicality, a prostitute working at home would do her best to shower after her sexual encounters?"

"I would say that would be a common and hygienic practice."

"Do you happen to know how much water is typically used by a person taking a shower?"

"Twenty gallons, depending."

Yuki nodded, said to Charlie, "Now, based on your general knowledge of prostitutes, and given that Ms. Moon worked at home, would you agree that she probably showered after having sex with each of her tricks, maybe six to ten times a day, seven days a week—"

"Objection," Davis called out. "Calls for speculation on the part of the witness, and furthermore, I strongly object to the way counsel is characterizing my client."

"Your Honor," Yuki protested. "We all know that Ms. Moon is a prostitute. I'm only asserting that she's probably a *clean* one."

"Go ahead, Ms. Castellano," Judge Bendinger said, snapping the rubber band on his wrist. "But get to the point *today,* will you?"

"Thanks, Your Honor," Yuki said, sweetly. "Lieutenant Clapper, could you tell us this?" Yuki drew a breath and launched into what was becoming her trademark—an uninterruptible run-on question.

"If a man was dismembered in a bathtub, and in the three months between the day the crime was committed and the time you examined the bathtub a large amount of soap and shampoo and water passed through that two-inch drain — by my calculations, 100 gallons of soapy water daily — and now let's double that for the johns who took a shower before going back to their dorm or office or home to their *wives* — so even if Ms. Moon practices 'Never on Sunday,' that would still be about 130,000 gallons by the time CSU examined the drains — could that activity have completely cleansed that bathtub of residual trace evidence?"

"Well, yes, that's very possible."

"Thank you, Lieutenant. Thank you very much."

Yuki smiled at Charlie Clapper as the judge told him that he could step down.

Chapter 74

YUKI SAT BESIDE the immense form of Len Parisi as Junie Moon's sleazebag pimp-boyfriend, Ricardo "Ricky" Malcolm, was sworn in.

Yuki was fully aware that Davis had hired a bounty hunter to drag Ricky Malcolm over the Mexican border for his court appearance, and as Malcolm swore to tell the whole truth, she wondered if Davis really thought this punked-out, tattooed, and homely creep could persuade the jury of anything. Davis's voice was confident as she asked Malcolm her preliminary questions, getting out ahead of the prosecution by getting Malcolm to say he'd served time for drug possession.

Then Davis started her direct examination in earnest.

"What's your relationship to Ms. Moon?"

"I was her boyfriend."

"No longer?"

"We're separated," Malcolm said drily. "I'm in Tijuana and she's in jail."

Titters arose in little pockets around the gallery.

"How long have you known Ms. Moon?" Davis asked.

"Gotta be three years."

"And did there come a time last January twenty-first when Ms. Moon called you at around eleven thirty at night and asked you to come to her house because one of her clients was having a heart attack?"

"No."

"Let me get this straight. You're saying Junie didn't call to tell you she needed help with Michael Campion?"

"No, ma'am. No, she did not."

"Did the police question you about the dismemberment and disposal of Michael Campion's body?"

"Yep. I told them I didn't do it."

"Were you telling the truth?"

Malcolm started to laugh. "Yeah, yeah, I told

them the truth. I never dismembered anybody.
I can't stand the sight of blood. I eat steak
well-done. It was one of the wackiest things I
ever heard."

"I agree," Davis said. "Pretty wacky."

Yuki jumped to her feet. "Objection, Your
Honor. Ms. Davis's opinions are totally irrele-
vant here."

"Sustained."

Davis spun on her heels, took a few paces
toward the jury, then turned back again. "And
yet," Davis said, her voice ringing out across
the oak-paneled courtroom, "according to
police testimony, Ms. Moon said that she
called you because Mr. Campion was having
a *heart attack,* and that when you arrived at
her place, Mr. Campion was *dead.*"

"It's totally bogus. Never happened," Malcolm said, clearly enjoying himself.

"The police further testified that Ms. Moon
told them that you dismembered Mr. Campion with a *knife* and that you and Ms. Moon
then transported Mr. Campion's remains and
disposed of them in a Dumpster.

"Did that happen?"

"*No way.* Crock a' shit. Plus, I've got no
skill with anything but power tools."

"Okay, Mr. Malcolm. So, in your opinion,

why would Ms. Moon say such a thing if it isn't true?"

"Because," Malcolm said, looking at Junie with his spacey green eyes, "she's simple, you know, like a special ed kid. She sucks up romance novels, daytime soaps—"

"Move to strike, Your Honor," Yuki said. "This whole line of questioning calls for speculation."

"Your Honor, Mr. Malcolm's testimony goes to the credibility of the defendant."

"I'll allow it. Go on, Mr. Malcolm."

Yuki sighed loudly, took her seat again between Gaines and Red Dog as Malcolm continued.

"Like I was saying, in my opinion, right? When the cops asked her if she'd done the deed with the famous Michael Campion, that was like lighting up a wide-screen, three-D fantasy starring Junie Moon, stupid little whore—"

"Thanks, Mr. Malcolm. Were you charged as an accessory in this crime?"

"The cops tried, but the DA knew they couldn't indict me on Junie's flaky confession, especially since she, whatchacallit, recanted."

"Thank you, Mr. Malcolm. Your witness," Davis said with a smirk to Yuki.

Chapter 75

YUKI READ LEN'S NOTES to her, his suggested line of questioning exactly what she planned to ask, but what was underscored in her mind was how important Malcolm was to the defense. And how important it was that she nullify his testimony.

Yuki stood, walked toward the witness stand, saying, "Mr. Malcolm, are you here today of your own volition?"

"Not exactly. The long arm of the *law* reached out and grabbed me out of a nice little titty bar in Tijuana."

"You have friends in Mexico, Mr. Malcolm?" Yuki asked over the laughter in the gallery.

"Or was this a case of 'you can run but you can't hide'?"

"A little of both." Malcolm shrugged, giving the jury a glimpse of his terrible, gappy smile.

"A few minutes ago you swore to tell the truth, isn't that right?"

"I got nothing against the truth," Malcolm said.

Yuki put her hands on the railing in front of the witness, asked, "How do you feel about the defendant? Ms. Moon."

"Junie's a sweet girl."

"Let's see if we can refine that answer, okay?"

Malcolm shrugged, said, "Refine away."

Yuki allowed a smile to show the jury she was a good sport, then said, "If you and Junie Moon were both free to walk out of here, Mr. Malcolm, would you spend the night with her?"

"Yeah. Sure."

"And if she needed a kidney, would you give her one of yours?"

"I've got two, right?"

"Yes. Odds are you have two."

"Sure. I'd give her a kidney." Ricky Malcolm grinned expansively, conveying what a generous guy he was.

"During your three-year-long relationship with the defendant, did you share things with her? Enjoy doing things with her?"

"Yeah. Sure."

"And how do you feel about her now?"

"That's a little personal, isn't it?"

Davis called out, "Your Honor, is this the Dr. Phil show? There's no relevance—"

"If the court would give me a moment to show relevance," Yuki interrupted.

"Overruled, Ms. Davis. Proceed, Ms. Castellano."

"Thanks, Your Honor," Yuki said. "Mr. Malcolm, your feelings aren't a secret, are they? Would you please roll up your right sleeve and show your arm to the jury."

Malcolm hesitated until the judge asked him to do it. Then he exposed his arm to the jury.

Called a "full sleeve" by tat aficionados, a dense collection of tattoos ran up Ricky Malcolm's pale skin from his wrist to his shoulder. Among the snakes and skulls was a red heart branded with the initials *R.M.* hanging from the hook of a feminized crescent moon.

"Mr. Malcolm, could you tell us what the letters underneath that heart tattoo mean?"

"You mean *T-M-T-Y-L-M-J-M*?"

"That's right, Mr. Malcolm."

Malcolm sighed. "It stands for 'Tell me that you love me, Junie Moon.'"

"So, Mr. Malcolm, is it fair to say that you love the defendant?"

Malcolm was looking at Junie now, his face heavy, having lost its wiseass expression, Junie looking back at him with her huge slate-gray eyes.

"Yes. I love her."

"Do you love her enough to lie for her?"

"Sure, I'd lie for her, what the hell?"

"Thanks, Mr. Malcolm. I'm done with this witness, Judge," said Yuki, turning her back on Ricky Malcolm.

Chapter 76

JACOBI CALLED THE MEETING to order at the crack of eight a.m. He asked me to come to the front of the room to brief the troops on our arson-homicide case and where we were with it—that is to say, nowhere. I was wearing jeans and a beaded tank top, a pair of moccasins, and a faded denim jacket that I'd left at Joe's place before the fire.

It was all that I had.

I got whistles, of course, one beefy old-timer shouting out, "Nice rack, Sarge."

"Shut up, McCracken," Rich shouted back, making me blush, extending the moment as my fellow cops laughed and made raunchy comments to each other. After Jacobi kicked a desk so that a hollow boom silenced the room, I filled everyone in on the Meacham and Malone homicides.

Assignments were divvied up, I got into the car with Conklin, and we drove to one of the dark and grubby alleys in the Mission. We were doing it again, more down-and-dirty detective work, hoping for clues in the absence of a single hard lead.

Our first stop was a pawnshop on Polk called Gold 'n' Things, a shop piled high with outdated electronics and musical instruments, and a half-dozen glass cases filled with tacky bling. The proprietor was Rudy Vitale, an obese man with thick glasses and thin hair, a marginal fence who used the pawnshop as his office while making his real deals in cars and bars, anywhere but here.

I let Conklin take the lead because my insides were still reeling from the sharp turn my life had taken only twelve hours before.

My mind was stuck in a groove of what the fire had cost me in emotional touchstones to my past: my Willie Mays jacket, my Indian pottery, and everything that had belonged to my mother, especially her letters telling me how much she loved me, a sentiment she'd only been able to write when she was dying but was never able to actually say.

As Conklin showed insurance photos to Vitale, I glanced at the display cases, still in a daze, not expecting anything, when suddenly, as if someone yelled *Hey* in my ear, I saw Patty Malone's sapphire necklace on a velveteen tray, right *there.*

"Rich," I said sharply. "Take a look at this."

Conklin looked, then told Vitale to open the case. Baubles clanked as Vitale pawed through them, handed the necklace up to Conklin with his catcher's mitt of a hand.

"You're saying these are real sapphires?" Vitale said innocently.

Conklin's face blanched around the eyes as he placed the necklace down on the photograph. It was clearly a match.

"Where'd you get this?" he asked Vitale.

"Some kid brought it in a week ago."

"Let's see the paperwork."

"Hold on," Vitale said, waddling back to his cage.

He moved a pile of auction catalogs and books on antique jewelry from his desk chair, then tapped the keys on his laptop.

"Got it. I paid the kid a hundred bucks. Here you go. Whoops. I just noticed his name."

I read the receipt over Conklin's shoulder, the name Clark Kent, an address somewhere in the middle of the bay, and the description of a "blue topaz necklace."

"Was he wearing a suit and eyeglasses?" Conklin yelled. *"Or maybe he'd changed into tights and a cape?"*

"I'll need the tape from that," I said, pointing to the video camera anchored in the corner of the ceiling like a red-eyed spider.

Vitale said, "That's got a twenty-four-hour loop. He's not on it anymore. Anyway, I dimly remember the kid, and I don't think he was the tights-and-cape type. More of a preppy look. I think maybe I sold him some comic books one time before."

"Can you do better than 'preppy look'?"

"Dark hair, I think. A little on the stocky side."

"We'll need you to come in and look at our mug books," I said. "Talk to a sketch artist."

"I'm no good at faces," said Vitale. "It's like a disorder I have. Some kind of dyslexia. I don't think I'd recognize you if I saw you tomorrow."

"Bull," Conklin snapped. "This is a homicide investigation, Vitale. Understand? If that kid comes in again, call us. Preferably while he's still here. And make a copy of his driver's license."

"Okay, chief," Vitale said. "Will do."

"It's something," Conklin said to me as he started up the car. "Kelly will be glad to have something from her mom."

"Yeah, she will," I said.

My mind flew to my own mom's death. I turned my head so that Conklin couldn't see the tears that came into my eyes.

Chapter 77

CHUCK HANNI STOOD with me and Joe in the dank basement of the building where I used to live, showing us the fine points of archaic knob-and-tube wiring as water dripped on our heads. The door to the fuse box was open, and Hanni held his Mag-Lite on a fuse he wanted me to see.

"See how this penny is annealed to the back of the fuse?"

I could just make out the dull copper blob.

"The college girls on the second floor—you know them?" Hanni asked.

"Just to wave hi."

"Okay, well, apparently they've been blow-

ing fuses every other day with their hair dry-
ers and air conditioner and irons and whatnot.
And your super got tired of running over here
to change the fuse, so he put this penny in
here."

"Which does what?"

Chuck explained everything that happened, how the copper penny overrode the
fuse so that the circuit didn't trip. Instead the
electricity went through the penny and melted
down the wiring at its weakest point. In this
case, the ceiling lights on the second floor
and the electric sockets in my apartment.

I visualized flames shooting out of the
socket, but I still didn't get it—so Chuck took
his time explaining to me and to Joe how my
building, like a lot of old buildings, had "bal-
loon construction," that is, the framing timbers ran from roof to ceiling without any fire
stops in between.

"The fire just races up through the walls,"
Hanni said. "Those spaces between the timbers act like chimneys. And so when the fire
reached your apartment, it came out the
sockets, set your stuff on fire, and just kept
going. Took out the roof and burned itself
out."

"So you're telling me this was an accident?"

"I was suspicious, too," Chuck told me.

He said that he'd questioned everyone himself: the building manager, the girls downstairs, and in particular our aging handyman, Angel Fernandez, who admitted he'd put the penny behind the fuse to save himself another trip up the hill.

"If anyone had died in this fire, I'd be charging Angel Fernandez with negligent homicide," Hanni said. "I'm calling this an accidental fire, Lindsay. You file an insurance claim and it will sail through."

I'd been trained to read a lie in a person's face, and all I saw was the truth in Chuck Hanni's frankly honest features. But I was jumpy and not quite ready to let my worst suspicions go. Walking out to Joe's car I asked for his point of view as a guy who'd spent a couple of decades in law enforcement.

"Hanni didn't do it, honey. I think he's suffering almost as much as you are. And I think he likes you."

"That's your professional opinion?"

"Yep. Hanni's on your side."

Chapter 78

YUKI WAS WIRED.

We were eating lunch at her desk, both of us picking through our salads as if we were looking for nuggets of gold instead of chicken. Yuki had asked me how I was feeling, but I didn't have much to say and she was pent up, so I said, "You first," and she was off.

"So, Davis calls her expert shrink, Dr. Maria Paige. Ever heard of her?" Yuki asked me.

I shook my head no.

"She's on Court TV sometimes. Tall? Blond? Harvard?"

I shook my head no again and Yuki said, "Doesn't matter. So, anyway. Davis puts this big-name shrink on the stand to tell us all about false confessions."

"Ahh," I said, getting it. "Junie Moon's 'false' confession?"

"Right. And she's a bright babe, this shrink. She's got it all down. How and why Miranda rights came into being so that cops can't coerce suspects. The landmark studies by Gudjonsson and Clark having to do with the suggestibility of certain subjects. And the Reid book for cops on how to get around Miranda.

"She sounds like she *wrote* the fricking book, Lindsay," Yuki continued, getting even more pissed off. "She says with *authority* how cops can browbeat and trick suspects into making false confessions."

"Well, some might do that—but I sure didn't."

"Of course not. And so then she says how certain people with low intelligence or low self-esteem would rather *agree* with cops than *disagree* with them. And so the jury looks at Junie."

"Junie confessed all on her *own*—"

"I know, I know, but you know what Junie looks like—*Bambi's baby sister.* So finally Dr. Paige wraps it up, and I'm wondering how

I'm going to cancel out her testimony without showing the whole two-hour tape of your interview with Junie."

"Well, you could've done that," I said, snapping the plastic lid closed on my salad and tossing it into the trash can. Yuki did the same.

"Two *hours,* Lindsay? Of Junie denying everything? So listen. I got up and said, 'Dr. Paige, did you ever meet Junie Moon?' 'No.' 'Ever see the tape of the interview with the police?' 'Yes.' So I said, 'Did the police browbeat the defendant or lie to her or trick her?' 'No, no, not really.'"

Yuki sipped her tea, then continued her reenactment of her cross-examination of Dr. Paige.

"So then I make a mistake."

"What did you do?"

"I was exasperated, Lindsay." Yuki grimaced. She raked her hair away from her lovely heart-shaped face.

"I said, 'So, what did the police do, exactly?' I know not to ask a question I don't have an answer to, but shit! I've seen the damned interview two dozen times and you and Conklin did nothing!

"And now Red Dog is glaring at me, and

the shrink is saying, 'In my opinion, Miss Moon not only has bottomless low self-esteem, she feels guilty because she's a *prostitute* and her confession was a way of *reducing her guilt.*'

"I couldn't believe she was asking the jury to swallow that, so I said, 'So you're saying she feels guilty that she's a prostitute and that's why she confessed to *manslaughter?*'

"'That's what I'm saying,' Paige says, so I say, 'That's all, Doctor.' And Bendinger tells her to step down, and I'm squeezing in behind Red Dog's chair, facing the gallery, and there's *Twilly,*" Yuki said.

"Isn't he there every day?" I asked my friend.

"Yeah, but now he's sitting right behind me. And I'm making eye contact with him because that's all I can do. And I hear Davis say she's calling Junie Moon to the stand, and the judge says, 'First we're going to recess for lunch.' And Red Dog pushes back his chair, pinning me chest to nose with that *creep,* Twilly.

"And Twilly sneers. And my stomach clenches and my skin gets cold and he whispers, 'Point, Davis.'

"Omigod, and so Red Dog turns and gives

me that withering look again, and I'm not going to lose this case over the testimony of
that shrink, am I, Lindsay, am I? Because I'll
tell you, that just can't *happen.*"

"It won't—"

"Right. It *won't,*" Yuki said through her
teeth, slamming her fist down on her desk.
"Because the jury's going to see the truth,
and they've got to come to one of two
conclusions.

"Either Junie Moon is *guilty.* Or she's guilty
as *sin.*"

Chapter 79

THE STANFORD MALL was an open-air dream market with shops grouped on narrow lanes, embedded in gardens. And what shops they were: the big stores Neiman and Nordstrom and Bloomingdale's, and the high-end boutiques Armani, Benetton, Louis Vuitton.

Hawk and Pidge had taken a seat on a bench outside the Polo shop, surrounded by a small forest of potted topiary, aromas of flowers and coffee wafting all around them. It was a Saturday, and great masses of designer-clad shoppers were out, parading down the little walkways past Pidge and

Hawk, swinging their shopping bags, stopping to admire Ralph Lauren's windows.

Pidge had a video camera about the size of a deck of cards and was filming the parade. If anyone asked what he was doing, he'd tell them the truth—or part of it, anyway. He was in the computer video lab at Stanford. He was making a documentary.

But what he wouldn't say is that he and Hawk were looking for the winners. The biggest, piggiest oink-oinks of the day.

They had two sets of contestants in mind.

Both couples had college stickers on the rear windows of their cars. They were primo candidates. It was going to be hard to choose, but once Hawk and Pidge had agreed on the winning couple, they would follow them to where they lived and check out their home.

Which one?

The rich and fatty couple loaded down with bags imprinted with designer logos? Or the older, more athletic pair, dressed ostentatiously, sipping lattes as they wandered along the avenues of gluttony.

Pidge was reviewing the footage when the security guard approached. He was late forties, blue uniform with a badge on his breast pocket, a hat, a gun, and a swagger. Every guy in a uniform these days thought he was a U.S. Marine.

"Hi, guys," the guard said affably. "You can't take pictures in here. Sign's right over there."

"Ah," said Pidge. He stood. At six two he towered over the guard, so that the smaller man had to step back. "These aren't pictures. This is a movie. A documentary for school. I can show you my student ID."

"Doesn't matter that you're in school," the guard said. "For security reasons, no picture taking is allowed. Now you have to either put that thing away or I'll have to escort you out of here."

"You dipshit rent-a-cop," Hawk muttered.

"We're sorry, sir," said Pidge, stepping in front of his friend. "We're going."

But it was annoying. Hours spent doing their surveillance and now, no winner.

"Gotta make a pit stop," Pidge said.

The two ducked into the men's facilities, and Pidge unzipped in front of a urinal. When he'd finished, Hawk took out a book of matches. He lit three or four of them together and tossed them into the waste bin.

They were out in the parking lot when they

heard the cry of the sirens on the freeway. They sat in Pidge's car and watched as the firefighters braked near the Frog Pond, un-furled their hoses, and streamed into the mall.

Many hundreds of customers streamed out.

"I sure love a good fire," Hawk said.

"Always makes my day," said Pidge.

Part Four

HOT PROPERTY

Chapter **80**

I WAS HEADING "HOME" to Joe's apartment, battling rush-hour traffic, when my cell phone rang. I jacked the phone off my hip, heard Yuki's voice screaming my name.

"*Lindsay!* He's *stalking* me."

"*Who? Who's* stalking you?"

"That freak! Jason Twilly."

"Slow down. Back up. What do you mean 'stalking'?"

I jerked the wheel left at the intersection of Townsend and Seventh instead of taking a right toward my former apartment on the Hill. It felt like I was swimming against the tide.

Yuki's voice was shrill. "*Stalking* as in *haunting* me, *dogging* me. Ten minutes ago, he was sitting in the passenger seat of my *car!*"

"He broke into your car?"

"I don't know. I can't remember if I locked it. I was carrying like a fifty-pound—"

The signal cut out. I hit speed dial, got Yuki's outgoing message, disconnected, tried again.

"Fifty-pound *what?*" I called into the crackle.

"Fifty-pound box of *files.* I just got my key into the door lock when this arm reached over from *inside* the car and pushed the door open for me."

"Before this car thing, did you tell him to leave you alone?"

"Yes! Did I ever!"

"Okay, then, it's illegal for him to be inside your car," I said, negotiating a lane switch, passing a rental car whose driver leaned on the horn and gave me the finger.

"You ready to swear out a complaint?" I asked Yuki. "He's going to go public. So think about it."

There was a moment of static-filled silence as Yuki considered the media ramifications.

"This guy is *sick,* Linds. He talks to me like

I'm a character in his book. He's *twisted* and maybe dangerous. He got into my *car.* What's next?"

"Okay," I said, pulling over to the curb. I took out my notepad and wrote down what Yuki had told me.

"You're going to have to go to civil court in the morning, get a restraining order," I said. "But effective *now* you've filed a police report."

"Tomorrow *morning?* Lindsay, Jason Twilly wants to scare the hell out of me—and he's *doing* it!"

Chapter 81

WHEN I REACHED Twilly's suite on the fifth floor of the St. Regis Hotel, he was waiting in the doorway, a cockeyed grin on his face, his hair disheveled and shirt untucked and unbuttoned. The fire exit door slammed at the end of the softly lit hallway. My guess, it was Twilly's paid-by-the-hour guest leaving in a hurry.

I showed Twilly my badge, and he fastened his eyes on the V of my tank top, skimmed the cut of my jeans, then took a slow return trip back to my face. Meanwhile, I was taking in his amazing room—leather-textured walls, a window seat with a great view of San Francisco. Very impressive.

"Working undercover, Sergeant?" Twilly leered.

He'd scared Yuki with this act, but it enraged *me.*

"I don't think we've met, Mr. Twilly. I'm Sergeant Lindsay Boxer," I said, putting out my hand. He grasped it in a handshake and I pulled his arm forward, twisted it high up behind his back, and pushed his face against the wall.

"Give me your other hand," I said. "Do it, *now.*"

"You're *joking.*"

"Other hand."

I cuffed him, frisked him fast and rough, saying, "You're under arrest for criminal trespass. Anything you say can be used against you in a court of law." When I finished informing Twilly of his rights, I answered his question: "What's this about?"

"It's about your illegal entry into ADA Yuki Castellano's car. She's filed a police report, and by noon tomorrow she'll have a restraining order against you."

"Whoa, whoa! This is the biggest deal about nothing I've ever heard. Her arms were full! I opened her car door to help her!"

"Tell it to your lawyer," I snapped. I had one

hand on Twilly's arm, my cell phone in my other, and was about to call for backup.

"Wait a minute," he said. "Is Yuki claiming that I'm harassing her? Because that's crap. I admit I provoked her a little, applied a little pressure just to get her going. I'm a *journalist. We do that.* Look. If I made a mistake, I'm sorry. Can we talk? Please?"

I'd checked Twilly out, and his record was clean. I had a moment of free fall as my anger evaporated. A stern warning would have been appropriate. Now that I'd cuffed him—that media flap Cindy had warned Yuki about?

It was going to go down.

I could already see Twilly spinning this "bust" to Larry King, Tucker Carlson, *Access Hollywood.* It would be bad news for Yuki, bad for me, but it would be stupendous publicity for Twilly.

"Sergeant?"

I had to hit rewind. I had to try.

"You want to avoid a court appearance, Mr. Twilly? Leave Yuki Castellano *alone. Don't* sit behind her in court. *Don't* tail her in supermarkets. *Don't* enter her car or premises, and we'll put this incident aside.

"Yuki files another complaint? I'm taking you in. Are we clear?"

"Totally," he said. "Crystal."

"Good."

I unlocked the cuffs and started to leave.

"Wait!" Twilly said. He stepped into the other room, with its aqua-striped wallpaper and canopied bed. He snatched a pen and pad from the bowlegged writing desk and said, "I want to make sure I got this right."

He scribbled notes, then recited my speech back to me, verbatim.

"That was really excellent stuff you just said, Sergeant. Who do you think should play you in the movie?"

He was screwing with me.

I left Twilly's suite feeling as though I'd been smacked in the face with a shit pie — and I'd done it to myself. Damn it to *hell.* Maybe I'd jammed myself up, and maybe I was wrong to cuff him, but it didn't mean that Jason Twilly wasn't crazy.

And it didn't mean he wasn't danger-ous.

Chapter **82**

JOE AND I had a takeout dinner from Le Soleil and were in bed by ten. My eyes flew open at exactly 3:04, the digits projected on the ceiling keeping track of the time as my sickening night thoughts churned.

An image of Twilly's sneer had awakened me, but his face dissolved, and in its place I saw the burned and twisted corpses on Claire's table. And I remembered the dulled eyes of a young girl who'd been orphaned by a nameless teenage boy who might now be lying awake in *his* bed, planning another horror show.

How many more people would die before we found him?

Or would he beat us at this sick game?

I thought of the fire that had consumed my home, my possessions, my sense of security. And I thought about Joe, how much I loved Joe. I'd wanted him to move to San Francisco so that we could make a life together—and we were doing it through thick and thin. Why couldn't I take him up on that big Italian wedding he'd proposed and maybe start a family?

I would be thirty-nine in a few months.

What was I waiting for?

I listened to Joe's breathing, and in a while my rapid nightmare heart thuds slowed and I started drifting off. I turned away from Joe, gripped a pillow in my arms—and the mattress shifted as Joe turned toward me. He enfolded me in his arms, tucked his knees up behind mine.

"Bad dream?" he asked me.

"Uh-huh," I said. "I forget the dream, but when I woke up, I thought about a lot of dead people."

"Dead people in general? Or real dead people?"

"Real ones," I said.

"Want to talk about it?"

"I would—but they've slunk back to the pit they came from. Hey, I'm sorry, Joe. I didn't mean to wake you up."

"It's okay. Try to sleep."

It took a second to understand that that was a *dare.*

Joe moved my hair away from the back of my neck and kissed me there. I gasped, shocked at the charge that his soft kiss sent through my body.

I hadn't expected to feel *this* tonight.

I rolled over, looked into Joe's face, saw the glint of his smile by the soft blue light of the clock. I put my hands on his face and kissed him hard, searching for an answer I couldn't find inside myself. He reached his arms around me, but I pushed them away.

"No," I said. "Let me."

I put all of my tormenting thoughts aside. I tugged off Joe's boxers, interlaced my fingers through his, pressed his hands against the pillows. He moaned as I lowered myself onto him and then I eased off, kissed him until he went crazy. Then I rode him, rode him, rode him, until he couldn't wait another second—and neither could I. There was the undeniable pull of the undertow, before I was released by great cascading waves of pleasure.

I collapsed onto Joe's chest, my knees still on either side of his body, my cheek resting over his pounding heart. He stroked my back and I told him I loved him. I remember him kissing my forehead, pulling the blanket up over my shoulders as I drifted off with him still inside me.

Oh, my God.

It was just so good with Joe.

Chapter 83

YUKI STUDIED JUNIE MOON as she was sworn in by the bailiff.

Defendants weren't required to testify. It couldn't be held against them if they didn't, and it rarely helped when they did. So it was very risky to put your client on the stand. No matter how well rehearsed, there was no way to know if your client was going to go rogue, or get flustered, or laugh at the wrong time, or in some unique way prejudice the jury against her.

But Davis was putting Junie Moon on the stand. And the citizens of San Francisco and trial watchers across the country were dying to hear what she would say. Junie's white blouse hung from her shoulders and her plain blue skirt billowed around her calves. She'd lost weight in jail—a lot of it—and when Junie raised her right hand to take the oath, Yuki saw vivid bruising on her forearm.

Spectators gasped and murmured. And now Yuki understood why Davis had risked everything she'd gained to have her client testify. Junie looked nothing like a whore and a ghoul.

She looked like a *victim.*

Junie swore to tell the truth, stepped up to the witness stand, and sat with her hands in her lap, smiling trustingly as Davis approached.

"How are you doing?" Davis asked.

"In jail, you mean?"

"Yes. Are you doing okay?"

"Yes, ma'am. I'm fine."

Davis nodded, said, "Good. And how old are you, Junie?"

"I'll be twenty-three next month."

"And when did you start turning tricks?" Davis asked.

"When I was fourteen," Junie said softly.

"And how did that come about?"

"My stepdad turned me out."

"Do you mean that your stepfather prostituted you? That he was your pimp?"

"I guess you could call him that. He was having sex with me from the time I was about twelve. Later on, he brought his friends over and they had sex with me, too."

"Did you ever report your stepfather for rape or child abuse, anything like that?"

"No, ma'am. He said it was how I paid my rent."

"Is your stepfather here today?"

"No. He died three years ago."

"And your mother? Where is she?"

"She's doing time. For dealing."

"I see," Davis said. "So, Junie, you're a bright enough girl. Did you really have to be a prostitute? Couldn't you have gotten a job in a restaurant or a department store? Maybe worked in an office?"

Junie cleared her throat, said quietly, "Doing sex is the only thing I've ever known, and I don't really mind. It's like, for a little time every day, I feel close to someone."

"Having sex with strangers makes you feel close?"

Junie smiled. "I know it's not real, but it makes me feel good for a while."

Davis paused to let the tragedy of the vulnerable young woman's story wash over the jury. Then she said, "Junie, please tell the jury: Did you ever have sex with Michael Campion?"

"*No, I did not. Absolutely never!*"

"So why did you tell the police that you did?"

"I guess I wanted to please them, so I told them what they wanted to hear. I...that's the kind of person I am."

"Thank you, Junie. Your witness," Davis said.

Chapter 84

YUKI HAD A THOUGHT. It was stark, simple, irrefutable.

When Junie took the stand in her own defense, she had come across so frail and so *helpless,* it would be best for Yuki to say, "I have no questions," get the woman off the stand. Then tear her apart in summation.

Nicky Gaines passed Yuki a note from Red Dog. She read it as Judge Bendinger snapped the rubber band on his wrist impatiently, then said, "Ms. Castellano? Are you planning to cross?"

Parisi's note was short. Three words. *"Go get her."*

Yuki shook her head no, whispered across Gaines to Parisi, "We should take a pass."

Parisi scowled, said, "Want me to do it?"

So much for irrefutable. Red Dog had spoken. Yuki stood, picked up the photocopy of the acknowledgment of rights form, and walked toward the witness stand.

"Ms. Moon," Yuki said without preamble, "this is an acknowledgment of rights form. Do you remember it?"

"Yes, I think so."

"And you *can* read and write, can't you?"

"Yes, I can."

"Okay, then. This form was presented to you by Sergeant Lindsay Boxer and Inspector Richard Conklin when you were interviewed at the police station on April nineteenth.

"It says here, 'Before we ask you any questions you must understand your rights. You have the right to remain silent. Anything you say can and will be used against you in a court of law.' And here's a set of initials. Are they yours?"

Junie peered at the document, said, "Yes."

Yuki read the entire form, stopping at each point to fire the question at Junie: "Did you understand this? Are these your initials?" *Bang, bang, bang.*

And after each question, Junie scrutinized the paper and said, "Yes."

"And here at the bottom is a waiver of rights. It says that you understand your rights, that you don't want a lawyer, that no threats have been made against you, that you weren't coerced. Did you sign this?"

"Yes, ma'am, I did."

"And did you tell the police that Michael Campion died in your house and that you disposed of his body?"

"Yes."

"Did you feel tricked or intimidated by the police?"

"No."

Yuki walked to the prosecution table, put down the form, collected a nod from Parisi, and turned back to the defendant.

"Why did you make this confession?"

"I wanted to help the police."

"I'm *confused,* Ms. Moon. You wanted to help them. So first you said you never *met* Mr. Campion. Then you said he died in your *arms.* Then you said you left his body parts in a *Dumpster.* Then you said you made up the story to please the police—because that's the kind of *person* you are.

"Ms. Moon. Which lie do you want us to believe?"

Junie shot a startled look to her attorney, then stared at Yuki, stuttered incoherently, her lips quivering, tears sliding down her pale face, before choking out, "I'm sorry. I don't know...I don't know what to say."

A woman's voice sounded out from the gallery, directly behind the defense table. *"STOP!"*

Yuki turned toward the voice, as did every other person in the courtroom. The speaker was Valentina Campion, wife of the former governor, mother of the dead boy. She was standing, resting a hand on her husband's shoulder for support.

Yuki felt her blood drain to her feet.

"I can't stand what she's doing to that poor child," Valentina Campion said to her husband. Then she edged past him to the aisle, and as two hundred people swiveled in their seats to watch her, Mrs. Campion exited the courtroom.

Chapter 85

YUKI HAD SPENT THE NIGHT flopping like a beached tuna, and she was still sweating this morning, thinking how first she'd been *sandbagged* by her fricking boss. And then Valentina Campion had thrown her under an eighteen-wheeler!

People bond during trials, Yuki knew that, and strange attachments were made. But Mrs. Campion protecting the defendant? That was crazy! Didn't she realize that Yuki was on her side? That she was trying to do the right thing by her son?

Now the buzz in the courtroom grew as spectators and reporters watched L. Diana

Davis take her seat. Davis looked smug, Yuki thinking that her opponent must've gotten drunk last night on self-congratulation.

Junie Moon was escorted into the courtroom. Davis stood, sat when her client sat, and immediately after they were both seated, the bailiff called out, "All rise."

There was a muffled whoosh of people standing as the judge limped to the bench. The jury filed in, dropped their bags, settled into their seats. Judge Bendinger spoke to the jury, reminded them of his instructions. Then he asked Yuki if she was ready to give her summation, and she said that she was.

But she wasn't sure.

She gathered her notes, stood tall in her Jimmy Choos, and walked to the lectern. She put her notes in front of her and blocked out everyone but the jury. She ignored Parisi's placid bulk, Twilly's mocking smile, Davis's hauteur, and the defendant's pathetic fragility. She even looked past Cindy, who gave her a thumbs-up from the back row.

Yuki stood a poster-sized photo of Michael Campion on the easel, turned it so it faced the jury. She paused to let everyone see the face of the boy who was so beloved that citizens of the world included him in their prayers at night.

Yuki wanted to be sure the jury understood that this trial was about Michael Campion's death, not the sad story of the prostitute who'd let him die.

Yuki put her hands on the sides of the lectern and began to speak from her heart.

Chapter 86

"LADIES AND GENTLEMEN, Junie Moon is a prostitute," Yuki said. "She's in violation of the law every time she works, and her clientele is made up largely of schoolboys below the age of consent. But we don't hold the defendant *less credible* because of what she does for a living. Ms. Moon has her reasons—and that doesn't make her guilty of the charges against her.

"So, please judge her as you would anybody else. We're all equal under the law. That's the way our system works.

"Ms. Moon is charged with tampering with evidence and with murder in the second degree.

"In my opening statement, I told you that in order to prove murder, we have to prove *malice.* That is, that the person acted in such a way as we can construe them to have had 'an abandoned and malignant heart.'

"What does an abandoned and malignant heart look like?

"Ms. Moon told the police that she ignored Michael Campion's pleas for help, she let him die, and then she covered up this crime by dismembering and disposing of that young man's body.

"Could any of you cut up a person's body?" Yuki asked. "Can you imagine what's involved in dismembering a human being? I have a hard time cutting up a *chicken.* What would it take to dismember a person who was living and breathing and speaking only hours before— someone who was sharing your bed?

"What kind of soul, what kind of character, what kind of person, what kind of *heart,* would it take to do that?

"Wouldn't that behavior *define* an abandoned and malignant heart?

"The defendant made this confession when she thought she was off the record and in the clear. But Junie Moon got it wrong. A *confession* is a *confession,* ladies and gentlemen, on tape or off. It's as simple as that. She made an admission of guilt, and we're holding her to it.

"Now, the People have the burden of proving our case beyond a *reasonable* doubt. So if you can't answer every question in your mind, that's normal. That's human. That's why your charge is to find the defendant guilty beyond *reasonable* doubt—but not beyond *all* doubt."

Yuki's voice was throbbing in her throat when she said, "We don't know where Michael Campion's body is. All we know is the last person to see him is sitting in that chair.

"Junie Moon confessed again and again and again.

"And that, ladies and gentlemen, is all you need to find her guilty and to give justice to Michael Campion and his family."

Chapter 87

NO ONE HAD YET DISCOVERED what the L. stood for in L. Diana Davis. Some said it was something exotic; Lorelei or Letitia. Some said that Davis had stuck the initial in front of her name to add mystique.

Yuki guessed the L. stood for "lethal."

Davis was wearing Chanel for her closing argument: a pink suit with black trim, calling up memories of Jackie Kennedy, although there was nothing of the former president's wife in Davis's strident voice.

"Ladies and gentlemen. You remember what I asked in my opening statement," she demanded rather than asked. "*Where's the beef?* And that's the bottom line here. Where's the body? Where's the DNA? Where's the confession? Where's the *proof* in this case?

"The prosecution is trying to convince us that a person confesses to a crime and the police have her in custody and they don't record her confession—and that doesn't mean anything? They say that there's no blood evidence and no body—and that doesn't mean anything either?

"I'm sorry, folks, but something is wrong here," Davis said, her hands on the railing of the jury box.

"Something is very wrong.

"Dr. Paige, a distinguished psychiatrist, got on the stand and said that in her opinion, Junie Moon falsely confessed because her self-esteem is so low it's off the charts, and that Ms. Moon wanted to please the police. She also said that in her opinion, Ms. Moon feels guilty about being a prostitute and so she confessed to discharge some of that guilt.

"Ladies and gentlemen, let me tell you the dirty little secret about false confessions. Every time a major crime is committed, false confessions pour into the hotlines. Hundreds of people confessed to the Lindbergh baby kidnapping. Dozens of people told police they killed the Black Dahlia. Maybe you remember when John Mark Karr caused an international brouhaha by confessing to the murder of Jon-Benet Ramsey ten years after her death.

"**He didn't do it.**

"People confess to crimes when they've been *cleared* by DNA evidence. Go figure. People confess for reasons you and I would find hard to understand, but it's the role of a good investigator to separate false confessions from real ones.

"Junie Moon's confession was *false.*

"The absence of evidence in this case is remarkable. If the name of the so-called victim was Joe Blow, there probably wouldn't have been an indictment, let alone a trial. But Michael Campion is a political *celebrity* and Ms. Moon is *at the bottom of the social totem pole.*

"It's *showtime!*

"But this isn't *Showbiz Tonight,* ladies and gentlemen. This is a court of *lawwww,*" Davis trumpeted. "So we're asking you to use your common sense as well as the facts in evidence. If you do that, you can only find Junie Moon *not guilty* of the charges against her, *period.*"

Chapter 88

IT WAS AFTER SEVEN when I got to Susie's. The patrons at the bar had achieved a high degree of merriment. I didn't recognize the plinky tune the steel band was playing, but it was all about sun and the sparkly Caribbean Sea.

Made me want to move to Jamaica and open a dive shop with Joe. Drink passion fruit mai tais and grill fish on the beach.

I reached our table in the back room as Lorraine was clearing away a plate of chicken bones. She took my order for a Corona and dropped off the menu. Claire was taking up one side of our booth, what she called "sitting for two," while Cindy and Yuki sat across from her—Yuki pressed up against the wall as if she'd been smushed there like a bug.

It looked like she'd lost a fight.

I dragged up a chair, said, "What'd I miss?"

"Yuki gave a *great* closing argument," Cindy said, and then Yuki broke in.

"But Davis *obliterated* it!"

"You are *nuts. You* got the final damned *word,* Yuki," Cindy said. "You *nailed* it."

I didn't have to beg. As soon as we ordered dinner, Yuki launched into her impeccable L. Diana Davis impression, screaming, *"Where's the beef? Where's the beef?"*

When Yuki paused for breath, Cindy said, "Do your rebuttal, Yuki. Do it like you *mean* it."

Yuki laughed a little hysterically, wiped tears from her eyes with a napkin, downed her margarita—a drink she could barely handle on a good day. And then she belched.

"I hate waiting for a verdict," she said.

We all laughed, Cindy egging Yuki on until she said, *"Okay."* And then she was into it, eyes glistening, hands gesturing, the whole Yuki deal.

"I said, 'Was a crime committed? Well, ladies

and gentlemen, there's a reason the defendant is here. She was indicted by a grand jury and not because of her relative social standing to the deceased. The police didn't throw a dart at a phone book.

"'Junie Moon didn't call the police and make a false confession.

"'The police developed *information* that led them to the last person to see Michael Campion. That person was Junie Moon — and *she admitted it.*'"

"That's gooood, sugar," Claire murmured.

Yuki smiled, continued on. "'We don't have Michael Campion's body, but in all the months since he saw Ms. Moon, he has never called home, never used his credit card, his cell phone, or sent an e-mail to his parents or friends to say he's all right.

"'Michael wouldn't do that. That's not the kind of boy he was. So where *is* Michael Campion? Junie Moon told us. He died. He was dismembered. And his body was dumped in the garbage. She did it.

"'Period.'"

"See?" Cindy said, grinning. "She totally nailed it."

Chapter 89

CLAIRE AND I were sitting up in her bed that night after our outing at Susie's, having a two-girl pajama party. Edmund was on tour with the San Francisco Symphony, and Claire had said, "I really, *really* don't want to go into labor here all by myself alone, girlfriend."

I looked over at her, lying in the huge divot she'd made in her memory-foam mattress with her rotund 260 pounds.

"I can't get any bigger," she said. "It's not possible. I wasn't this big with two boys, so how can this little girl-child turn me into the blimp that ate the planet?"

I laughed, thinking it was possible that when

she'd had her first baby twenty years ago, she was a few sizes smaller than when she'd conceived Ruby Rose, but I didn't say so.

"What can I get you?" I asked.

"Anything in the freezer compartment," Claire said.

"Copy that," I said, grinning at her. I returned with a carton of Chunky Monkey and two spoons, climbed back into the bed, saying, "It's cruel to call an ice cream Chunky Monkey when that's what it turns you into."

Claire cackled, pried off the lid, and as we took turns dipping our spoons in, she said to me, "So how's it going with you and Joe?"

"What do you mean?"

"Living together, you idiot. Are you thinking of getting seriously hooked up? As in married?"

"I like the way you kind of edge into a subject."

"Hell. You're not such a subtle creature yourself."

I tipped my spoon in her direction—*touché, my friend*— then I started talking. Claire knew most of it: about my failed marriage, about my love affair with Chris, who'd been shot dead in the line of duty. And I talked about my sister, Cat, divorced with two young kids, holding down a big job, and having a bitter relationship with her ex.

"Then I look at you, Butterfly," I said. "In your grown-up four-bedroom house. And you have your darling husband, two great kids off into the world, and now you have the guts and love enough to make another baby."

"So where are you in all this, sugar?" Claire said. "You going to let Joe make the decision you don't love him enough to marry him? Let some other girl make off with Joe, the perfect man?"

I threw myself back against the pillows and stared at the ceiling. I thought about the Job, about working with Rich seventeen hours a day and loving that. How little time I had for anything but work; hadn't done Tai Chi in ages, stopped playing the guitar, even turned the nightly run with Martha over to Joe.

I put my mind on how different it would all be if I were married and had a baby, if there were people who worried about me every time I left the house. And damn—what if I got shot?

And then I considered the alternative.

Did I really want to be alone?

I was about to run all this by Claire, but I'd

been quiet for so long, my best friend picked that moment to jump in.

"You'll figure it out, sweetheart," she said, capping the empty ice-cream container, resting her spoon in a Limoges saucer on the nightstand. "You'll work on it and then, snap. You'll just *know* what's right for you."

Would I?

How could Claire be so sure, when I was without a clue in the world?

Chapter 90

ONLY THREE BLOCKS from the Hall, Le Fleur du Jour is a popular morning hangout for cops. At 6:30 a.m. the smell of freshly baked bread made noses quiver up and down the flower market. Joe, Conklin, and I were at one of the little tables on the patio with a view of the flower stalls in the alley. Having never been with Joe and Conklin together, I felt an uneasiness I would have hated to explain.

Joe was telling Conklin some of his thoughts about the arson-homicide cases, saying he agreed with us, that one person couldn't have subdued the victims alone.

"These kids are show-offy smart," Joe said. "Quidquid latine dictum sit, altum videtur."

"And that means what?" I asked, raising an eyebrow. Did everyone know Latin but me?

Joe flashed me a grin. "It means, 'Anything said in Latin sounds profound.'"

Conklin nodded, his brown eyes sober this morning. I'd seen this precise look when he interrogated a suspect. He was taking in everything about Joe, and maybe hoping that my boyfriend with his high-level career in law enforcement might actually have a theory.

Or better yet, Joe might turn out to be a jerk.

No doubt, Joe was appraising Richie, too.

"They're definitely smart," Conklin said, "maybe a little smarter than we are."

"You know about Leopold and Loeb?" Joe asked, sitting back as the waiter put strawberry pancakes in front of him. The waiter walked around the table distributing eggs Benedict to me and to Conklin.

"I've heard their names," Conklin said.

"Well, in 1924," Joe said, "two smart and show-offy kids who were also privileged and sociopathic decided to kill someone as an intellectual exercise. Just to see if they could get away with it."

Joe had our attention.

"Leopold had an IQ that went off the charts at around 200," Joe said, "and Loeb's IQ was at least 160. They picked out a schoolboy at random and murdered him. But with all their brilliance they made some dumb mistakes."

"So you're thinking our guys could have a similar motive. Just to see if they could get away with it?"

"Has the same kind of feel."

"Crime TV has been educational for this generation of bad guys," Conklin said. "They pick up their cigarette butts and shell casings....Our guys have been pretty careful. The clues we're finding are the ones they're leaving on purpose."

Right about then, I stopped listening and just watched body language. Joe, directing everything to Conklin, coming on a little too strong. Conklin, deferring without being deferential. I was so attached to them both, I turned my head from one to another as if I were courtside at Wimbledon.

Blue eyes. Brown eyes. My lover. My partner.

I pushed my eggs to the side of my plate.

For probably the first time in my life, I had nothing to say.

Chapter 91

YUKI SAT AT the prosecution table between Nicky Gaines and Len Parisi, waiting for court to convene. It was Friday. The jurors had deliberated for three days, and word had come down late last night that they'd arrived at their verdict. Yuki wondered if the jurors had rushed their decision so they could have a weekend free of responsibility and tension. And if so, would that be good or bad for the People?

She felt overcaffeinated because she was. She'd been swigging coffee since six this morning and hadn't slept more than two hours the night before.

"You okay?" she asked her second chair. Nicky was breathing through his mouth, the odor of VapoRub coming off him in waves.

"I'm good," he said. "You?"

"Peachy."

To Yuki's right, Red Dog was writing a memo on a legal pad. He appeared blasé, carefree, a mountain of calm. It was an act. In fact, Parisi was a volcano resting between explosions. Across the aisle, L. Diana Davis looked fresh, powdered, and coiffed. She put a mothering arm around her client's frail shoulders.

And then, at nine on the dot, the bailiff, a sinewy man in a green uniform, called out, "All rise." Yuki stood, then sat back down as the judge took the bench. Nicky coughed into his handkerchief. Parisi capped his pen and put it in his breast pocket. Yuki clasped her hands in front of her, swung her head to the right as the door to the jury room opened and the jurors entered the courtroom.

The twelve men and women were wearing church clothes today, hair combed and sprayed into place, men in jacket and tie, the women sparkling with jewelry.

The foreperson, a woman named Maria Martinez, was about thirty, Yuki's age, a sociology teacher and mother of two. Yuki couldn't see Martinez coming out in favor of a prostitute who would let a boy die, then cover up the fact with a body dump.

Martinez put her handbag on the floor next to her chair.

Yuki felt a prickling sensation on the back of her neck and her arms as Judge Bendinger opened his laptop, made a joke to the court reporter that Yuki couldn't hear. Then he swiveled his chair face-forward and said, "Order, please."

The room quieted, and Bendinger asked if the jury had a verdict.

Martinez said, "We do, Your Honor."

The verdict form moved from Martinez to the judge and back again to Martinez. Nicky Gaines coughed again, and Parisi reached behind Yuki and flicked Gaines on the back of his head, frowned a rebuke.

"Will the foreman please read the verdict?" Bendinger asked. Martinez stood, looking small in her charcoal-gray suit. She cleared her throat.

"We, the jury, find the defendant, Junie Moon, *not guilty* in the charge of murder in the second degree.

"We find the defendant, Junie Moon, *not*

guilty in the charge of tampering with evidence..."

The packed courtroom erupted in loud exclamations punctuated by the sharp slams of Bendinger's gavel.

"What did she say? What did she say?" Gaines asked Yuki, even as the judge thanked the jury and dismissed them.

Yuki felt sick, physically ill. *She'd lost.* She'd lost, and she'd let everyone down — the police, the DA's office, the Campions, and even Michael. Her job and her passion had been to get justice for the dead boy, and she'd failed.

"I shouldn't be doing this kind of work," Yuki said to herself. She stood abruptly.

Without speaking to Parisi or Gaines, she turned around and said to the Campions, "I'm very sorry."

Lowering her eyes, Yuki pushed her way into the crowded aisle and left the courtroom.

Chapter 92

YUKI SAW TWILLY RISE from his seat in the gallery and move to follow her out of the courtroom and into the hallway, that *bastard*. She worked her way through the knots of people in the corridor, shoved open the door to the ladies' room, found an empty stall, and locked it. She sat with her head in her hands for long minutes, then went to a sink, washed her face, and slipped on her sunglasses.

Once back in the hallway, she headed for the fire exit, heart still knocking inside her chest as she walked quickly down the staircase, her mind circling the verdict, still shocked that the jury had found Junie Moon not guilty. The public would go berserk when they learned that Junie Moon was going to get out of jail free. They'd blame the verdict on *her,* and they'd be right to do it.

It was her case and she'd lost.

Yuki opened the door into the lobby and, with her head down, walked out of the gray cubical building into the equally gray morning. Len Parisi was on the top step of the courthouse, standing like a red-haired sequoia inside a clump of journalists who were reaching their mics and cameras forward, shouting questions.

She saw star TV reporters, Anderson Cooper and Rita Cosby, Diane Dimond and Beth Karas. Cameras rolled as Parisi told the press whatever politically correct blah-di-blah a public servant with a coronary in his history and probably another one in his future would say.

Fifty feet away from Parisi, three steps down, Maria Martinez and several of the jurors were also surrounded by reporters.

Yuki heard Martinez say, "We were overwhelmed with reasonable doubt." And then the video cameras shifted as L. Diana Davis exited the big steel-and-glass double doors with her arm still sheltering Junie Moon.

Yuki ran down the remaining steps to the street. She saw Connor Campion and his wife at the curb, Campion's driver holding open the door to a Lincoln sedan. Jason Twilly was standing beside Campion, the two men deep in conversation as Yuki passed.

Yuki crossed Bryant against the light, eyes focused on the All Day parking lot, glad to be invisible in the morning crush of pedestrians, especially relieved that Twilly was busy with a bigger fish than she. Keys in hand, she found her Acura toward the back of the lot.

She heard someone call her name. She turned with a scowl, saw that Jason Twilly was coming toward her, his dark jacket flying open like the wings of a vulture.

"Yuki! Hang on."

Jason Twilly was following her again!

Chapter 93

YUKI JAMMED THE CAR KEY into the key slot, heard the soft *thwick* as the locks opened.

"Yuki, wait."

She turned again, one hand clutching the strap of her handbag, the other clenched around the handle of her briefcase.

"I've got *nothing* to say to you, Jason. *Go away.*"

Twilly scowled, his expression murderous, the look of a man who could go violently out of control.

"You listen to *me*, little girl," Twilly said.

"Be glad that you *lost,* because Junie Moon didn't kill Michael Campion. But I know who *did.*"

What? What had he said?

"*Look* at me, Yuki. Look at *me.* Maybe it was *me.*"

Yuki got behind the wheel and yanked the door shut in Twilly's face. Twilly bent down, rapped on her window, *bap-bap-bap,* losing it, desperate, yelling through the glass, *"We've got unfinished business, Yuki. Don't drive away!"*

Yuki threw the car into gear, jammed down the accelerator, and with tires squealing, she left the lot. She called Lindsay from the car, her voice shrill over the sound of traffic.

"Jason Twilly just told me he *knows* who killed Michael Campion, Lindsay, but he wants me to think that *he* did it. That *he* killed Michael. Lindsay! Maybe he *did.*"

Twilly's rented Mercedes was in her rearview mirror as Yuki circled the block. She ran a red light, took a sudden turn into an alley—and when she was sure she was no longer being followed, she parked in a fire zone outside the Hall.

She flashed her ID at the security guard, ran through the metal detectors, then took the stairs to the squad room on the third floor. She was panting when she found Lindsay waiting for her at the gate.

"Don't worry," Lindsay told her. "I've got your back."

Chapter 94

TWO HOURS after leaving the Hall of Justice, Yuki packed an overnight bag and headed out of town. She tried to shake the echo of Twilly's voice as she drove over the Golden Gate Bridge toward Point Reyes.

Could Twilly really have killed Michael Campion? If so, *why* would he do it?

And why would he tell *her?*

She turned on the radio, found a classical station, dialed it up loud, and the music filled the car and her mind. It was a beautiful afternoon. She was going to Rose Cottage, to walk in the surf and remember that she wasn't a quitter.

That she wouldn't quit on *this.*

As she got onto Highway 1, she let the incomparable beauty of the place take her over. She switched off the radio, buzzed down all the car windows so she could hear the thundering waves break over the huge rocks below her. Moist ocean air whipped her hair away from her eyes and brought blood into her cheeks. She looked out over the blue, blue sea that stretched out to the horizon—no, out to *Japan*—and she breathed in the fresh air, consciously exhaled, letting the tension go.

In the small town of Olema, she turned off Highway 1, passed the little shops at the intersection, and from there negotiated the back roads by memory. She glanced down at her new wristwatch. It was only two thirty in the afternoon, plenty of sunlight left in the day.

The sign spelling out ROSE COTTAGE ¼ MILE was almost hidden by the roadside flora, but Yuki caught it and made the turn through a forested glen and up an unpaved road that climbed the hillside. The rutted road became a driveway that looped in front of the manager's cabin just ahead.

The manager, a tall, blond-haired woman

named Paula Vaughan, welcomed Yuki back to Rose Cottage. They exchanged pleasantries as Vaughan ran Yuki's credit card through the machine. And then the manager made the connection, saying, "I was just watching the news. Too bad you didn't win."

Yuki looked up, said, "You've got takeout menus, right? The Farm House does takeout?"

Minutes later, she opened the front door to Rose Cottage, dropped her bags in the larger of the two bedrooms, and opened the sliders to the deck. The Bear Valley hiking trail passed to the right of the cottage, climbed upward four hundred feet through a wooded area, opening at the top of a ridge to a brilliant ocean view.

She'd hiked this trail with Lindsay.

Yuki changed into jeans and hiking shoes. Then she unsnapped the locks on her briefcase, took out her new Smith & Wesson .357 handgun, slipped it into one pocket of her Windbreaker, put her cell phone in the other. But before she could leave for her nature walk, there was an insistent knock on the door.

And the booming in her chest started all over again.

Chapter **95**

JASON TWILLY WAS WEARING chinos and a navy blue sweater and had a leather bag hooked over his right shoulder. He looked handsome, urbane, as if he'd just stepped from the pages of *Town & Country,* and his crooked smile had lost its menace.

"What are you doing here, Jason?"

Yuki kept the door open about four inches, just enough to see and hear him. And she clamped her hand around the gun in her pocket, felt the power of that little weapon, knowing what it could do.

"Hey, you know, Yuki, if I didn't like you so much, I'd be really hurt. I spend most of my life fending women off, and you keep slamming doors in my face."

"How'd you find me?"

"I waited for you to leave your apartment and followed you. Wasn't that hard. Look, I'm sorry I got rough this morning." He sighed. "It's just that I'm in trouble. I took a huge advance on this book and the money's gone."

"Oh, really?"

"Yeah. Sports betting. A little weakness of mine." Twilly added a dash of boyish charm to his smile. "To be honest, it's more than a little weakness—and it's kind of snowballed lately. See, I'm telling you this so you understand. Really nasty people want their money back. And they don't care if my book crashes."

"Not my problem, Jason."

"Wait. Wait. Just listen, okay? I can't give back the advance, you understand, and I've got these *debts.* All I need is your feelings, your insight, your own true words—that's where we'll find a satisfying ending to the Michael Campion story."

"Are you serious? After all the crap you've dished out? I have nothing to say to you, Jason."

"Yuki, this isn't personal. It's *business.* I'm

not going to touch you, okay? I need one crummy hour of your time, and you're going to benefit. You're the devoted prosecutor whose conviction was snatched from you by the little whore with a heart of stone. Yuki, you were robbed!"

"And if I don't want to be interviewed?"

"Then I'll have to write around you, and that'll really suck. Don't make me beg anymore, okay?"

Yuki took the gun out of her pocket. "This is a .357," she said, showing it to him.

"So I see," Twilly said, his smile becoming a grin, the grin turning into laughter. "This is priceless."

"I'm glad you find me amusing."

"Yuki, I'm a reporter, not a freaking mobster. No, this is good. Bring your gun. God knows I want you to feel safe with me. Okay if we go for a walk?"

"This way," Yuki said.

She stepped outside and closed the door behind her.

Chapter 96

YUKI KEPT HER HAND gripped around the gun in her pocket as she walked beside Twilly up the path through the woods. He did most of the talking, asking her opinion of the jury, of the defense counsel, of the verdict. For a moment she saw the charming man she'd been attracted to a few weeks ago—then she remembered who he *really* was.

"I think the verdict was completely off the wall," Yuki said. "I don't know what I could have done differently."

"Not your fault, Yuki. Junie *is* innocent," Twilly said amiably.

"Really? And you know she's innocent how?"

They'd reached the ridgeline, where a rocky outcropping overlooked the best view of Kelham Beach and the Pacific Ocean. Twilly sat down on the rock, and Yuki sat a few feet away. Twilly opened his bag, took out two bottles of water, twisted off the cap of the first and handed the bottle to Yuki.

"Don't you think it's strange that there was no trace evidence at the so-called crime scene?" he asked her.

"Strange, but not impossible," Yuki said, taking a deep chug-a-lug from the water bottle.

"That information that the police 'developed.' That was an anonymous caller, right?"

"How did you know that?"

"I was writing a *book* about Michael, Yuki. I followed him all the time. *I* followed Michael to Junie's house that night. After Michael went into Junie's house, I felt great. Michael Campion spent time with a hooker! Good meat for my story. I waited, and then I saw him leave—alive.

"Of course, I didn't know he'd never be seen again."

"Hmmm?" Yuki said.

She'd come here to hear Twilly tell her who'd killed Michael or confess that he was the one who had done it—but suddenly she felt as though there was plastic foam inside her head.

What was happening?

Shapes shifted in front of her eyes, and Twilly's voice ballooned out of his mouth, volume rising and falling. What was *that?* What was Twilly *saying?*

"Are you okay?" he asked her. "Because you don't look so good."

"I'm *fine,*" Yuki said. She was nearly overcome with dizziness and nausea. She gripped the rock she was sitting on with both hands, held on tight.

She had a gun!

What time was it?

Wasn't she supposed to keep track of the time?

Chapter **97**

TWILLY LEERED, his face very big in front of hers. Big nose, teeth like a Halloween jack-o'-lantern, his words so elastic, Yuki became fascinated with the sounds more than the sense of what he was saying.

Get a grip, she told herself. *Get a grip.*

"Say that again?"

"When Michael went missing," Twilly spoke patiently, "the cops came up with *nothing.* No *clues.* No *suspects.* I waited for months."

"Uh-huh."

"The Campion story was getting stale — so I did what I had to do. Good citizen thing, right? I called in a tip. I gave the cops a suspect. Completely legitimate. I'd seen Michael at the house of a little hooker named Junie Moon."

"You ... did that?"

"Yep, it was *me*. And like an answered prayer, Junie Moon *confessed*. Man, sometimes I even think she did it. But you didn't convict her, did you, Yuki? And now I have a shitty ending for my book. And whoever killed Michael is *free*. And I'm up to my neck in knee-breakers, so I can only think of one way to get a big-bang ending and bring it on home.

"And that's where you come in, little girl," Twilly said. "I think you're going to appreciate the drama and the poetry."

There were flashes in the sky behind Twilly, bright colors and images she couldn't make out. There was a whooshing in her ears, blood racing or animals running through the underbrush. *What was going on?*

"What's ... happening ... to me?"

"You're having a mental breakdown, Yuki, because you're so depressed."

"Me?"

"*You.* You ... are ... very ... depressed."

"Nooooo," Yuki said. She tried to stand, but her feet couldn't hold her. She looked at

Twilly, his eyes big and as dark as black holes.

Where was her gun?

"You're *morbidly* depressed, Yuki. That's what you told me in the parking lot this morning. You said that you have no love in your life. That your mother is dead because you didn't save her. And you said you can't get over blowing this trial—"

He was bending her mind.

"Craaaazzzy," she said.

"Crazy. Yes you *are!* You were on camera, Yuki. *Thousands* of people saw you *run* from the courthouse," Twilly said, each of his words distinct and powerful—yet senseless.

"That's the way I'll tell the story, how you ran to the parking lot and I ran after you, and you said that you wanted to kill yourself, you were so ashamed. One of those Japanese honor things. Hara-kiri, right?"

"Nooooo."

"Yes, little girl. That's what you told me. And I was so worried about you, I followed you in my car."

"You...?"

"*Meeeeee.* And you showed me your gun that you'd gotten so that you could end your

life and give me the freaking megawatt ending my book so richly deserves!"

Gun! Gun! Her arm was made of *rubber.*
She couldn't move her hand off the rock.
Lights flashed in the dark.

"I didden...nooooo."

She started to slip from her perch, but
Twilly hauled her up roughly by her arm.

"The prosecutor lost her case," he said,
"and took her own freaking loser life. It's the
money shot. Get it? Bang. Clean shot to the
temple and another big chunk of dough goes
into my bank account—thanks to your dramatic, *tragic,* movie ending.

"Plus, Yuki, it *is* personal. I've really come
to hate you."

"What time is it?" Yuki asked, blinking up
at the starburst pattern that was somehow
Twilly's face.

Chapter 98

I WAS FRANTIC.

The audio had been coming in loud and clear from the transmitter in Yuki's wristwatch, but now we'd lost her! We'd gone out of range! I grabbed Conklin's arm, stopped him in the path that had petered out onto a small clearing before snaking out in three directions.

"I've lost the transmission!"

"Hold it," Conklin said into his mic to the SWAT team that was moving through the woods in a grid formation.

And then the static cleared. I couldn't hear Yuki, but Twilly's voice was tinny and clear.

"See, when I was thinking about this earlier," Twilly was saying, "I thought I could get you to spread your wings and fly off this cliff. But now I'm thinking, you're going to *shoot* yourself, Yuki."

Yuki's scream was high-pitched. Wordless.

Twilly was threatening to kill her! Why didn't Yuki use her gun?

"Up there. Top of the ridge," I shouted to Conklin.

We were at least two hundred yards away from the summit. Two hundred yards! It no longer mattered if he heard us. *I ran.*

Brambles grabbed out at me, branches snapped in my face. I stumbled on a root, grabbed out and hugged a tree. My lungs burned as I ran. I saw their forms between the tree trunks, silhouetted against the sky. But Twilly was so close to Yuki, I couldn't get a clean shot.

I yelled out, *"Twilly! Stand away from her now."*

There was the crack of gunshot.

OH, GOD, NO! YUKI!

Birds broke from the trees and flew up like scattershot as the report echoed over the hillside. Eight of us boiled out of the woods into the clearing at the ridgeline. That's where

I found Yuki, on her knees, forehead touching the ground.

The gun was still in her hand.

I got down on the ground and shook her shoulders.

"Yuki! Yuki! Speak to me! *Please.*"

Chapter 99

TWILLY HELD HIS HANDS in the air. He said, "Thank God you showed up, Sergeant. I was trying to stop her, but your friend was determined to kill herself."

I pulled Yuki into my arms. The smell of gunpowder was in the air, but there was no blood, no wound. Her shot had gone wild.

"Yuki. I'm here, honey, I'm *here*."

She moaned, sounded and looked dopey. There was no liquor on her breath. Had she been drugged?

"What's wrong with her?" I shouted at Twilly. "What did you do to her?"

"Not a thing," Twilly said. "This is how I found her."

"You're under arrest, scumbag," Conklin said. "Hands behind your back."

"What are the charges, if you don't mind me asking?"

"How do you like attempted murder for starters?"

"You've got to be *kidding.* I didn't touch her."

"Yuki was wired, buddy. You teed her up for a dive off this cliff. We've got it all."

Conklin squeezed the bracelets tight enough to make Twilly yelp. I called for a medevac, sat with my arms around Yuki as we waited for the chopper to arrive.

"Lindsay?" Yuki asked me. "I got it...on my watch... didn't I?"

"You sure did, honey," I said, hugging my friend, so very grateful that she was alive.

While I held her, another part of my mind was turning it all over. We had Twilly in custody for the attempt on Yuki's life, but the *reason* we'd tailed him was because of what he'd hinted to Yuki this morning: that *he'd* killed Michael Campion.

What he'd told Yuki in the last ten minutes contradicted that.

Conklin stooped beside us, said, "So this was all a trap? He set Yuki up to create an ending for his *book?*"

"That's what that psycho said."

And he'd almost done it. Now the ending was *him.* His arrest, his trial, and, we could always hope, his conviction.

Yuki tried to speak, but ragged sounds came from her throat.

She was struggling to breathe.

"What did he give you, Yuki? Do you know what drug?"

"Water," she said.

"The medics will give you water in a minute, honey."

Yuki's head was in my lap when the chopper's arrival sounded overhead.

I looked down to shield my eyes—and saw a glint in the path. I shouted over the racket.

"Twilly drugged the *water.* Is that what you mean, Yuki? He put it in the *water?*"

Yuki nodded. Moments later Conklin had bagged the evidence, two plastic water bottles, and Yuki was in a carry-lift up to the chopper's belly.

Part Five

BURNING DESIRE

Chapter **100**

HAWK AND PIDGE left the car around the corner from the huge Victorian house in Pacific Heights, the biggest in a neighborhood of impressive, multi-multimillion-dollar homes, all with stunning views of the bay.

Their target house was imposing and yet inviting, so American it was iconic—and at the same time, completely out of reach for everyone but the very wealthy.

The two young men looked up at the leaded windows, the cupolas, and the old trees banked around the house, separating it from the servant quarters over the garage and the neighbors on either side of the yard.

They had studied the floor plans on the real estate brokers' Web site and knew every corner of every floor. They were prepared, high on anticipation, and still cautious.

This was going to be their best kill and their last. They would make some memories tonight, leave their calling card, and fade out, blend back into their lives. *But this night would never be forgotten.* There would be headlines for weeks, movies, several of them. In fact, they were sure people would still be talking about this crime of all crimes into the next century.

"Do I look okay?" Pidge asked.

Hawk turned Pidge's collar up, surveyed his friend's outfit down to the shoes.

"You rock, buddy. You absolutely *rock.*"

"You too, man," Pidge said.

They locked arms in the Roman forearm handshake, like Charlton Heston and Stephen Boyd in *Ben-Hur.*

"Ubi fumus," said Hawk.

"Ibi ignis," Pidge answered.

Where there's smoke, there's fire.

Pidge twisted the gold foil tight around the bottle of Cointreau, and then the two boys advanced side by side up the long stone walkway toward the front porch. There was a card taped to a glass panel on the front door. "To the members of the Press: Please, leave us alone."

Hawk rang the bell.

Bing-bong.

He could see the gray-haired man through the small-paned living room windows, followed his silhouette as the famous figure walked through the house, turning on the lights in each room, making his way to the front door.

And then the door opened.

"Are you the boys who called?" Connor Campion asked.

"Yes, sir," Pidge said.

"And what are your names?"

"Why don't you call me Pidge for now, and he's Hawk. We have to be careful. What we know could get us killed."

"You've got to trust us," Hawk said. "We were friends of Michael's, and we have some information. Like I said on the phone. We can't keep quiet any longer."

Connor Campion looked the two boys up and down, decided either they were full of crap or maybe, just maybe, they'd tell him something he needed to know. They'd want money, of course.

He swung the door open wide and invited them inside.

Chapter 101

THE SIXTY-FIVE-YEAR-OLD MAN led the two boys through the vestibule and living room, into his private library. He switched on some lights: the stained-glass Tiffany lamp on the desk he'd used in the governor's mansion, the down-lighting above the floor-to-ceiling bookcases of law books.

"Is your wife at home?" the one called Hawk asked him.

"She's had a very stressful day," Campion said. "She couldn't wait up. Can I get you boys something to drink?"

"Actually, we brought you this," Pidge said, handing over the bottle of Cointreau. Connor thanked the boy, slid down the foil bag, and looked at the label.

"Thanks for this. I'll open this for you if you like, or maybe you'd like something else. I'm having scotch."

"We're good, sir," said Pidge.

Campion put the bottle next to Michael's picture on the ornately carved mantelpiece, then bent to open the bowed glass doors of the vitrine he used as a liquor cabinet. He took out a bottle of Chivas and a glass. When he turned, he saw the gun in Hawk's hand.

Campion's muscles clenched as he stared at the revolver; then he looked up at the smirk on Pidge's face.

"Are you crazy? You're holding me up?"

Behind Pidge, Hawk's eyes were bright, smiling with anticipation, as he took a reel of fishing line out of his back pocket. Horror came over Campion as suspicion bloomed in his mind. He turned his back to the boys, said neutrally, "I guess I won't be having this." He made a show of putting the Chivas back inside the cabinet, while feeling around the shelf with the flat of his hand.

"We have to tie you up, sir, make it look like a robbery. It's for our own protection," Pidge said.

"And you need to get Mrs. Campion down here," Hawk added firmly. "She'll want to hear what we have to say."

Campion whipped around, pointed his SIG at Hawk's chest, and squeezed the trigger. *Bang.*

Hawk's face registered surprise as he looked down at his pink shirt, saw the blood.

"Hey," said Hawk.

Didn't these punks know that a man like him would have guns stashed everywhere? Campion fired at Hawk again, and the boy dropped to his knees. He stared up at the older man and returned fire, his shot shattering the mirror over the fireplace. Then Hawk collapsed onto the rug facedown.

Pidge had frozen at the sound of the shooting. Now he screamed, *"You shit! You crazy old shit! Look what you did!"*

Pidge backed out of the room, and when he cleared the library's doorway, he turned and raced for the front door. Campion walked over to Hawk, kicked the gun out of his outstretched hand, lost his footing, and fell, hitting his chin against the edge of the desk. He pulled himself up using the desk leg, then stumbled out to the vestibule and pressed the intercom that connected to the caretaker's cottage.

"Glen," he yelled. "Call 911. I shot some-one!"

By the time Campion reached the front walk, Pidge was gone. The caretaker came running across the yard with a rifle, and Valentina stood in the front doorway, her eyes huge, asking him what in God's name had happened.

Lights winked on in neighboring houses, and the wolfhound next door barked.

But there was no sign of Pidge.

Campion clamped his fist around the grip of his gun and shouted into the dark, *"You killed my son, you son of a bitch, didn't you? You killed my son!"*

Chapter 102

I ARRIVED AT the Campions' home within fifteen minutes of getting Jacobi's call. A herd of patrol cars blocked the street, and paramedics bumped down the stone steps with their loaded gurney, heading out to the ambulance.

I went to the gurney, observed as much of the victim as I could. An oxygen mask half covered his face, and a sheet was pulled up to his chin. I judged that the young man was in his late teens or early twenties, white, with well-cut, dirty-blond hair, maybe five ten.

Most important, he was alive.

"Is he going to make it?" I asked one of the paramedics.

She shrugged, said, "He's got two slugs in him, Sergeant. Lost a lot of blood."

Inside the house, Jacobi and Conklin were debriefing the former governor and Valentina Campion, who sat together on a sofa, shoulder to shoulder, their hands entwined. Conklin shot me a look: something he wanted me to understand. It took me a few minutes to get it.

Jacobi filled me in on what had transpired, told me that there was no ID on the kid Campion had shot. Then he said to the former governor, "You say you can identify the second boy, sir? Help our sketch artist?"

Campion nodded. "Absolutely. I'll never forget that kid's face."

Campion looked to be in terrible pain. He'd shot someone only minutes before, and when he asked me to sit down in the chair near the sofa, I thought he wanted to tell me about that. But I was wrong.

Campion said, "Michael wanted to be like his friends. Go out. Have fun. So I was always on his case, you know? When I caught him sneaking out at night, I reprimanded him, took away privileges, and he hated me for it."

"No he *didn't,*" Valentina Campion said

sharply. "You did what I didn't have the courage to do, Connor."

"Sir?" I said, wondering where he was going with this.

Campion's face sagged with exhaustion.

"He was being irresponsible," Campion continued, "and I was trying to keep him safe. I was looking ahead to the future—a new medical procedure, a pharmaceutical breakthrough. *Something.*

"I told him, straight up, 'When you decide to act like an adult, let me know.' I wasn't *angry,* I was *afraid,*" Campion said, his voice cracking. "So I lost him before I lost him."

His wife tried to calm him, but Connor Campion wouldn't be soothed. "I was a tyrant," Campion said. "Mikey and I didn't speak for the whole last month of his life. If I'd known he had a month to live... Michael told me, '*Quality* of life, Dad. That's what's important.'"

Campion fixed me with his bloodshot eyes.

"You seem to be a caring person, Sergeant. I'm telling you this so you understand. I let those hooligans into my house because they said they had information about Michael—and I *had* to know what it was.

"Now I think they killed him, don't you? And tonight they were going to rob us. But why? *Why?*"

"I don't know, sir."

I told Campion that as soon as we knew *anything,* we'd let him know. That was all I had for him. But I got it now, why Conklin had given me that look when I'd walked in the door. My mind was running with it.

I signaled to my partner and we went outside.

Chapter 103

CONKLIN AND I leaned against the side of my car, facing the Campion house, staring at the lights glowing softly through a million little windowpanes. Campion and his wife didn't know what kind of death Hawk and Pidge had planned for them tonight, but *we* knew—and thinking about that near miss was giving me the horrors.

If Connor Campion hadn't fired his gun, Hawk and Pidge would have roasted him and his wife alive.

Rich pulled out a pack of cigarettes and offered me one—and this time I took him up on it.

"Might be some prints on that foil around the bottle of booze," he said.

I nodded, thinking we'd be lucky if those kids had records, if their prints were in AFIS, but I wasn't counting on it.

"Hawk. Pidge. Crazy names," Conklin said.

"I got a pretty good look at Hawk," I said. "He matches Molly Chu's description of the so-called angel who carried her out of the fire."

Conklin exhaled a long stream of smoke into the night. He said, "And the governor's description of Pidge sounds like the kid who pawned Patty Malone's necklace."

"And of course there's the fishing line. So...what are we thinking?" I said to Conklin. "That Hawk and Pidge *also* killed Michael Campion? Because I don't see two guys killing a kid when their MO is to tie up rich couples, leave a few words in Latin inside a book, and then burn the house down."

Conklin said, "Nope. That doesn't work for me, either. So why do you think these birds targeted the Campions?"

"Because the Campions are in the news. Big house. Big fire. Big headlines. Big score."

Conklin smiled, said, "Only they screwed up."

I smiled back, said, "Yeah."

We were both starting to feel it, the kind of incomparable exhilaration that comes when after nothing but dead ends, A leads to B leads to C. I was sure that Hawk and Pidge were the sadists who did the arson killings, but not only couldn't we prove that, we didn't know who Hawk and Pidge *were.*

I stamped out my cigarette on the street, said to Conklin, "That Hawk bastard had better live."

"At least long enough to *talk,*" said my partner.

Chapter **104**

HAWK'S SURGEON, Dr. Dave Hammond, was a compact man with rusty hair and the tight manner of a perfectionist who'd spent the night stitching his patient's guts back together. Conklin and I had spent the same eight hours in a small, dull waiting room at St. Francis Hospital, waiting for Hammond's report.

When the doctor entered the waiting room at 6:15 a.m., I shot to my feet, asked, "Is he awake?"

Hammond said, "Right now, the patient's condition defines touch-and-go. He was bleeding like a son of a bitch when he came in. One slug punctured his lung and nicked his aorta. The other damn near pulverized his liver."

Conklin said, "So, Doctor, when can we talk to him?"

"Inspector, you understand what I just said? We had to inflate the kid's lungs, transfuse him, and remove a chunk of his *liver.* This is what we like to call major surgery."

Conklin smiled winningly. "Okay. I hear you. Is he awake?"

"He just opened his eyes." Hammond sighed with disgust. "I'll give you one minute to get in and get out."

One minute was all we'd need, enough time to wring two words from that bastard—his first name and his last. I pushed open the door marked RECOVERY and approached Hawk's bed. It was a shocking sight.

Hawk's body was lashed down in four-point restraints so that he couldn't flail and undo the work his surgeons had just done. Even his head was restrained. IV bags dripped fluids into his body, a chest tube drained ooze out of his lungs, a catheter carried waste into a canister under the bed, and he was breathing oxygen through a cannula clipped to his nose.

Hawk looked bad, but he was alive.

Now I had to get him to talk.

I touched his hand and said, "Hi there. My name is Lindsay."

Hawk's eyes flickered open.

"Where . . . am I?" he asked me.

I told him that he'd been shot, that he was in a hospital, and that he was doing fine.

"Why can't . . . I move?"

I told him about the restraints and why he was tied down, and I asked for his help. "I need to call your family, but I don't know your name."

Hawk scanned my face, then dropped his gaze to the badge on my lapel, the bulge of my gun under my jacket. He murmured something I had to strain to hear.

"My work here is finished," Hawk said.

"No," I shouted, gripping the kid's hand with both of mine. "You are *not* going to die. You've got a great doctor. We all want to help you, but I have to know your *name.* Please, Hawk, tell me your *name.*"

Hawk pursed his lips, starting to form a word—and then, as though an electric current had taken over his body, his back bowed and he went rigid against his restraints. Simultaneously, the rapid, high-pitched beeping of an alarm filled the room. I wanted to *scream.*

I held on to Hawk's hand as his eyes rolled back and a noise came from his throat like soda water pouring into a glass. The monitor tracking his vital signs showed Hawk's heart rate spike to 170, drop to 60, and rocket again even as his blood pressure dropped through the floor.

"What's happening?" Conklin asked me.

"He's crashing," Hammond shouted, stiff-arming the door. The rapid beeping turned into one long squeal as the green lines on the monitor went flat.

Hammond yelled, *"Where's the god-damned cart!"*

As the medics rolled it in, Conklin and I were pushed away from the bed. A nurse closed the curtain, blocking our view. I heard the frenzy of doctors working to shock Hawk's heart back into rhythm.

"Come on, come on," I heard Dr. Hammond say. Then, "Crap. Time of death, 6:34 a.m."

"Damn it," I said to Conklin. "Damn it to *hell.*"

Chapter **105**

AT 7:45 THAT MORNING, I took off my jacket, hung it over the back of my chair, opened my coffee container, and sat down at my desk across from Conklin.

"He died on purpose, that monster," I said to my partner.

"He's dead, but this is not a dead end," Conklin muttered.

"Is that a promise?"

"Yeah. Boy Scout's honor."

I opened my desk drawer, took out two cello-wrapped pastries, not more than a week old. I lobbed one to Rich, who caught it on the fly.

"Oooh. I love a woman who bakes."

I laughed, said, "Be glad for that coffee cake, mister. Who knows when we'll see food again."

We were waiting for phone calls. A blurry photo of Hawk being wheeled out of the Campion house was running in the morning *Chronicle.* It was unlikely someone could ID him from that, but not impossible. At just after eight, my desk phone warbled. I grabbed the receiver and heard Charlie Clapper's voice.

"Lindsay," he said, "there were a dozen prints on that bottle and the foil it was wrapped in."

"Tell me something good."

"I'd love to, my friend," Clapper said. "But all we've got for sure is a match to Hawk's prints, and he's not in AFIS."

"There's a shock. So he's still a John Doe and, I take it, so is Pidge."

"Sorry, kiddo. The only other match I got was to Connor Campion."

I sighed, said, "Thanks anyway, Charlie," and stabbed the blinking button of my second line.

Chuck Hanni's voice sounded wound-up, excited.

"Glad I got you," Hanni said. "There's been a fire."

I pressed the speaker button so Conklin could hear.

"It just happened a few hours ago in Santa Rosa," Chuck said. "Two fatalities. I'm on the way out there now."

"It's arson? You think it's related to our case?"

"The sheriff told me that one of the vics was found with a book in his lap."

I stared at Conklin, knowing he was thinking the same thing: that SOB Pidge hadn't wasted any time.

"We'll meet you there," I said to Hanni.

I wrote down the address and hung up the phone.

Chapter 106

THE HOUSE WAS TUDOR-STYLE, surrounded by tall firs and located in a develop-
ment of million-dollar-and-up homes bordering
on a golf course in Santa Rosa. We edged
our car into the pack of sheriff's cruisers and
fire rigs, all of which had been on the scene
for hours. The firefighters were wrapping up
as the ME and arson investigators came and
went, ducking under the barrier tape that had
been looped around the premises.

I was furious that Pidge had killed again,
and once again, he'd taken his hellacious
arson spree to a county where Rich, Chuck,
and I had no official standing.

Chuck called out to us, and we walked toward the house.

"The fire was contained in the garage," he said, massaging the old burn scar on his hand.

Hanni held the garage door open, and Conklin and I stepped inside. It was a three-car garage, tools and lawn equipment against the walls, and in the center of the floor was a late-model minivan that had been seared by flames, the exterior scorched black, blue, and a powdery gray. Hanni introduced us around to Sheriff Paul Arcario, to the ME, Dr. Cecilia Roach, and to the arson investigator, Matt Hartnett, who said he was a friend of Chuck's.

"The homeowner is a Mr. Alan Beam," Hartnett told us. "He's still inside his vehicle. And there's a second victim, a female. She was found on the floor next to the van. She's in a body bag for safekeeping. Otherwise, everything is just as we found it."

Hanni shined his light into the carcass of the van so that Conklin and I could get a better look at the victim's incinerated body in the driver's seat. The seat was tilted back. A heavy chain lay across the victim's legs, and a small book rested on his lap, right above the pink and protruding coils of his large intestine.

I went weak at the knees.

The smells of burned flesh and gasoline were overpowering. I could almost hear the screaming, the pleading, the soft *whick* of a match, and the boom of the consuming fire. Rich asked me if I was okay, and I said that I was. But what I was thinking was that what had happened here in the small hours of the morning had been the ultimate in terror and agony.

That it had been nothing less than the horror of hell.

Chapter 107

DR. ROACH ZIPPED the body bag closed and asked her assistants to carry the female victim out to the van. Roach was petite, in her forties, wore her thick graying hair in a ponytail and her glasses on a beaded chain.

"There was no ID on her," Dr. Roach told me. "All I can say is that she looks to be a juvenile, maybe a teenager."

"Not Beam's wife?"

"The ex–Mrs. Beam lives in Oakland," said the sheriff, closing his cell phone. "She'll be here in a few."

Hanni began a run-through of the fire for our benefit.

"The fire started inside the passenger compartment," he said. "Paper and wood were piled up in the backseat directly behind the driver. And this is a tow chain," he said of the heavy links lying across the victim's lap.

He pointed to a metal bar down in the driver-side foot well, explained that it was a steering wheel lock, like The Club, and that it had been passed through the chain and locked around the steering column. Hanni theorized that first the chains and The Club were locked, then the newspapers and wood were doused with gasoline.

"Then, probably, the gas was poured over the victims and the can was wedged behind the seats—"

"Sorry, folks, but I've got to start processing this scene," Hartnett said, opening his kit. "I'm getting shit from the chief."

"Hang on just a minute, will you please?" I asked the arson investigator. I borrowed a pen from Hanni, reached into the van, and as Hanni aimed his light over my shoulder, I used the pen to open the book resting on Alan Beam's lap.

What kind of message had Pidge left for us?

The usual fortune cookie nonsense?

Or was he mad now? Would he slip up and give us something that made sense? I stared at the title page, but all I saw were the printed words *The New Testament.* That was all. No scribbling in Latin, not even a name. I was backing out of the van when Rich said, "Lindsay, check that out."

I went back in for a second look and this time saw a bit of fire-blackened ribbon trailing out from the pages. Using the pen again, I opened the Bible to the bookmark. Matthew 3:11.

A few lines of text had been underlined in ink.

My cheek was nearly resting on the victim's parched and naked bones as I read the underlined words out loud.

"I baptize you with water for repentance. But after me will come one who is more powerful than I, whose sandals I am not fit to carry. He will baptize you with the Holy Spirit and with fire."

Chapter 108

CONKLIN GRUNTED, said, "Purification by fire. It's a major biblical theme."

Just then the garage door opened behind us and I turned to see a chic forty-something woman wearing a business suit limned in the sunlight behind her. Her face was stretched in anger and fear.

"I'm Alicia Beam. Who's in charge here?"

"I'm Paul Arcario," the sheriff said to her, stretching out his hand. "We spoke earlier. Why don't we go outside and talk?"

Mrs. Beam pushed past him to the van, and although Conklin put an arm out to stop her, it was too late. The woman stared, then shrank away, screaming, *"Oh, my God! Alan! What happened to you?"*

Then she snapped her head around and locked her eyes on *me.*

"Where's Valerie? *Where's my daughter?"*

I introduced myself, told Mrs. Beam that she had to leave the garage, and that I would come with her. She became compliant as soon as I put my hand on the small of her back, and we walked together out of the garage to the front of the house.

"It's my daughter's weekend with her father," she said.

She opened the front door, and as she stepped over the threshold, she broke away from me, running through the rooms, calling her daughter's name.

"Valerie! *Val.* Where *are* you?"

I followed behind her, and when she stopped she said to me, "Maybe Val spent the night with a friend."

The look of sheer hope on her face pulled at my heart and my conscience. Was that her daughter in the body bag? I didn't know, and if it was, it was not my job to tell her. Right now I had to learn whatever I could about Alan Beam.

"Let's just talk for a few minutes," I said.

We took seats at a pine farm table in the kitchen, and Alicia Beam told me that her marriage of twenty years to Alan had been dissolved a year before.

"Alan has been depressed for years," Alicia told me. "He felt that his whole life had been about money. That he'd neglected his family and God. He became very religious, very repentant, and he said that there wasn't enough time..."

Alicia Beam stopped in midsentence. I followed her eyes to the counter, where an unfolded sheet of blue paper was lying beside an envelope.

"Maybe that's a note from Val."

She stood and walked to the counter, picked up the letter, began to read.

"Dear Val, my dearest girl. Please forgive me. I just couldn't take it any longer..."

She looked up, said to me, "This is from *Alan*."

I turned as Hanni leaned through the doorway and asked me to step outside.

"Lindsay," he said. "A neighbor found a message from Alan Beam on her answering machine saying he was sorry and goodbye."

It was all coming clear, why there were no

Latin come-ons. No fishing-line ligatures. And the victims were not a married couple.

Pidge hadn't done this.

Pidge had nothing to do with these deaths. Any hope I had of tripping him up, finding a clue to his whereabouts, was dead — as dead as the man in the car.

"Alan Beam committed suicide," I said.

Hanni nodded. "We'll treat it as a homicide until we're sure, but according to this neighbor, Beam had attempted suicide before. She said he was terminal. Lung cancer."

"And so he chained himself to the steering wheel and set himself on *fire?*"

"I guess he wanted to make sure he didn't change his mind this time. But whatever his reason," said Hanni, "it looks to me now like his daughter tried to save him — but she never had a chance.

"The poisonous gas and the superheated air brought her down."

Chapter 109

BY THE TIME I got home that evening, I had too much to tell Joe and hoped I could stay awake long enough to tell him. He was in the kitchen, wearing running shorts and a T-shirt, what he wore when he went for a run with Martha. He was holding a wineglass, and from the scrumptious smell of garlic and oregano, it seemed he'd cooked dinner, too.

But the look on Joe's face stopped me before I could reach him.

"Joe, I was at the hospital all night—"

"Jacobi told me. If I hadn't found wet footsteps on the bathmat this morning, I wouldn't have even known you'd been home."

"You were sleeping, Joe, and I only had a few minutes. And is this a house rule? That I have to check in?" I said.

"You call it checking in. I call it being thoughtful. Thinking of *me* and that I might worry about *you*."

I hadn't called him. Why hadn't I called?

"I'm drinking merlot," he said.

Joe and I rarely fought, and I got that sickening gut-feel that told me that I was in the wrong.

"I'm sorry," I said. "You're totally right, Joe. I should have let you know where I was." I walked over to him, put my arms around his waist — but he pulled away from me.

"No flirting, Blondie. I'm steamed."

He handed me a glass of wine and I took it, saying, "Joe, I said I'm sorry, and I am!"

"You know what?" he said. Martha whimpered and trotted out of the room. "I saw more of you when I lived in DC."

"Joe, that's not true."

"So, I'm going to ask you flat out, Lindsay. One question. And I want the truth."

I thought, *No, please, please don't ask me if I really want to marry you, please don't. I'm not ready.* I looked into the storm raging in Joe's deep blue eyes.

"I want to know about you and Conklin. What's going on?"

I was flabbergasted.

"You think I'm—Joe, you can't think *that!*"

"Look. I spent an hour with the two of you. You've got a little something special going on between you, and please don't tell me you're partners.

"I worked with you once, Lindsay," Joe went on. "*We* were partners. And now, here we are."

I opened my mouth, closed it without speaking. I felt so guilty I couldn't even act offended. Joe was right about everything. That Rich and I had a special feeling for each other, that I was neglecting Joe, that the time we spent together was more focused on each other when Joe lived a couple of time zones away than it was now.

Once Joe had made the commitment to move to San Francisco, he'd been mine, mine, totally mine. And I'd taken him for granted. I was wrong. And I had to admit it. But my throat was backed up with tears. This was the very thing that broke up cop marriages.

The Job. The obsession and commitment to the Job.

That's what this was about—wasn't it?

I felt sick with shame. I never wanted to make Joe feel bad, never wanted to hurt him at all. I set my glass down on the counter and took Joe's glass out of his hand, put that glass down, too.

"There's nothing going on, Joe. It's just the Job."

He looked into my eyes, and it was as though he was patting down my brain. He knew me that well.

"Give the sauce a stir in a couple of minutes, okay, Linds? I'm going to take a shower."

I stood up on my toes and wrapped my arms around Joe's neck, held on to the man I thought of as my future husband, pressed my cheek to his. I wanted him to hold me. And finally he did. He closed his arms around my waist and pulled me tight against him.

I said, "I love you so much. I'm going to do a better job of showing you, Joe, I swear, I will."

Chapter 110

RICH WAS ALREADY at the computer when I got to my desk. He looked like he was in fifth gear, his index fingers tapping a fast two-step over the keys. I thanked him for the Krispy Kreme he'd parked on a napkin next to my phone.

"It was my turn," Rich said, not looking up as I dragged out my chair and sat down. "Dr. Roach called," Rich continued. "Said there were fifty-five ccs of gasoline in Alan Beam's stomach."

"What's that? Three ounces? Geez. Is she saying he *drank* gasoline?"

"Yeah. Probably directly out of the can.

Beam really wanted to make sure he got it right this time. Doctor says the gas would've killed him if the fire hadn't. She's calling it a suicide. But look here, Lindsay."

"Whatcha got?" I said.

"Come over here and see this."

I walked around our two desks and peered over Conklin's shoulder. There was a Web site on his screen called Crime Web. Conklin pressed the enter key and an animation began. A spider dropped a line from the top of the page, made a web around the blood-red headline over the feature story, then skittered back to its corner of the page. I read the headline.

Five Fatal Shootings This Week Alone When are the cops and the DA going to get it together?

The text below was a sickening indictment of San Francisco's justice system—and it was all true. Homicides were up, prosecutions were down, the result of not enough people or money or time.

Rich moved the cursor to the column listing the pages on the site.

"This one—here," Rich said, clicking on a link called Current Unsolved Murders.

Thumbnail photos came up.

There was a family portrait of the Malones. Another of the Meachams. Rich clicked on the thumbnail of the Malones and said, "Listen to this."

And then he read the page to me:

"'Were the murders of Patricia and Bertram Malone committed by the same killers of Sandy and Steven Meacham?

"'We say yes.

"'And there have been other killings just as heinous with the same signature. The Jablonskys of Palo Alto and George and Nancy Chu of Monterey were also killed in horrific house fires.

"'Why can't SFPD solve these crimes?

"'If you have any information, write to us at CrimeWeb.com. Diem dulcem habes.'"

My God, it was Latin!

"We never told the press about the Latin," I said. "What does it mean?"

"Diem dulcem habes means 'Have a nice day.'"

"Yeah, okay," I said. "Let's hope it's going to be even better than that."

I called the DA's office, asked for Yuki, got Nick Gaines, told him we needed a warrant to get an Internet provider to give us the name of the Web site holder.

"I'll buck it up the line," Gaines said. "Just asking, Sergeant: You've got probable cause?"

"We're working on it," I said. I hung up, said, "Now what?" as Rich clicked on a box labeled Contact Us.

He typed with two fingers: "Must speak with you about the Malone and the Meacham fires. Please contact me." Conklin's e-mail address showed that he was with the SFPD. If the Webmaster was Pidge, we could be scaring him off.

On the other hand—there was no other hand.

I needn't have worried. Only a couple of minutes after firing off his e-mail, Rich had a response in his inbox.

"How can I help you?" the e-mail read.

It was signed Linc Weber, and it contained his phone number.

Chapter 111

THE MEETING WITH WEBER was set for four that afternoon. Conklin and I briefed Jacobi, assigned our team, and set out at two o'clock for a bookstore in Noe Valley called Damned Spot. Inspectors Chi and McNeil were in the van parked on Twenty-fourth Street, and I was wired for sound. Inspectors Lemke and Samuels were undercover, loitering in front of and behind the store.

My palms were damp as I waited with Conklin in the patrol car. The Kevlar vest I was wearing was hot, but it was my racing mind that was causing the heat.

Could this be it? Was Linc Weber also known as Pidge?

At three thirty Conklin and I got out of the car and walked around the corner to the bookstore.

Damned Spot was an old-fashioned bookstore, dark, filled with mystery books, secondhand paperbacks, a two-books-for-one section. It bore no resemblance to the air-conditioned chain stores with latte bars and smooth jazz coming over the speakers.

The cashier was an androgynous twenty-something in black clothes, hair buzzed to a bristle, and multiple face piercings. I asked for Linc Weber, and the cashier told me in a sweet feminine voice that Linc worked upstairs.

I could almost hear the scratching sound of mice nesting in the stacks as we crept along the narrow aisles and edged past customers who looked psychologically borderline. In the back of the store was a plain wooden staircase with a sign on a chain across the handrails reading NO ENTRY.

Conklin unlatched the chain, and we started up the stairs, which opened into an attic room. The ceiling was cathedral-style, but low, only eight feet high under the peak, tapering to about three feet high at the side walls. In the back of the room was a desk where high piles of magazines, papers, and books surrounded a computer with two large screens.

And behind the desk was a black kid, maybe fifteen, reed-thin, with black-rimmed glasses, no visible tattoos, and no jewelry, unless you counted the braces on his teeth, which I saw when he looked up and smiled.

My high hopes fell.

This wasn't Pidge. The governor's description of Pidge was of a stocky white kid, long brown hair.

"I'm Linc," the boy said. "Welcome to CrimeWeb dot com."

Chapter 112

LINC WEBER SAID he was "honored" to meet us. He indicated two soft plastic-covered cubes as chairs, and he offered us bottled water from the cooler behind his desk.

We sat on his cubes, turned down the water.

"We read your commentary on the Web site," said Conklin, casually. "We were wondering about your take on whoever set the Malone and Meacham fires."

The kid said, "Why don't I start at the beginning?"

Normally that was a good idea, but today my nerves were so close to the snapping point, I just wanted two questions answered, and as succinctly as possible: *Why did you use a Latin phrase on your Web site? Do you know someone who goes by the name of Pidge?*

But Weber said he'd never had a visit from cops before, and meeting in his office had legitimized his purpose and his Web site beyond his expectations. In fifteen minutes, he told us that his father owned Damned Spot, that he'd been a crime-story aficionado since he was old enough to read. He said that he wanted to publish crime fiction and true-crime books as soon as he got out of school.

"Linc, you said 'Have a nice day' in Latin on your Web site. Why did you do that?" I said, breaking into his life's story.

"Oh. The Latin. I got the idea from *this*."

Linc shuffled the piles on his desk, at last finding a soft-cover book, about 8½ by 11, with an elegant font spelling out the words *7th Heaven*. He handed the book to me. I held my breath as I flipped through the pages. Although it resembled a big, fat comic book, it was a graphic novel.

"It was published first as a blog," Weber told us. "Then my dad staked the first edition."

"And the Latin?" I asked again, my throat

tightening from the strain and the possibilities I could almost see.

"It's all in there," Weber told me. "The characters in this novel use Latin catchphrases. Listen, can I say on my Web site that you used me as a consultant? You have no idea what that would mean to me."

I was looking at the title page of the book I held in my hands. Under the title were the names of the illustrator and the writer.

Hans Vetter and Brett Atkinson.

There was an icon under each of their names.

Hans Vetter was the pigeon and Brett Atkinson, a hawk.

Chapter 113

BY FIVE THAT EVENING, Conklin and I were back at our desks in the squad room. Conklin clicked around the Internet, researching Atkinson and Vetter—and I couldn't stop turning the pages of their novel.

I was hooked.

The drawings were stark black and white. The figures had huge eyes, and called to mind the manga style of violent borderline pornography imported from Japan. The dialogue was edgy, all-American slang punctuated by Latin sayings. And the story was actually *crazy* but somehow compelling.

In this book, "Pidge" was both the brains

and the muscle. "Hawk" was the dreamer. They were depicted as righteous avengers, their mission to save America from what they viewed as an obscene fantasy world for the very rich. They referred to this American "piggishness" as 7th Heaven and described it as a never-ending spiral of gluttony, gratification, and waste. The Pidge-Hawk solution was to kill the rich and the greedier wannabes, to show them what *real* consumption was—consumption by fire.

Pidge and Hawk dressed all in black: T-shirts, jeans, riding boots, and sleek black leather waist jackets with logos of their name-birds front and back. Sparks flew from their fingertips. And their motto was "Aut vincere aut mori."

Either conquer or die.

Hawk—the boy, not the character—had done both.

My guess? They never expected any of their victims to live long enough to give away their pseudonyms.

The motives and the methods the killers used were clearly drawn in their book, but it was all disguised as make-believe. And that was making me crazy with anger. Eight *real people* had died because of this arrogant nonsense, and we had virtually no evidence to prove that the real-life Hawk and Pidge were their killers.

I flipped the book to the back cover, scanned the rave reviews from social critics and the high-profile bloggers. I said to Rich, "The sickest part yet? This book has been picked up by Bright Line."

"Hmmm?" Rich muttered, still tapping his keyboard.

"Bright Line is an indie studio," I said. "One of the best. They're turning this screed into a *movie*."

"Brett Atkinson," Rich said, "is a junior at Stanford U, majoring in English lit. Hans Vetter also goes to Stanford. He's in the computer department. These creeps both live at home, only two blocks apart in Mountain View, a couple of miles from Stanford."

Rich turned his computer monitor around, saying, "Check out Brett Atkinson's yearbook photo."

Brett Atkinson was Hawk, the boy Connor Campion had shot, the handsome, blond-haired boy with patrician features we'd seen in the hospital just before he died.

"And now," Rich said, "meet Pidge."

Hans Vetter was a good-looking tough, an

illustrator, computer sciences major, now polishing his extracurricular activities as a serial killer.

"We *will* get warrants," I croaked. I cleared my throat and said, "I don't care who I have to beg."

Rich looked as serious as I'd ever seen him.

"Absolutely. No mistakes allowed."

"Aut vincere aut mori," I said.

Rich smiled, reached over the desk, and bopped my fist. I called Jacobi, and he called Chief Tracchio, who called a judge, who reportedly said, "You want an arrest warrant based on a comic book?"

I barely slept that night, and in the morning Rich and I went to the judge's chambers with *7th Heaven,* the crime scene photos of the Malones, the Meachams, and the Jablonskys, and the morgue photos of the Chus. I brought Connor Campion's statement that the boys who'd come to his house with a gun and fishing line had said their names were Hawk and Pidge, and I showed the judge their yearbook photos, captioned with their real names.

By ten a.m. we had signed warrants and all the manpower we'd need.

Chapter 114

STANFORD UNIVERSITY, an A-list university for the best and brightest, is located 33.5 miles south of San Francisco, just off Highway 280, near Palo Alto.

Hans Vetter, AKA Pidge, spent his days in the video lab of the Gates Computer Science Building, a pale five-story, L-shaped building with a tiled roof and a rounded bulge at the entranceway. The labs and research offices were clustered around three major classrooms, and the building itself was isolated on an island of its own, separated from other school buildings by service roads.

Conklin and I had gone over the floor plans

of the Gates Building with the U.S. marshals, who were coordinating with campus security. With windows on all sides of the building, the law enforcement team would be seen by anyone sitting near a window.

We parked our vehicles out of sight on the curve of a service road and moved in on foot. Conklin and I wore Kevlar under our SFPD jackets and had our guns drawn, but we were taking direction from U.S. marshals.

Adrenaline surged through me as we were given the signal to go. While others stood by side entrances, twelve of us charged up the front steps and entered the high-ceilinged lobby, then went to the stairwells and landings.

Pairs of marshals peeled off as we took each floor, clearing the open spaces, locking classrooms down.

My thoughts raced ahead.

I was worried that we were too loud, that we'd already been seen, and that if Vetter had smuggled a weapon past the metal detectors, he could take his classmates hostage before we could bring him down. Conklin and I reached the top-floor landing and marshals took up stances on both sides of the doorway to the video lab. Conklin peered through the sidelight of the door, then turned the knob, swung the door wide open.

Backed by Conklin and the U.S. marshals armed with automatic rifles, I stepped through the doorway and bellowed, *"FREEZE. Everyone stay still and no one will get hurt."*

A female student screamed, then the room erupted into chaos. Kids bolted from their stools and hid under workstations. Cameras and computers crashed to the floor. Glass shattered.

Kaleidoscopic images spun around me, and shrieks of terror ricocheted off the walls. The situation went from bad to out of control. I kept scanning the room, trying to pick out a stocky boy with long brown hair, square jaw, the eyes of a killer—but I didn't see him.

Where was Hans Vetter?
Where was he?

Chapter 115

THE LAB INSTRUCTOR stood transfixed at the front of the room, his blanched face going livid as shock turned to outrage. He was in his thirties, balding, wearing a green cardigan and what looked like bedroom slippers under the cuffs of his trousers. He shoved his hands out in front of himself as if to push us out of his classroom. He announced his name—Dr. Neal Weinstein—and demanded, *"What the hell? What the hell is this?"*

If it weren't so damned terrifying, it would've been almost funny to watch Weinstein, armed with only his flapping hands and his PhD, face down adrenaline-pumped federal law enforcement officers primed to blow the place apart.

"I have a warrant for the arrest of Hans Vetter," I said, holding both the warrant and my gun in front of me.

Weinstein shouted, *"Hans isn't here."*

A white female student with black dreads, a ring in her lower lip, peeked out from behind an overturned table. "I spoke to Hans this morning," she said. "He told me he was going away."

"You saw him this morning?" I asked.

"I talked to him on his cell."

"Did he say where he was going?"

She shook her head. "He only told me because I wanted to borrow his car."

I left marshals behind to interview Weinstein and his students, but as Conklin and I left the building, I felt terra firma shimmy beneath my feet.

Hawk's death last night had sent Pidge underground.

He could be anywhere in the world by now.

In the parking lot across from the Gates Building, some kids were clinging together in clumps, others dazed and wandering. Still others were laughing at the unexpected excitement. News choppers circled over-head, reporting to the world on an incident that was a total disaster.

I called Jacobi, covered one ear, and summed up the situation. I didn't want him to know how scared I was that we'd blown it and that Vetter was still out there. I tried to keep my voice even, but there was no fooling Jacobi.

I heard him breathing in my ear as he took it all in.

Then he said, "So, what you're saying, Boxer, is that Pidge has flown the coop."

Chapter 116

THE SHERIFF'S DEPARTMENT and their SWAT team rolled up alongside our squad car as we braked on a crisp, well-shorn lawn. In front of us was a three-story colonial-style house only a couple of miles from the Stanford campus. The detailing on the house was authentic to the period, and the neighborhood was first class. The mailbox was marked VETTER.

And Hans Vetter's car was in the driveway.

Walkie-talkies chattered around us, and radio channels were cleared. Perimeters were set up, and SWAT got into position. Conklin and I got out of our car. I said, "Everything about this place reminds me of the homes Hawk and Pidge burned to the ground."

Using a car door as body armor, Conklin called out to Hans Vetter with a bullhorn. *"Vetter. You can't get away, buddy. Come out, hands on your head. Let's end this peacefully."*

I saw movement through the second-story windows. It was Vetter, moving from room to room. He seemed to be shouting to someone inside, but we couldn't make out his words.

"Who's he talking to?" Conklin asked me over the roof of the squad car.

"Has to be his mother, goddamn it. She's gotta be inside."

A TV went on in the house and was turned up loud. I could hear the announcer's voice. He was describing the scene we were *living.* The announcer said, "A tactical maneuver that began two hours ago at Stanford University has changed location and is centered in the upscale community of Mountain View, a street called Mill Lane—"

"Vetter? Can you hear me?" Rich's voice boomed out through the bullhorn.

Sweat rolled down my sides. The last pages in *7th Heaven* depicted a shootout with cops. I recalled the images: bloody bodies on the ground, Pidge and Hawk getting away. *They had shielded themselves with a hostage.*

Conklin and I conferred with the SWAT captain, a sandy-haired pro and former U.S. Marine named Pete Bailey, and we worked out a plan. Conklin and I moved quickly to the Vetter house and flanked the front door, prepared to grab Vetter when he opened it. SWAT was positioned to take the kid out if anything went wrong.

As I neared the house, I caught a whiff of smoke.

"Is that fire?" I asked Rich. "Do you smell it?"

"Yeah. Is that stupid *fuck* burning his house down?"

I could still hear the sound of the TV inside the Vetter house. The news announcer was getting a feed from the chopper overhead and was keeping up with the action on the ground. It made sense that Vetter was watching the television coverage. And if Rich and I were in the camera's-eye view, Vetter knew where Conklin and I were standing.

Captain Bailey called to me on our Nextels, *"Sergeant, we're going in."* But before he could give the order, a woman's voice cried out from behind the front door.

"Don't shoot. I'm coming out."

"Hold your fire," I shouted to Bailey. "Hostage coming out."

The knob turned.

The door opened and gray smoke swirled out into the dull, overcast day. There was the sound of a well-oiled motor, and under the shifting plume of pale gray smoke, I saw the leading edge of a power chair bump and maneuver, then stall on the threshold.

The woman in the chair was small and frail, maybe palsied. She wore a long yellow shawl draped over her head, fanning out over her shoulders, bunched loosely across her bony knees. Her face looked pinched, and diamonds sparkled on the fingers of her hand.

She turned her frightened blue eyes on me.

"Don't shoot," she pleaded. *"Please don't shoot my son!"*

Chapter 117

I STARED INTO Mrs. Vetter's ice-blue eyes until she broke the spell. She turned her head to the side and cried out, "Hans, do what they tell you!" As she turned her head, the yellow shawl dropped away. My heart bucked as I realized that there were *two people* sitting in that wheelchair.

Mrs. Vetter was sitting in her son's lap.

"Hans, do what they tell you," Vetter mimicked.

The chair rolled forward onto the lawn. I saw clearly now. Vetter's huge right hand was on the chair's power controls. His left arm crossed his mother's body, and he held the muzzle of a sawed-off, double-barreled, twelve-gauge shotgun hard against the soft underside of his mother's jaw.

I lowered my Glock 9 and forced a level of calm into my voice that I didn't remotely feel.

"Hans, I'm Sergeant Boxer, SFPD. We don't want anyone to get hurt. So just throw that gun down, okay? There's a safe way out of this situation, and I want to get there. I won't shoot if you put down that gun."

"Yeah, right," Vetter said, laughing. "Now listen to me, both of you," he said, pointing his chin at me and then at Conklin. "Stand between my mom and the cops. Now, drop your guns, or people are going to die."

I wasn't afraid. I was terrified.

I tossed my gun to the ground, and Conklin did the same. We stepped in front of the wheelchair, shielding Mrs. Vetter and her wretched son from the SWAT team at the edge of the lawn. My skin prickled. I felt cold and hot at the same time. We stood locked in this horrifying vignette as the smoke around us thickened.

With a muted *boom,* flames broke through the windows at the front of the house as the living room flashed over. Shards of glass exploded into the front yard, and sparks rained down on our heads. Conklin held his hands out so that Vetter could see them.

He shouted, "Vetter, we've done what you said. Now, *drop your damned gun, man.* I'll take care of you. We'll surround you all the way in, make sure you're okay. Just put down the gun."

There was the roar of the backdraft and then the whine of sirens as fire trucks neared the scene. Vetter wasn't giving up. Not if I was right that the wild glint in his eye was defiance.

But Pidge had given himself no exit.

What the hell would he do?

Chapter 118

VETTER LAUGHED LOUDLY.

For a split second, all I could see were the beautiful, open-mouthed choppers of a kid who'd had the best dentistry in the world. He said to Conklin, "Can't you just see Francis Ford Coppola directing this scene?"

I heard a faint click and then a thunderous *KABOOM*.

I'd never seen anything like it before.

One minute I was looking into Mrs. Vetter's eyes, and in the next moment her head exploded, the top of her skull opening like a flower. The air darkened with a bloody mist that coated me and Conklin and Vetter with a red sheen.

I screamed, *"No!"*

And Vetter laughed again, his smile blinding white, his face a mask of blood. He used the barrel of his gun to shove his mother's body out of the chair so that she tumbled and rolled, coming to a stop at my feet. Vetter aimed through the space between me and Conklin and fired again, the second horrific boom of double-aught buck sailing over the heads of cops and SWAT twenty yards away at the edge of the lawn.

I tried to wrap my mind around the horror of what I'd just seen. Instead of using his mother as a ticket to safety, Vetter had blown her up. And SWAT couldn't get a bead on Vetter without hitting us.

Vetter thumbed the breech release, cracked the muzzle, and reloaded. He flipped his gun shut with a snap of his wrist and it clacked as it closed. It was a sharp and unmistakable sound.

Vetter was ready to shoot again.

There was no doubt in my mind. I was in the last moments of my life. *Hans Vetter was going to kill us.* I'd never reach my gun in time to stop him.

The air was heavy with smoke. The fire blazed. Flames leaped from the second floor up through the roof. The heat dried my sweat and the dead woman's blood on my face.

"Step aside," Vetter said to me and Conklin. "If you want to live, step aside."

Chapter 119

FEELING CAME BACK into my fingertips, and hope rushed into the chambers of my heart. Now I understood. Vetter wanted SWAT to take him down in a superhero-style blaze of glory. He wanted to *die,* but I wanted him to *pay.*

As if my thoughts had caused it, Vetter suddenly screamed and jerked in the wheelchair like he was having a grand mal seizure.

I saw the wires and looked up at Conklin.

While Vetter's attention had been focused on the SWAT team, Rich had unhooked his Taser from his belt and fired. The Taser's electrified prongs had pierced Vetter's right arm and thigh. Conklin kept the juice flowing as he shoved the wheelchair onto its side, kicked Vetter's shotgun downhill.

While Vetter jerked in agony, SWAT swarmed up the slope to where we stood. I choked out to Rich, "You're smart. Anyone ever tell you that?"

"Never."

"Are you okay?"

He grunted. "Not yet."

I fumbled in the grass for my Glock, then held the muzzle to Vetter's forehead. Only then did Rich let up on the Taser. Still twitching, Vetter grinned up at me, said, "Am I in heaven?"

I was panting, my pulse beating a deafening tattoo against my eardrums, the smoke making my eyes stream with tears.

"You *asshole*," I screamed.

Fire rigs drove up to the curb, and the SWAT team surrounded us. Captain Bailey saw the look of fury in Conklin's eyes. He said slowly, deliberately, "I've got something in the van you can use to clean yourselves up."

He turned his back and so did the rest of his team. With the rising blanket of smoke blocking out the news chopper's view, Rich kicked Vetter in the ribs.

"*This* is for the Malones," he said. He kicked Vetter again and again, until that psycho stopped grinning and started spitting teeth.

"*That's* for the Meachams and the Jablonskys and the Chus," Rich said. He kicked Vetter hard in the hams.

"*This,* you *scum.* This one's for *me.*"

Chapter **120**

CONKLIN AND I had scrubbed at our faces with damp paper towels, but the stench of fire and death clung to us. Jacobi stood up-wind and said, "You two smell like you've been wading through a sewer."

I thanked him, but my mind was churning.

Two blocks away, a raging fire was burn-ing the Vetter house to the ground. There might have been evidence inside that house, something that would have tied Hans Vetter and Brett Atkinson to the arson murders.

Now all of that was gone.

We stood in front of the house where the dead boy, Brett Atkinson, had lived with his parents. It was a soaring contemporary with cantilevered decks and hundred-mile views. Very, *very* wealthy people lived here.

Hawk's parents, the Atkinsons, hadn't answered repeated knocks by patrolmen, never returned our calls, and their son's body was still lying unclaimed in the morgue. A canvass of the neighborhood had confirmed their absence. No one had seen or heard from the Atkinsons in days, and they hadn't told anyone they were leaving home.

The engines on the Atkinsons' cars were cold. There was mail in the mailbox a couple of days old, and the fellow who'd stopped mowing the lawn when we arrived said he hadn't seen Perry or Moira Atkinson all week.

While Vetter's house was a total loss, I still had hope that the Atkinsons' house might hold evidence of the horrific killings the boys had done. Thirty-five minutes had passed since Jacobi phoned Tracchio for a search warrant.

Meanwhile, Cindy had called me, saying that she and a handful of TV news vans were parked behind the barricade at the top of the street. Conklin pushed a bloody clump of his hair away from his eyes, said to Jacobi, "If this isn't 'exigent circumstances,' I don't know what is."

Jacobi growled, "Cool it, Conklin. Understand? If we blow this, we're freakin' buried. I'll be retired, and you two will be working for Brink's Security. If you're lucky."

Fifteen more minutes crawled by.

I was about to lie and say I smelled decomp when an intern from the district attorney's office arrived in a Chevy junker. She sprinted up the front walk a half second before Conklin caved in the front window of the Atkinson house with a tire iron.

Chapter 121

THE INSIDE OF the Atkinson house was like a museum. Miles of glossy hardwood floors, large modern canvases hung on two-story-high white walls. Lights came on when we stepped into a room.

It was like a museum after hours: no one was home.

And it was creepy. No pets, no newspapers or magazines, no dishes in the sink, and except for the food in the refrigerator and a precise lineup of clothing in each closet, there was little sign that anyone had ever lived in this place.

That is, until we reached Hawk's room in a wing far from the master suite.

Hawk's roost was large and bright, the windows looking west over the mountains. The bed was the least of the room. It was single, with a plain blue bedspread, speakers on each side, and a headset plugged into a CD player. One long side of the room was lined with a built-in Formica desk. Several computers and monitors and high-tech laser printers were set up there and the adjacent wall was lined with thick corkboard.

Pidge's drawings, many of which I recognized from *7th Heaven,* were pinned to the board. But there were new drawings, too, and they looked to be works in progress for a second graphic novel.

"I'm thinking that this was their workshop," I said to Conklin. "That they cooked it all up in here."

Conklin took a seat at the desktop, and I examined the corkboard. "Book number two," I said to Conklin. *"Lux et Veritas.* Got any idea what that means?"

"Easy one," Rich said, lowering the seat of the hydraulic chair. "Light and truth."

"Catchy. Sounds like more fires in the making—"

Rich called out, "Hawk's got a journal. I touched the mouse and it came up on the screen."

"Fantastic!"

As Rich scrolled through Brett Atkinson's journal, I continued my study of the drawings on the wall. One of them nailed me as if I, too, were pinned to the corkboard. The drawing depicted a middle-aged man and woman, arms around each other's waist, but their faces were flat, expressionless. A caption was written beneath the drawing.

I recognized the handwriting.

It was the same as the printing we'd seen on the title pages of the books left at the houses of the arson victims.

"Requiescat in leguminibus," I said, sounding out the syllables. "Rest in what?"

Rich wasn't listening to me.

"This map on Atkinson's computer," he said. "He's starred San Francisco, Palo Alto, Monterey. Unreal. Look at this! Photos of the houses they burned down. *This is evidence, Lindsay.* This is *frickin' evidence.*"

It *was.*

I peered over Conklin's shoulders as he opened Web pages, scanned research on each of the victim couples, including the names of their kids and the dates of the fires. Long minutes went by before I remembered the peculiar drawing pinned to the corkboard and was able to grab Rich's attention.

"Requiescat in leguminibus," I said again.

Rich came over to the wall and looked at the drawing of a couple who might be the Atkinsons. He read the caption.

"Leguminibus," Rich said. "Means legumes, I think. Aren't they a kind of vegetable? Like beans and peas?"

"Peas?" I yelled. "Jesus Christ! Jesus Christ!"

"What?" Conklin asked me. "What is it?"

I hollered out to Jacobi, who was working the rest of the house with the sheriff's department. With Conklin and Jacobi behind me, I found the stairs to the basement. The freezer was of the trunk variety, extra large.

I opened the lid and cool air puffed out.

"Requiescat in leguminibus," I said. "Rest in peas."

I started moving the bags of frozen vegetables aside until I saw a woman's face.

"This freezer is deep enough for two," Jacobi muttered.

I said, "Uh-huh," and stopped digging.

From her approximate age, I was pretty sure I was looking at Moira Atkinson, dressed in her finest, frozen to death.

Chapter 122

I WAS WEARING my new blue uniform, and I'd washed my hair thirteen times and once more for good luck when I walked into the autopsy suite the next day. Claire was standing at the top of a six-foot ladder, her Minolta focused down on Mieke Vetter's decapitated and naked body. Claire looked huge and wobbly up there.

"Can't someone else do that?" I asked her.

"I'm done," she said. She climbed down the ladder, one ponderous step at a time.

I gestured to the woman on the table. "I can save you some time," I said to Claire. "I happen to know this victim's cause and manner of death."

"You know, Lindsay, I still *have* to do this for evidentiary purposes."

"Okay, but just so you know. Yesterday, your patient sprayed me with blood, bone fragments, hair, not to mention brains. You have any idea what dripping brains feel like?"

"Warm gummy bears? Am I right?" Claire said, grinning at me.

"Uh. Yeah. Exactly."

"One of my first cases was a suicide," Claire said, getting on with her work, drawing a Y incision with her scalpel from each of Ms. Vetter's clavicles to her pubis.

"This old soldier ends it all with a twelve-gauge shotgun under his chin. So I come into his RV, fresh out of training, ya know? And I'm leaning over his body in the La-Z-Boy, taking photos, and the cops are yukking it up."

"Because?"

"I had no idea. You see, that's the *point,* girlfriend."

I started laughing for the first time in a long while.

"So as I'm leaning over the body, about a

quarter of the guy's brain has been slowly peeling off the ceiling—it falls and smacks me right behind my ear."

She slapped her neck to show me, and I rewarded her story with a good guffaw.

"Like I said, warm gummy bears. So, how'd it go?" she asked me.

"How did which go? The interview with your patient's devil spawn? Or the meeting with the mayor?"

"Both of 'em, baby girl. I'm going to be here all night, thanks to your bird friends filling up my vault all over again."

"Well, Vetter first, short and to the point," I told Claire. "He lawyered up, pronto. Got nothing to say. But when he *does* get around to saying something, I'll bet you a hundred bucks he says his buddy tortured and killed all those people and he just watched."

"Won't really matter, will it? Killer or accessory, he still gets the needle. Plus, you witnessed him killing this poor woman."

"Me and thirty other cops. But for the sake of the victims' families, I still want him convicted for killing them all."

"And your meeting with the mayor?"

"Hah! First Conklin and I get the high fives and Jacobi almost cries, he's so proud of us, and I think, 'Whoa, we're gonna pull our horrible crime-solution rate out of the basement up to maybe the ground floor'—when the whole conversation devolves into which jurisdiction has the first bite at Vetter since the killings took place in Monterey and Santa Clara Counties as well as—Claire? Honey? What is it? What's wrong?"

Claire's face had twisted in pain. She dropped her scalpel, and it rang out against the stainless steel table. She grabbed her belly, looked at me with shock in her eyes.

"My water just broke, Lindsay. I'm not due for three weeks."

I called for an ambulance, helped my friend into a chair. A minute later the doors to the ambulance bay banged open and two brawny guys strode into the autopsy suite carrying a stretcher.

"What's up, doc?" said the biggest one.

I said, "Guess who's having a baby?"

Chapter **123**

BECAUSE LITTLE RUBY ROSE was premature, we all wore sterile pink paper hospital gowns, hats, and masks for the occasion. Claire looked like she'd been dragged a quarter of a mile in a tractor pull, but the baby-glow was there under her pallor. And since baby-glow was contagious, we were all euphoric and giggly.

Cindy was crowing about her interview with Hans Vetter's uncle, and Yuki, having put on a couple of ounces since recovering from being drugged with LSD and almost killed by Jason Twilly, chortled at Cindy's jokes. The girls told me that I looked hot and possibly happy, the way I *should* look, since I was living with the perfect man.

"How long is she going to keep us waiting?" I asked Claire again.

"Patience, girlfriend. They'll roll her in when they're good and ready. Have another cookie."

I'd just folded a gooey double chocolate chip with walnuts into my maw when the door to Claire's room opened—and Conklin came in. He was wearing matching gown, hat, and mask in blue, but he was one of the few men I'd ever known who could look goofy and great at the same time. I could see his gorgeous brown eyes, and they were shining.

Rich held a big bunch of flowers behind his back, and he went around the room saying hello, kissing Cindy and Yuki on their cheeks, squeezing my shoulder, kissing Claire, and then he dramatically produced red roses.

"They're *ruby roses,*" he said, with a shy version of his brilliant smile.

"My God, Richie. Three dozen long stems. You know I'm married, right?"

When the laughter stopped, Claire said, "I thank you. And when my little girl gets here, she'll thank you, too."

Cindy was looking at Conklin like she'd never seen a man before. "Pull up a chair," she said. "Richie, we're going to Susie's for dinner in a while. Why don't you come with?"

"Good idea," I said. "We've got to toast our little associate member of the Women's Murder Club—and you can be the designated driver."

"I'd like to help you guys out," Rich said. "But I've got a plane to catch in"—he looked at his watch—"in two hours."

"Where're you going?" Cindy asked.

I wondered, too. He hadn't mentioned a trip to me.

"Denver. For the weekend," Rich told Cindy.

I looked away, my eyes sliding across Claire's face. She caught it. Saw that I'd taken an unanticipated blow.

"Going to see Kelly Malone?" Cindy asked, the reporter in her refusing to just shut up.

"Uh-huh," Rich said. And unless he'd caught the baby-glow from Claire, he was excited.

"I'd really better go. Don't want to get caught in traffic. Claire, I just wanted to congratulate you on this great news. I'll want a picture of Ruby as a screen saver."

"Sure thing," Claire said, patting Conklin's hand, thanking him again for the flowers.

I said, "Have a good weekend."

And Rich said, "You too. All of you guys."

And then he was gone.

As soon as he was out of the room, Cindy and Yuki started talking about what a rock star Rich was and wasn't Kelly Malone his high school sweetheart? And then the door opened again. A nurse rolled a tiny cart up to Claire's bed and all of us peered inside.

Ruby Rose Washburn was a beauty.

She yawned, then opened her dark, long-lashed eyes and looked straight at her mom, my glorious, beaming friend Claire.

We four held hands, made a circle around the cart, each saying a silent prayer for this new child. Claire released our hands so she could hold her baby.

"Welcome to the world, little girl," said Claire, hugging and kissing her everywhere.

Cindy turned to me, asked, "What did you pray for?"

I snorted a laugh. "Is *nothing* sacred, you bulldog? Can't I even talk to *God* without you asking for a *quote?*"

Cindy cracked up, put a hand over those cute overlapping front teeth of hers. "Sorry.

Sorry," she said, tears coming out of her eyes.

I put my hand on Cindy's shoulder and said, "I prayed that Ruby Rose would always have good friends."

Chapter **124**

YUKI GOT OUT of Lindsay's car, saying, "Now I know what they mean about feeling no pain."

"We couldn't stop you from downing two margaritas, sweetie, and God knows we tried. You're way too little for that much octane. I'll walk you inside."

"I'm okay, I'm okay." Yuki laughed. "I'm going straight to bed. So I'll talk to you on Monday, 'kay?"

She said good night to Lindsay and walked into the lobby of the Crest Royal, said hello to Sam, the doorman, and wobbled up the three steps to the mail alcove. On the third try, she managed to get the tiny key into the tiny lock, pulled out the banded packet of mail, and took the elevator up to her apartment.

The apartment was empty, but since the ghost of her mother lingered in the furnishings, Yuki talked to Mommy as she dropped the mail on the console in the foyer. An envelope slipped out of her fingers onto the floor. Yuki peered down at it. It was a padded envelope, not very big, dark brown with a handwritten label.

She kicked off her high heels and said, "Mommy, whatever it is, it can wait. Your daughter is smashed."

But the envelope was intriguing.

Yuki put one hand on the console, bent and picked up the envelope, stared at the unfamiliar handwriting in ballpoint pen. But the return address on the left-hand corner grabbed her. It was just a name: Junie Moon. Yuki ripped open the envelope as she walked unsteadily to her mom's green sofa.

Junie had been acquitted of Michael Campion's death. Why would Junie be writing to her?

Sitting on the sofa, Yuki shook the contents of the envelope out onto the glass coffee table.

There was a letter and a *second* envelope with her name on it.

Yuki unfolded the letter impatiently.

Dear Ms. Castellano,

By the time you get this I will be on the road somewhere, I don't even know where. I want to see America because I have never been outside of San Francisco.

I guess you're wondering why I'm writing to you, so I'll get to the point.

The evidence you wanted is in the second envelope, and you'll probably want to use it to give the Campions some closure.

I hope you understand why I can't say any more.

Take care,
Junie Moon

Yuki read the letter again.

Her mind was swimming, trying to follow what Junie had said. "The evidence you wanted is in the second envelope."

Yuki tore open the plain white envelope and emptied two items onto the tabletop. Item one was a shirt cuff, ripped from its sleeve,

monogrammed with Michael Campion's initials. The cuff was saturated with dried
blood.

Item two was a small clump of dark hair,
about three inches long, roots attached.

Yuki's hands were shaking, but she was
sobering up, starting to think about the call
she would make to Red Dog. Wondering, if
they put a rush on it, how much time it would
take for the lab to process the DNA that would
surely match to Michael Campion.

And she thought about how even if they
were able to find Junie Moon and bring her
in, the law was clear: she couldn't be tried for
Campion's death again. They could charge
her with *stuff*—perjury, obstruction, hinder-
ing prosecution. But unless they could estab-
lish how the evidence came into Junie's
possession, odds were that the DA wouldn't
even try to indict her.

Yuki looked at the gruesome evidence that
had now dropped literally into her lap. She
picked up the phone and called Lindsay. As
she listened to the phone ring, she thought
about Jason Twilly.

He was charged with attempted murder
on the life of a peace officer, and if convicted
he could go to prison for the rest of his life

without possibility of parole. Or he could hire the best criminal defense attorney money could buy and maybe win.

Maybe he'd go free.

Yuki saw Twilly in her mind, sitting in some café in LA writing his book with everything he needed for his big-bang, gazillion-dollar ending. The news would get out about the bloody cuff, the hank of hair, the DNA matching to Michael Campion.

Who dunnit?

Twilly wouldn't have to prove it. He could make her a character in his book. And then he could simply point his finger at Junie Moon.

The ring tone stopped.

"Yuki?" she heard Lindsay say.

"Linds, can you come back? I've got something you have to see."

Chapter 125

JUNIE MOON LOOKED out the window and marveled again at the feeling of flight and at the amazing bright turquoise water below. And there, just coming into view, was a little town by the sea. She couldn't even pronounce its name.

The pilot's voice came over the speaker. Junie put up her tray table and tightened her seat belt, still staring out the window, seeing the beaches now, and the little boats and the people.

Oh, my God, this was just too fantastic.

She started to think again about that long-ago night when Michael Campion wasn't a client anymore. They'd talked about their love and how hopeless it all was.

Michael had playfully tugged at the little braid hanging down the back of her neck.

"I have an idea," he said. "A way for us to be together."

"I'd do anything," she'd said. *"Anything."*

"Me too," Michael had said.

It was a pledge.

They'd made plans over the next few weeks, plans that would take place six months in the future. And one night when everything was in place, Michael left her house and just disappeared. Three months later, someone called the police saying he'd seen Michael at her house. And then the police had come and she'd gotten confused and made up a story—and talked herself into a huge mess.

It had been hell: jail and the trial and especially not being able to get mail or phone calls. But she'd known he would wait for her. And if she'd been convicted, he would have come forward. But Junie had hung in, used the brains and the lawyer God had given her, and played her role to the hilt.

And thank you, God, she'd been acquitted.

Three days ago she'd taken the blood and hair he'd sent her and put it into that letter to Yuki Castellano. Now the hard part was over and Junie was traveling light. She had worn boy's clothes on the bus from San Francisco to Vancouver, the flight to Mexico City, and now she was on another plane, on her way to a little village on a beach in Costa Rica.

This remote and enchanted place would be their new home, and Junie Moon hoped with her whole being that someday Michael's heart would be fixed and that paradise would last for-fricking-ever.

She'd changed into a cute little sundress in the bathroom, fluffed up her newly straightened dark brown hair, put on the chic cat's-eye glasses. The wheels of the plane bounced on the landing strip and all the passengers began to clap. Junie clapped, too, as the plane rolled to a stop.

Moments later the cabin door opened and Junie stepped carefully down the steps that had been wheeled up to the aircraft. Junie scanned the many faces peering out at the plane from the small outdoor terminal.

And there he was.

He'd shaven his head, had grown a goatee, and he was brown all over from the sun. He was wearing a bright striped shirt and cutoffs, grinning and waving, calling, "Baby, baby, over here!"

No one would ever recognize him, no one but her.

This was her real life.

And it was starting now.

The Novels of James Patterson

FEATURING ALEX CROSS

Double Cross
Cross
Mary, Mary
London Bridges
The Big Bad Wolf

Four Blind Mice
Violets Are Blue
Roses Are Red
Pop Goes the Weasel
Cat & Mouse

Jack & Jill
Kiss the Girls
Along Came a Spider

THE WOMEN'S MURDER CLUB

7th Heaven (coauthor Maxine Paetro)
The 6th Target (Maxine Paetro)
The 5th Horseman (Maxine Paetro)

4th of July (Maxine Paetro)
3rd Degree (Andrew Gross)
2nd Chance (Andrew Gross)
1st to Die

THE JAMES PATTERSON PAGETURNERS

The Dangerous Days of Daniel X
The Final Warning: A Maximum Ride Novel
Maximum Ride: Saving the World and Other Extreme Sports

Maximum Ride: School's Out — Forever
Maximum Ride: The Angel Experiment

OTHER BOOKS

You've Been Warned (coauthor Howard Roughan)
The Quickie (Michael Ledwidge)

Step on a Crack (Michael Ledwidge)
Judge & Jury (Andrew Gross)

For more information about James Patterson's novels, visit **www.jamespatterson.com**.